"I'll go first," Jenks whispered. "You watch my back."

Mandrake nodded and drew his snub-nosed .38 from where it'd been clipped to his waist.

Jenks shook his head. "You're going to want more stopping power than that."

"You do things your way," Mandrake said, "and I'll do them mine. I'm getting really sick and tired—" he began, then Jenks shoved him and yelled, "Get down!"

A tall, dark, lean figure had appeared in the mouth of the corridor not twenty paces in front of them and cut loose with a burst of gunfire that ripped across Jenks's chest and flung him to the floor.

Mandrake glanced back at him, then at the steadily approaching figure who was goose-stepping forward inexorably while ejecting his used clip and fumbling for another to ram home into the Uzi he carried.

Mandrake blanked his mind. There was no time to worry about Jenks now. He rose to one knee and extended his pistol in a two-handed firing stance. Taking careful aim, he squeezed off a shot.

The .38 bucked in his hand and his shot struck home. *The target stumbled. But still he came on.*

Book of Justice by Jack Arnett
  Book 1: Genocide Express
  Book 2: Zaitech Sting
  Book 3: Death Force
  Book 4: Panama Dead

Eagle Force by Dan Schmidt
  Book 1: Contract for Slaughter
  Book 2: Death Camp Columbia
  Book 3: Flight 666
  Book 4: Red Firestorm

Overload by Bob Ham
  Book 1: Personal War
  Book 2: The Wrath
  Book 3: Highway Warriors
  Book 4: Tennessee Terror
  Book 5: Atlanta Burn
  Book 6: Nashville Nightmare

BOOK OF JUSTICE

#3

DEATH FORCE

By
Jack Arnett

BANTAM BOOKS
NEW YORK • TORONTO • LONDON • SYDNEY • AUCKLAND

To Gail, for love and patience
beyond the call of duty

THE BOOK OF JUSTICE, BOOK 3
DEATH FORCE
A Bantam Book / May 1990

ISBN 0-553-28455-X

Published simultaneously in the United States and Canada

PRINTED IN THE UNITED STATES OF AMERICA

RAD   0 9 8 7 6 5 4 3 2 1

DEATH FORCE

I.

HAVEN
28TH SEPTEMBER—9:30 A.M.

William Justice fell on his back and wriggled under the network of barbed wire that was just inches above his nose. The sweat poured off his body as he pushed himself through the sand, cleared the last of the wire, rolled, and came to his feet.

He sprinted a hundred yards with the smooth, graceful lope of a trained athlete, not even breaking stride when he hit the rope at the edge of the water. He hauled himself up thirty feet using just his arms, then went hand over hand on the rungs of the rope ladder stretching above the peaceful lagoon. The ladder was a hundred feet long. When it ended, Justice let go and plummeted into the water below.

He came up swimming for the opposite shore two hundred yards away. He was breathing hard but evenly when he hit the sand and tackled the obstacle course that had him leaping over rails like a steeplechaser.

He flung himself over the finish line and Joachim One Eagle punched the stopwatch. He looked at the result and smiled.

"New course record, William." He looked at the men gathered around him.

Justice smiled back. "Not bad for a desk jockey," he said.

Joachim nodded, and his smile widened at their own private joke. Justice just played at being a desk jockey. True, he was a politician and businessman, but he was also a man of action whose passionate devotion to physical activity bordered on the religious.

He and Joachim were trying to make a point to the men watching his exhibition of awesome physical conditioning. They were all new recruits for the Haven commando team, which was led by One Eagle, a slim, muscular Mescalero Apache. One Eagle and Justice wanted to show them right from the start that this was a hard, tough unit, and the toughest of all was the man ultimately in charge, William Justice.

A tall, slim man dressed in an impeccable white Nehru jacket and light powder blue turban stepped forward from the group and tossed Justice a towel.

Justice caught it and vigorously wiped his face. "Thanks, Sardi."

Sardi bowed. Once an important politician in India, Sardi had long ago thrown in his lot with Justice and was now his right-hand man. He knew Justice's mind better than anyone, sometimes better than Justice himself. Now, as he watched his chief, he looked worried.

Justice saw—and correctly interpreted—Sardi's expression. "What's bothering you now?" he asked.

"The car has arrived," Sardi said softly. "It's been delivered to the laboratory at Diamond Rock."

Justice stood perfectly still for a moment. His gaze grew far and unfocused. He remembered first seeing the car as if it had been yesterday, not almost ten years before.

It was a warm California night in the late spring, and Justice was running on Malibu Beach with a friend, a stockbroker named Ed Barkes. For a man who had once been paralyzed from the neck down, the smooth play of muscles in legs and arms gave Justice a heady, intoxicating feeling. Running—any kind of exercise—was like an irresistible drug that Justice couldn't refuse.

Justice and Barkes had just made the turn back to Justice's beachfront home when the first explosion shattered the quiet night and Justice saw a column of flame erupt through the roof of his home. His mind was seized by blind panic, and his body went on automatic. He sprinted toward the house, knowing that his wife, Allie, and her mother were in the house, alone, unaware, and undefended.

He had reached the macadam driveway when another explosion rocked the night, its hot breath blowing over him with fiery violence. He threw his hand up to protect his face, and a car gunned down his driveway with its headlights off and motor roaring. Silhouetted by the flames that were engulfing his house, Justice could see that it was a big Ford, less than a year old. There were two men inside. The driver was an older man with a lined face, thick mustache, and short, gray hair. The passenger was a young guy. Laughing and excited, he pounded the dashboard in his glee. As the car shot by them, Justice's mind had taken a mental snapshot of the license plate, but it wasn't until just a year ago, under the influence of Ugandan priestess Mama Alice, that Justice had remembered the plate's letters and numbers. California, XJS–4379.

Back then, the night it had happened, the car had shot by him and lost itself in the night. Justice raced up the driveway just in time to see his mother-in-law, dress and hair flaming, crash through the living room window and hit the front lawn screaming. She was dead before he reached her side, and Ed Barkes tackled him before he could throw himself into the raging inferno after his wife.

It was nearly ten years ago, but William Justice remembered it as if it were yesterday. . . .

"You should not expect too much," Sardi cautioned him. "The car has been . . . damaged."

Justice started, drawn out of his reverie. He nodded. "I've seen a picture of it."

It had taken several months to track down the car used by the hit men who'd firebombed Justice's house. It had finally been found in a Florida junkyard and was purchased by Justice's agents.

Justice tossed the towel to One Eagle. "Put them through their paces, Joachim. A thousand-dollar bonus to anyone who breaks my new course record." He turned to Sardi. "Let's take the chopper over to Diamond Rock."

Sardi nodded and followed Justice through a patch of palm trees and jungle. It was a beautiful late summer Caribbean day. It was warm, but the edge of the heat was dulled by the cooling, salt-scented breezes blowing in from the ocean. After a short walk through undeveloped jungle, they found themselves on the outskirts of Schoelcher, Haven's only city. They jumped into the jeep Sardi had left waiting and drove through the town to the heliport on the east side. Haven natives, of a remarkable number of races and nationalities, greeted Justice with cordial respect as he and Sardi passed by.

Haven was a unique island, and Justice, its leader, a unique man. A former French colony in the French West Indies, Haven was now home for the dispossessed of the earth, for the teachers and intellectuals and refugees of all political and philosophical stripes who'd been thrown out of nearly every country in the world. They were all stockholders in the island, which was organized like a great international corporation. Justice was their CEO.

Haven was a subsidiary of Lambert International, through which Justice, under the alias of William Lambert, owned or controlled half a hundred corporations throughout the world. Lambert sold and manufactured anything and everything except material unsafe to the environment and armaments. He hated to support arms manufacturers, but he couldn't endanger his people by asking them to do dangerous jobs without the proper equipment. Justice had specialists running the various branches of his gigantic corporation. He took a direct hand only in very special cases that piqued his personal interest.

Diamond Rock, located two miles offshore of Haven, was Justice's personal headquarters. The only rock ever commissioned into the British navy, it thrust six hundred feet upwards from the ocean floor. It had once held off a siege for over a year. The way Justice had armed and armored, it could now hold off anything short of a nuclear attack for a lifetime.

Justice and Sardi buzzed over in Justice's private chopper and landed on the helicopter pad that had been carved from the cliff face about two-thirds of the way up the rockside. They got into the large elevator, passed the command center on the upper level, and went straight down to Research. The car was sitting in a lab, surrounded by technicians who were waiting for Justice's order to take it apart.

"Christ," Justice swore. "The thing's been turned into a doorstop."

Seeing a picture of the car was one thing; having it standing there before your eyes was another. Justice could still see its original outlines, sort of, but the car had been compressed into a huge metallic cube, about six feet on each side. The California plate hanging crookedly on the front of the cube read XJS–4379.

He looked at the technicians who were watching him expectantly. "All right," he said. "Do your stuff. Be careful and be thorough. I want to wring every ounce of information we can out of this baby. There's no telling what may be important."

The technicians nodded and attacked the wreck with crowbars and metal snips and buzz saws under the watchful eye of Justice and Sardi.

"Look there," Sardi suddenly said. "In the front, right behind the windshield frame, you can see a bit of the front seat."

Justice nodded, his gaze following Sardi's lean, pointing finger. "Looks like a stain," he said. "A big one. Sort of dark brownish red."

Justice and Sardi looked at each other. "Blood," they said.

"The son of a bitch who owned this car had better not be dead," Justice said in a low voice. He looked at Sardi. "Where's Bob Jenks? I thought he brought the car in."

"He supervised the airlift from Florida," Sardi told him, "but hopped right back on the transport that brought the car in and returned to Florida to do some more investigating himself."

One of the technicians had been prying at the squashed front driver-side door. It fell to the concrete with a dull clang. The technician looked inside and pulled something off the crumpled front seat.

"Hey, look at this."

It was a bundle of white feathers. Their tips were bloodstained. Tied together at the quill end, they were attached to a large bird foot. Stuck in the foot's claws was a small leather pouch closed tightly by a drawstring.

"What in the world is this?" the technician asked.

"Be careful how you handle that," Sardi barked. "It's a *wanga.*"

"*Wanga?*" Justice asked.

Sardi nodded seriously. "A Haitian voudou charm meant for evil purposes. That pouch may contain a deadly poison."

"I hope," Justice said after a moment, "that Jenks is being careful."

Sardi shook his head and sighed. "Well," he said, "I suppose there's a first time for everything."

II.

GATOR GROVE, FLORIDA
28TH SEPTEMBER—1:15 P.M.

The Florida afternoon was so hot and humid that the junkyard dog didn't even bare his teeth at Bob Jenks as Jenks passed by. The hound just looked up with a pitiful expression and quickly covered his eyes with his paws as Jenks snarled at him.

Jenks was a lean, muscular six-four with pale blond hair and faded blue eyes. Once a Kansas lawman, Justice had busted him out of Leavenworth's death row where he'd been awaiting execution on trumped-up murder charges. He'd been Justice's strong right arm since then, going where Justice told him to go and doing what Justice told him to do, which usually involved kicking ass. Jenks truly loved William Justice and he truly loved kicking ass.

A wiry old black man in faded, meticulously patched overalls was dozing in the junkyard's cramped office, his feet on the battered desk. Every inch of wall space in the office was covered by *Playboy* centerfolds, some dating back to when Jenks was in diapers. The old man jerked awake when Jenks knocked on the sagging screen door.

"Afternoon," Jenks said. "Got a minute?"

"Got more time than I know what to do with, son. Come on in."

The old man swung his legs off the desk and rolled the ancient swivel chair back in the corner, making room for Jenks. There was nowhere for Jenks to sit, so he perched on the edge of the desk. He surveyed the unique wallpaper for a moment, then turned back to the old man.

"You sold an associate of mine a car the other day—"

"Say, son," the old man said, a look of concern on his face. "We sell 'em, we don't guarantee 'em. Once they's out of the lot—"

Jenks held up his hand. "No, no, it's all right. It wasn't running. It'd been crushed. Turned into a big paperweight."

"Oh, that one."

"Yeah. What I need to know is who you bought it from."

The old man shifted uneasily in his chair and focused his eyes on Miss February 1965. "What you need to know that for, son?"

Jenks reached into his pocket and drew out a roll of twenties. He counted off five and dropped them on the old man's desk. "Business," he said. "Just business."

The old man looked from Miss February's hooters to the bills, back to Miss February, and back to the bills again. He sighed and reached out a thin, veined hand, and stashed the bills in a pocket of his coveralls.

"You don't want no business with Ti Albert Moreau, son, none at all." He shook his head almost mournfully. "He's a crazy mother."

"Tough, huh?" Jenks asked. This was beginning to look good. As far as Jenks was concerned, there was no better way to pass time than busting heads. "Was it his car?"

The old man shook his head. "Nope. Belonged to some feller was a business 'sociate of Ti Albert."

"What happened to this fellow?"

"Took sick."

Jenks frowned. "Is he still around?"

The old man just shook his head.

"So you junked his car because he got sick?"

"He didn't have no more use for it. And nobody else would want it."

"I never heard of a disease you could catch from a car seat."

The old man just shrugged.

"All right." Jenks slid off the desk. Miss December 1979 caught his eye, and he gazed at her for a moment. "How do I find this Moreau?"

"Hard not to. He owns about half the south side of town."

"Any particular place he hangs out?"

The old man glanced at the wristwatch hanging loosely on his scrawny wrist. "This time of day prob'ly at his place on South Main. Maybe at the Lifeline Medical Supply place if he's got any business."

"What's he look like?"

"Black feller," the old man said. "Wears an eye patch. Bald. Tall. Big. Mean."

Jenks nodded. "You're a man of few words, gramps," he said as he opened the screen door and stepped from the office.

"And all my words is true. Be careful, young feller, be real careful."

Jenks nodded. This was starting to sound up his alley after all. He went by the junkyard dog, who was snoring and chasing dream-rabbits, and climbed into his rented Blazer. Gator Grove was a flyspeck of a town on Florida's east coast. There wasn't much to it besides bars and bait shops, so Moreau's place shouldn't be too hard to find.

The junkyard was on the northern outskirts of town. Jenks took the highway, which quickly narrowed down to become Main Street, passing the whitewashed bungalows of the residents and the mom-and-pop stores that were the town's major industry. It looked like a small, friendly burg that survived by servicing tourists.

Once he crossed the railroad tracks that bisected the town into north and south, its character seemed to change. There were a lot more men lounging before the stores, even though this was the middle of a workday. It seemed to Jenks that they watched him closely as he drove by. He could almost feel their eyes bore into the back of his head. It was an uneasy kind of feeling that made Jenks wish he'd had firepower with him.

It was getting hotter as the day wore on, and Jenks felt a powerful need for a cool drink. He was about to check out one of the local watering holes, when he saw a place called *Ti Albert's* and figured it had to be Moreau's place. He pulled the Blazer into the potholed parking lot. The bar's whitewashed facade was chipped and dirty, but it was cool and dark inside.

Jenks felt all the customers—all eight of them—turn and stare as he came in. Two old men were sitting near the front playing dominoes. The other six customers were grouped at two tables in a back corner. Three men sat at one of the tables. Two looked like your average goon. The third was small and nattily dressed. Two women flanked a man at the other table. One of them was blond, the other black. Both had long, lean legs and outstanding physical attributes. The man who sat between them was tall. And bald. And mean looking. He also wore an eye patch.

Bingo! thought Jenks. I've hit the jackpot.

The bartender looked at Jenks with an expression that was somewhat less than friendly and continued to wipe down the bar with a dirty rag as Jenks perched on a bar stool.

"I'll have a draft," Jenks said.

The man continued to wipe the bar for a moment, then left the dirty rag in a heap right in front of Jenks and turned in slow motion to fill his order. Jenks stared at the glass when the man placed it in front of him. It was mostly foam.

"Three dollar," the bartender said.

Jenks looked at him for a moment, then shook his head. "No wonder this place is almost empty." He reached into his jeans and pulled out his roll of bills. He put a five down on the bar. "Keep the change," he said.

The bartender took the bill and trudged to the cash register.

"Hey, you're welcome," Jenks said.

The bartender got another dirty rag from under the counter and started to wipe down the other end of the bar. Jenks took a short pull at the beer, downing most of it. It was as cool and tasty, Jenks thought, as, well, a cool beer on a hot day.

He heard a sound on his left and swiveled on his stool to see that the short, well-dressed guy was standing next to him. He was wearing an impeccable white linen suit, white shirt, and dark tie. He carried a three-foot-long walking stick of dark, polished wood that he continually fingered with neat little hands adorned with half a dozen sparkling rings.

He was one of those men, Jenks thought, who went through life showing how tough they were because they stood about five feet nothing. The two guys standing behind him, though, didn't have to worry about an inferiority complex, at least when it came to size. They were both bruisers showing off huge biceps in sweat-stained muscle-man T-shirts.

"What do you want here, *mon*?" Shorty asked. His English was tinged with French, but also with a lilting, liquid tongue that Jenks couldn't identify.

"Just a cool drink and a little chat," Jenks told him.

Shorty frowned. "You had your drink. Shove off."

Jenks wasn't going to be brushed off so easily. "Sure, pal," he said. "Just as soon as I talk with Albert Moreau." He nodded toward the big guy at the corner table, who was watching the scene impassively.

"What for, *mon*?" Shorty asked suspiciously.

"Business." Jenks wasn't sure where this conversation was heading, so he decided to be as closemouthed as possible.

"Whyn't you say so? But Ti Albert is ver' busy now. He can't talk to you now. Come back tomorrow."

Jenks decided to push a little. "I can see that your boss is a busy guy, but I can't wait, my friend. I'm only in town for the day, and I can't afford to sit around on my butt. Have to be elsewhere tomorrow."

Shorty nodded. "Maybe you should come around tonight, just before dark. Maybe Ti Albert will see you then."

Jenks looked steadily at Moreau, and after a moment he returned Jenks's gaze. His one visible eye stared back at Jenks with an unblinking gleam. His gaze suggested strange power, as if he could almost read minds. Jenks shrugged the feeling off with difficulty.

"Okay. Here?"

Shorty looked at him with eyes that were suddenly narrowed in suspicion. "No. The Lifeline plant. Everybody does business there."

"Oh." Jenks supposed the guy was talking about the plant the geezer at the junkyard had mentioned, but he couldn't be sure. "Oh, yeah."

"You know how to get there, *mon*?" Shorty asked, and Jenks had the awful feeling that a lot was riding on his answer.

"Sure," he said, vaguely. "It's right outside of town?"

"No one sent you here on business," Shorty said suddenly. "You don't know near enough. You don't know shit."

Jenks sighed and drained his glass of beer. "Well," he drawled, "I know one thing. I know when it's time to fish and when it's time to cut bait."

"What?"

Jenks smiled at the little guy and slammed the glass into his face.

It shattered and Shorty screamed and spun away, dropping his walking stick and falling against the goons who were standing behind him. Jenks slid off the stool and scooped up the stick in his right hand. One of the thugs was twisted up in Shorty, who was clawing at his bloody face. The other was reaching for Jenks.

Jenks gave him the stick right in the gut. He swung it like a baseball bat and connected like Mickey Mantle belting a high fastball. The goon went down with a rasping gasp, the breath driven from his lungs. Shorty was screaming in a language that sounded like French, but wasn't, Jenks realized. The other goon was trying to get around him to get at Jenks, but wasn't having much luck because Shorty was wriggling on the floor like a gaffed fish.

Jenks smiled at the second goon. "Nighty-night," he said.

The thug saw what was coming and tried to jerk away, but only managed to duck into the blow. Jenks caught him on the side of the head, and he went out like a light.

Shorty made it to his knees. His face was a bloody mask, but it looked as if he were bleeding from only a forehead cut that wasn't too serious.

"Nice bat," Jenks said. "So far I'm two for two with it."

Then he slammed the walking stick down hard on Shorty's head. Shorty crumpled, his eyes glazed over. "Three for three," Jenks amended. "Guess I haven't lost my batting eye after all."

He tucked the stick under his arm and dusted off his palms in a self-satisfied manner. He nodded at Moreau, who was still watching like a great, impassive spider from the darkness of his corner table.

Jenks thought about buying another drink and sipping it at the bar, but that, he decided, would only be showy bravado. He turned and sauntered out of the bar, nodding at the old men playing dominoes by the door.

III.

HAVEN
28TH SEPTEMBER—9:37 P.M.

"That's all that was found in the car?" Justice asked, gesturing at the bundle of feathers that Sardi was toying with. The bag had been removed from the charm so the powder it contained could be analyzed, but Sardi had kept the rest of the object for study.

"That's all, boss man," Kim Bouvier said. Bouvier was

a Eurasian, originally from Vietnam, with a delicate, beautiful face, a slight body, and long silken black hair that fell unbound to her waist. Even in repose, she looked like a lithe cat ready to pounce . . . and she could be, Justice reflected, as dangerously vicious as a cat, or as cuddly and purrful. Justice knew she was half in love with him. Sometimes he dreamed of her lithe body squirming against him, her hot tongue probing his mouth demandingly. He dreamed of it, but could never allow it to happen. The hit men who had killed his wife had also taken away his ability to give himself fully to anyone. It was another thing they had to pay for.

"That's not much," Justice heard himself say, as if it were all Kim's fault. He immediately regretted his words, but could not bring them back. And he would not, even if he could. Being occasionally abrupt with Kim was the only way he could keep their relationship cool and professional, the only way he could keep himself from giving in and sweeping her off to his bed.

"Sorry," Kim said, dropping her eyes.

"It may be enough," Sardi said softly, almost dreamily.

"What," Justice asked, "could that bundle of junk tell you?"

Sardi turned the talisman over in his hands, examining it closely.

"First of all," he said in a professorial tone that commanded their attention, "it is called, as I've said, a *wanga*."

"*Wanga*," Kim repeated, making a funny face. "It sounds obscene. *Wanga, wanga*," she gestured at Justice.

"It is obscene," Sardi assured her, "in the broadest, most vile sense of the word. It is a charm made to bring harm to someone. Perhaps," Sardi conjectured, "to the owner of the car."

Kim almost giggled, but took one look at the serious expression on Sardi's face and contained herself.

"It was made by a *bokor*, a practitioner of black voudou magic."

This time Kim couldn't contain her smile. "Oh, come on," she said. "Voudou! Next you'll be talking about little dolls with needles stuck in them, and women sleepwalking at night in their underwear. I've seen all of that in old movies on television."

Sardi shook his head. "Hollywood has debased many things for the sake of cheap entertainment. Voudou is an ancient religion, first practiced in Haiti by the slaves brought to the island in the late 1600s. The word 'voudou' itself means 'spirit' among the Fon people of Benin, but parts of the voudou religion have been borrowed from dozens of tribes from all over West Africa."

"Can you explain the basis of this religion?" Justice asked.

Sardi shrugged. "Can you explain Hinduism, or Catholicism, in a few words? Well, I shall try." He took a deep breath and looked seriously at Justice and Kim. "In the voudou religion there is but one god, who sits far apart from everything. But there are many—literally hundreds—of divine spirits, called *loa*. These *loa* are said to live beneath the great water, that is, the ocean. Some of the *loa* are good, some of them are evil, but they all touch the lives of the people. The people pray to them for help or give sacrifices to placate them. At times the *loa* are even said to possess their worshipers during voudou ceremonies and walk among the celebrants in the bodies of those whom they've taken."

"You don't really believe that!" Kim said.

"I have never seen it with my eyes," Sardi retorted, "but not everything—"

The door to Justice's office suddenly swung wide open, and a panic-stricken woman wearing a technician's white lab coat stuck her head into the room. "I-I'm sorry to interrupt—" she stammered.

Justice stood up. "What is it?"

"Trouble—trouble in the lab. The tech who was analyzing the powder in that pouch . . ."

"Take your time," Justice said soothingly, noting the tremendous fear on the woman's face. "Choose your words carefully. Speak slowly and precisely."

The woman caught her breath and nodded once vigorously. "O-okay. There was an accident. Some of the powder blew on his face, and, and he fell over and stopped breathing!"

"What!" Kim and Sardi rose to stand beside Justice.

"We've called the medical team—" she said, but Justice and the others had already pushed by her and were running down the corridor.

Justice won the dash to the laboratory. He burst into the lab with Sardi and Kim on his heels and pushed through a knot of techs who had surrounded the unfortunate man lying faceup on the floor.

Justice kneeled down before him. The tech's face was flushed, his eyes were shining, his forehead was glistening with sweat. His mouth hung open, and a line of drool dripped over his blue, swollen lips.

Justice grabbed his hand. It was sweaty and felt cool and clammy. His pulse was rapid, weak, and intermittent.

"How do you feel?" Justice asked gently.

"Ants," the man said in a husky voice. "Ants, crawling all over me. Biting me. Ants . . ."

His eyes, staring at Justice, became fixed. His face turned pale and sweat covered. As Justice held him his eyes glazed and his laboring breath stopped with a great, hoarse shudder.

Justice stared over the tech's body at Sardi and Kim, his expression of grief and rage mingled in an inseparable mask.

IV.

GATOR GROVE
28TH SEPTEMBER—9:49 P.M.

Jenks parked the Blazer off the road some distance from Lifeline's parking lot and killed the headlights. He drained the beer can with one long swallow and tossed the empty into the backseat with the others.

Finding Lifeline had been easy. After leaving *Ti Albert's*, Jenks had cruised around a while, making sure Shorty and his pals weren't on his tail, then he systematically quartered the south half of the city. Lifeline Medical Supply stood out like a sore thumb. It was the only business complex that had a parking lot without a jungle of weeds poking through cracks in the asphalt, that had whitewashed walls which were still white, and that looked as if it employed more than half a dozen people.

It shone like a beacon through the poverty of south Gator Grove, the ten-foot-tall letters across its wrought-iron fenced entrance proudly spelling "Lifeline Medical Supply." The parking lot had been jammed, and a constant stream of people were moving from the building to the lot and back again. It was not the time to investigate.

It *was* time to find something to eat. Jenks was starved. He didn't want to hang around Gator Grove making himself available to Shorty and his friends, so he drove to the next little town, grabbed himself a big steak and a couple of ales, and sacked out for a while as he considered his options. There weren't a lot of them, and they all led back to Lifeline Medical Supply.

He'd come back at night expecting to find the plant deserted. But the parking lot was still full. At least the building seemed deserted. The windows were all shut, and there were no lights on behind them. He could hear, though, a throbbing noise coming from somewhere in the distance, somewhere in the darkness beyond the plant.

He slid out of the Blazer, the walking stick he'd taken from Shorty tucked under his arm. The heat and humidity dragged at him like fifty-pound ankle weights. It was still as hot and sticky as it had been during the day, only now there were also mosquitoes seemingly the size of hummingbirds buzzing him like miniature dive bombers. He slapped at them and cursed at them, but they kept after him as if he were the day's blue plate special.

"Vile little critters," he muttered under his breath as he darted across the open road and slunk up against the gatepost. The gate was chained with a huge padlock, but the chain was only looped around the gate-halves, and the padlock was open.

"Expectin' customers this time of night?" Jenks wondered aloud as he slipped into the parking lot and dropped down behind a battered old Chevy. He quietly crossed the lot, keeping to cover as best he could, but his stealth proved unnecessary. There was no one in the lot to hide from.

He plastered himself against a wall of the Lifeline building and listened. The mosquitoes kept circling him, but above their annoying buzzing he heard the sounds he had heard before.

It was a strange throbbing of drums, pounding out a complex, convoluted rhythm. There were at least half a dozen of them, big ones that boomed across the night and small ones that interwove a pitter-pat counterpoint. Their beat was hypnotic, and suggestive of a multitude of sinful things. An eerie wailing slid and tumbled through the drumbeat like the dying cry of an unearthly animal. Jenks suddenly realized that he was standing glassy-eyed, swaying to the beat.

He pulled himself upright, scowling, then slipped around the corner of the building, going fast and low for the first available cover.

He dived behind a low-lying palm and parted the

fronds to peer out at a scene from some jungle version of Dante's *Inferno*.

There was a large level clearing about the size of a football field bordering the back of the plant. A drainage canal led into a mangrove swamp on one side of the clearing and dense growths of mangrove lurked on all others. In the center of it a huge bonfire sent crackling flames into the steamy night. The bonfire surrounded a concrete dais. In the center of the dais a carved pole thrust ten feet into the night like a monstrous, erect penis.

Twenty or thirty people danced counterclockwise around the pole to the music of three conch-shell trumpets, which produced the thin, eerie wailing, and half a dozen wooden, hand-beaten drums.

About sixty people were watching the dancers with rapt attention as they moved widdershins around the pole. The dancers were in no particular formation. They simply danced as the whim took them, performing fantastic pirouettes and gyrations in time to the staccato beat of the drums. Sometimes two dancers would come face-to-face and have a dance-off, trying to outdo each other in agility and improvisation to the complex rhythms of the drums.

It suddenly struck Jenks what he was watching, and he rocked back on his heels and whispered, "Jesus, Joseph, and Mary. This must be some kind of voudou ceremony."

As he watched the dancers, his eyes fastened on a tall woman who was holding the hem of her long skirt with both hands and raising and lowering it in time to the music. The white of her underwear stood out starkly against the smooth blackness of her skin. Suddenly she was struck by a fit of continuous trembling, and she shook visibly from head to toe like a leaf caught in a hurricane-force wind.

The drumming continued, seemingly redoubling in volume and complexity of rhythm, but she still kept pace with it while voicing strange, high-pitched cries. The other dancers, no matter how frenzied their motions, seemed to realize that something special was happening to the woman. They moved away from her, giving her

her own private space in which to leap, pirouette, and shake.

Her inarticulate cries turned to words shouted in a language Jenks had never heard before. She tore at her clothing in a frenzy. Her blouse came off first, exposing magnificent breasts with hard, pointed nipples covered by a sheen of sweat. She pulled off the dress encumbering her legs and continued to dance in only panties, her head thrown back and masses of unbound hair tumbling down her back in wild abandon.

Her cries became demanding, as if she were ordering something from the crowd, and a man stepped forward to hand her a bottle filled with a clear liquid. The bottle was half filled. She put it to her lips and drained it in one long, continuous swallow. Then she stooped, and broke the bottle against the ground. A collective gasp went up from the spectators as she bit off a piece of glass from the bottle and chewed it eagerly.

Jenks was impressed. That much liquor would kill most people if drunk that fast. And eating glass was something that Jenks had certainly never seen before. It made him feel queasy, but it didn't seem to affect the woman. She dropped what was left of the bottle and danced on, but now her movements were slow and sensual, her pelvic thrusts an alluring invitation that promised incredible pleasure.

After a moment a man joined her in the circle. He was a huge, thickly built man who looked as if he had plenty of muscle hidden under his fat. He wore a patch over his left eye, and Jenks suddenly realized that this was Albert Moreau.

He approached the woman and held out his right hand, which had a black-feathered chicken in it, struggling to get free. The woman sank to her knees before him and accepted the chicken as if it were a great gift. She took it by its bound feet and caressed its feathers for a moment, then with a sudden, vicious, totally unexpected move, ripped off its head.

Blood fountained from the chicken's neck, splattering over her breasts. She held it until its blood stopped pumping, and then tossed it away. She rose lithely to her feet and ran her hands over her breasts, sweat and blood forming a glistening film over them.

She threw herself into Moreau's arms, and he crushed her against him in a squirming, wriggling embrace. After a moment they pulled apart, and Moreau began to lick the mixture of sweat and blood from her firm, heaving breasts. She moaned in guttural pleasure, her eyes had rolled back into her head so that only their whites were showing.

"Who-eee," Jenks muttered to himself. "This is getting damn strange." He scuttled back and faded into the shadows cast by the plant. "But it's not telling me a damn thing, except these people *really* party heavy on a Friday night."

He slunk around to the front entrance of the Lifeline building. "And if they're so busy partying, maybe no one's guarding their cookies."

The door was locked, but it yielded immediately to the picklock Jenks always carried. The reception area was dark and quiet. He moved through it slowly, flashing a penlight over the chrome and black leather furniture. He stopped to check the framed photos on the walls.

"Other Lifeline plants," he muttered. "LA, New Orleans, New York, and . . . Haiti? Hmmm."

He moved through the reception area into a corridor running right and left. He turned left. After going down a short ways, he found himself in what looked like the shipping-receiving department. It was neat and orderly and looked as innocent as hell. He went by what was apparently several different shipments left half unpacked for the next workday. Everything seemed in order.

Lifeline, apparently, dealt mostly in over-the-counter pharmaceuticals, all pretty routine stuff. There were bottles of pain relievers, cold medicines, decongestants, and sleeping pills all arrayed on shelves and counters, ready for packing into smaller containers. Past the racks of pill bins was a huge cold-locker.

Jenks stopped, stepped backward a step, and looked at the locker.

"This could be interesting," he said to himself. Its door was locked—the only locked interior door Jenks had come across so far. It yielded quickly to his skilled use of the picklock, and when he swung the door open, he was hit square in the face with a blast of frigid air that felt cool and welcome in the hot, humid night.

He sniffed, wrinkling his nose. There was a taint to the air. A hint of corruption overlaid by a powerful chemical odor. He pulled the chain dangling before his face, and a naked light bulb flicked on, illuminating the interior of the locker.

It was filled with stack upon stack of plain pine boxes, coffin-sized and coffin-shaped. Jenks approached one gingerly and read the shipping label stapled to its side. The label was in French, but he could make out enough of it to realize that the body inside had come from Haiti and was bound for an American medical school. All the bodies in the stack were headed for the same school, while those in other stacks were being shipped to other schools.

Jenks made a grimace of distaste. Bodies could be, and often were, used to smuggle various illicit goods. He had to check this out thoroughly.

He went to one of the stacks that was only about four feet high. He set aside Shorty's walking stick and yanked the lid off the top box. It had been hammered in with only a couple of nails, but they made loud, screeching noises as they came out of the wood. Jenks listened for a moment, but heard no one coming to investigate the noise.

He set the lid aside and looked in the box.

There was a body inside, all right, an old, withered man who looked as if he'd gone through more misery in his life than anyone ever should. His face was lined and sad looking, his eyes were still open. They seemed to stare at Jenks in frozen anguish.

"Sorry, old-timer, I got to check things out here." He gingerly touched the old man's jaw. The flesh was cold and had a rubbery feel to it. He pulled down the jaw and looked into the mouth. The end of a plastic bag filled with white powder filled his mouth cavity. Jenks pulled on it, removing a long, narrow bag that had been stuffed down his throat. It was full of white powder.

"Oh-ho," Jenks said. He didn't have to analyze the stuff to know what it was. "Cocaine."

He dropped the bag back into the box, and then put the lid back on. The smugglers were careless about hiding their illicit goods. This probably meant that customs agents had been bribed to look the wrong way or to make only the most cursory examinations.

"Now that I know what Moreau's got his fingers in," Jenks told himself, "it's time to visit the man's office."

He picked up the walking stick and went back out into the corridor. This time he followed it from the reception room to the other end and found the executive suites. The one at the far end of the corridor had "Albert Moreau" inlaid in golden letters on the door.

Jenks peered carefully into the suite, flashing his light cautiously around the room before entering. He whistled softly to himself. It was quite a place.

The carpet, when he stepped inside and closed the door after him, was a luxurious, deep pile that he sank in to his ankles. The huge desk looked like teak, as did the magnificently stocked bar set at right angles to it. The walls were covered by strange but beautiful paintings done in a naive style. They were mainly jungle scenes with people being menaced by weird beasts, or ethereal landscapes of some eerie heaven with glowing saints and black angels.

The room had an elegance and richness to it that contrasted sharply with the poverty of Gator Grove. Lifeline Medical Supply, Jenks decided, must have a pretty good profit margin.

He moved over to the desk. The blotter was clear. The gold pen-and-pencil set were planted securely in their marble holders. The silver letter opener was positioned on the opposite side of the blotter. There were no letters that had been opened, no documents that had been written. The desk's surface was totally devoid of any sign of use, and it had no drawers to check.

Either, Jenks thought, Moreau doesn't do any work, or else he gathers it all up at the end of the day and locks it away somewhere.

The latter seemed more likely. Jenks could pick simple locks, but he wasn't prepared for a safe-busting operation. He went to the wet bar, picked up the bottle of

Jack Daniels, and removed the top. He took a long swig, then wiped his lips with the back of his hand. He had to take a leak. The door off the wet bar looked like a likely place for an executive bathroom.

He took another swig from the bottle, set it back in place among the other waiting soldiers and opened the bathroom door.

Only the door didn't lead into a bathroom.

"Holllll-y," Jenks whistled appropriately. He was looking into a little room that seemed to be a shrine.

There was a small bench, or altar, that ran across the back wall of the room, about waist high and three feet wide. It was covered with black candles and odd knick-knacks. There were empty and partially full liquor bottles and playing cards and bundles of feathers and dried gourds standing among what looked like pictures of Catholic saints and bones and skulls. Some of the bones looked human. One of the skulls definitely was.

Jenks shook his head. This was some weird shit.

Various pictures were also tacked up on the walls around the altar. Most were cheap lithographs of Christ and a panoply of saints like those that reposed on the altar, but a couple of other pictures caught Jenks's eye. These were snapshots. Polaroids. Jenks leaned forward to look at them more closely.

One was of a blondish young guy smiling in a smirky way. He was standing before an early eighties model Ford with California plates.

Jenks took the photo down. It was the car, all right, before it'd been turned into a two-ton paperweight. He slipped the photo in his pocket, hoping no one would miss it from the irregularly spaced photo montage tacked up on the wall.

He turned to go, but stopped as the light from his penlight slashed across another photo that suddenly caught his eye.

It was another snapshot of the same guy, but with just some trees in the background. The guy wasn't smiling this time. In fact, he didn't look good at all. He was thin to the point of gauntness, with hollow cheeks and great staring eyes. He reminded Jenks of photos he'd seen of

people liberated from concentration camps. Or of AIDS
sufferers.

"What the hell," Jenks muttered to himself. Maybe,
he thought to himself, they crushed his car because he'd
come down with AIDS. But that still made no sense at
all. You couldn't catch AIDS from a car seat. He reached
out and took the second photo from the wall. "If they
don't miss one," he said aloud, "they ain't gonna miss
two."

He put the photo in his pocket, wondering how things
were going at the orgy outside, turned, and started at
the sight of the tall, cadaverous man looming before him.
The man towered above Jenks. He stared at him with
empty, burning eyes and reached out with hands that
looked big enough to strangle bears.

"Jesus," Jenks swore.

The tall black man said nothing.

V.

HAVEN
28TH SEPTEMBER—11:05 P.M.

It was a beautifully cool tropical night, but Justice
could not sleep.

He always had too much on his mind to have internal
peace, but this night was worse than most. Memories of
Allie, never far from the surface of his thoughts, had
returned with a vengeance. He would have been dead
without her, dead twice over. First she'd rescued him
from the bullet of a CIA assassin, come to destroy one of
their own because the company was afraid Justice would
spill his guts about government participation in drug
deals and civilian massacres.

Then she'd saved him from an even worse death, a living death of paralysis. For Justice had been wounded in the massacre he'd witnessed. His spinal cord had been severed by a bullet in the back, a bullet so closely joined to the cord that Justice's doctors, afraid to risk further damage to his nervous system, had to leave it in place.

But Justice, despite the impossibility of his desire, was determined to beat his paralysis and walk again. His burning will convinced Allie that it could be done. She in turn held him together the times he was too weary to believe in himself anymore. She gave Justice every bit of her mind, spirit, and body as he fought with the dogged determination of a monomaniacal zealot to become whole again.

He succeeded, with Allie at his side, and as he rebuilt his body, he took the name William Lambert so he could live in safe obscurity, and built Lambert International, becoming one of the richest men in the world. Then, with his life and happiness seemingly complete, Allie was torn from him by the firebombers. He teetered on the edge of total madness until Sardi gave direction to his life by convincing him to serve humanity.

But the madness was still there, peering out from the corners of Justice's eyes, threatening to burst forth like a slavering dog and tear apart everything in its path. It was never far away. Justice fought it constantly. Sometimes he gave in to it.

"The technician will be all right."

"What—!" Justice jerked his head up from the book that was open and unseen before him.

If Sardi recognized the madness whirling in Justice's eyes, he said nothing. He just repeated in his gentle, soothing voice, "I said that the lab man will recover. Fortunately he has a strong constitution, and even more fortunately he inhaled only a microscopic portion of the dust. The powder that momentarily paralyzed him contained," and here Sardi consulted a little slip of paper, "pulverized bone—probably human—fish scales, and traces of tetrodotoxin of unknown organic origin."

"Tetrodotoxin?"

"One of the most poisonous substances known. A neurotoxin one hundred and sixty thousand times stronger than cocaine. Five hundred times more potent than cyanide. A lethal dosage of this substance would fit on the head of a pin."

"That was in the voudou charm bag?"

Sardi nodded seriously. "Some Haitians know potent folk medicines—and poisons—that have yet to appear in a scientific context in Western society." He paused. "This could be a very lucrative field to explore."

Justice smiled. "You've been reading my mind again, while I've been reading up on Haiti." He gestured at the book that lay open before him. "It's a fascinating, if sometimes morbid story."

Sardi settled down into the chair across from Justice's desk and let Justice talk on, almost to himself.

"Haiti has a long history. Columbus landed there in 1492. In fact, his flagship, the *Santa Maria*, ran aground off the island. The French took it from the Spanish in the early 1600s, and by 1700 it was the richest colony in the New World.

"Think of it, Sardi! There was sugarcane, coffee, cotton, and indigo in such abundance that the French plantation owners were living a life of decadent luxury unguessed at even in Europe. But," Justice said, shaking his head, his voice sinking low, "that incredible luxury was bought with the price of human misery and suffering the likes of which the world has rarely seen. Saint-Domingue, as the colony was called, was of course a slave colony, but its slaves were treated with a savagery incredible for even that unenlightened age.

"It says here," Justice said, thumping the book, "that the plantation owners found it cheaper to work the slaves to death and then buy new ones than to allow them to have families and reproduce themselves. Work conditions were utterly miserable. The slaves worked in the fields under the lash from sunup to sundown. They were fed little food of poor quality and had no medical care.

"That slave revolt was inevitable is not surprising. That it succeeded is."

Justice suddenly leapt up and began to pace around the room.

"But the fools who succeeded the slavers had learned too much hatred from their decadent masters, and Haiti has been continually torn by civil war, political corruption has rotted her heart, and economic exploitation has crippled her citizens."

He stopped to stare at Sardi, the madness snapping in his eyes.

"A tropical paradise, the richest, lushest island in the New World is now the poorest! And all because of greed."

"But," Sardi said quietly, soothingly, "the potential for prosperity is still there. All it needs is a little breath to kindle it."

"Yes," Justice said between clenched teeth.

"Haiti does present an interesting, if daunting problem. Shall we look into it after our schedule clears, after the economic summit we're attending later this week at the UN?"

Justice shook his head. "Economic summit!" he growled. "What a waste of time! A group of useless politicians babbling lies to each other, telling each other only what they want to hear."

"I take it then," Sardi said with his gentle smile, "that we are about to play hooky from the conference in New York and embark upon a little vacation."

"Yes," Justice said, pacing around his desk and throwing himself in his chair. He picked up the bundle of chicken feathers that had been sitting on the desk next to his book. "A Haitian holiday."

The man was big and mean looking, but so slow that Jenks easily ducked under his reach, chopped him hard in the throat, then backed off. But Jenks's smile quickly turned into a frown as the man kept advancing at a steady pace, arms outstretched and eyes staring.

"What the hell—" Jenks said. He backed off, staring at his opponent, knowing that the throat chop would have brought any normal man to his knees in agony.

He danced in under his opponent's reach again, planning a fast right-left combination to his midsection. He landed the first punch, then jumped back in pain, trying to shake the sudden numbness out of his hand. His foe's stomach had felt as hard as three-inch-thick oaken board.

In a sudden change of tactics, Jenks's expressionless opponent suddenly brought one of his long arms straight down like a club, smashing Jenks at the juncture of his neck and shoulder. Jenks felt as if he'd been slapped by a baseball bat. He fell to his knees, dazed by the blow. He knew that he was in trouble. His opponent looked like a refugee from a diet center, but he was inhumanly tough and strong. Just the way Jenks liked his foes.

Jenks made a growling sound deep in his throat and launched himself at his antagonist's knees, bringing him down with a crashing thud on the thick pile carpet. Pressing his advantage, Jenks swarmed up his foe's body until he was straddling his waist. He clenched his hands together into a double-handed fist and smashed his foe's jaw. The man's head jerked at the impact, but his eyes never lost their burning stare.

"Shit," Jenks spit out. He ducked another awkward, flailing blow, but couldn't avoid it entirely. His opponent clipped him on the side of the head and sent him rolling across the carpet, where he landed dazed against the altar. "You're one brutal mother," he said, shaking his head to clear it.

The man was on him before he could move away from the altar. His long arms reached out and grabbed Jenks by the shoulders. His fingers were tough and strong as steel cable as they bit into Jenks's thick shoulder muscles and pulled him to his feet. Jenks grabbed for his opponent, but could only snatch his shirt as he was lifted off the ground. He kicked out wildly, hitting his antagonist's shins hard, but the blows seemed to have no effect. The man lifted Jenks effortlessly over his head and threw him halfway through the wall.

Jenks crashed through the paneling and the plasterboard underneath, and hit hard against studs and piping. He fell to his knees, groaning, still gripping the shreds of his foe's shirt.

The impact of Jenks's body against the wall had rattled the altar, and many of the candles fell over, some rolling onto the floor where they started smoldering in the deep pile carpet.

Jenks had more to worry about than the possibility of a fire. He looked up at the man looming over him like an avalanche ready to fall. Jenks was panting desperately, trying to get his breath back, when, in the intensity of the moment, he noticed something that chilled him to his core.

His antagonist was standing stock still over him, as if waiting for Jenks to make the next move. *Stock* still. He wasn't even breathing.

"What the hell are you?" Jenks asked through clenched lips, but his foe didn't answer.

Fear stabbed at Jenks like an ice pick through his brain. He drew back from the creature towering over him, and as he did, his eyes fell on the carved wooden staff he'd left leaning against the altar. He reached for it as pain shot through his back where he'd struck the pipe in the wall space. He grimaced and did his best to ignore the agony shooting through his back. His hand closed on the staff.

"All right, motherfucker," he muttered. "Let's see how tough you really are."

Jenks stayed crouched on the floor and swung out low with the hardwood staff. He struck his antagonist solidly on the knee, but the stony face didn't change expression. It was as if he felt no pain or fear. But the blow made him sway a little.

Jenks took heart and struck at the knee again and again, connecting solidly each time. His gaunt antagonist tried to reach him, but the staff was longer than his lean, muscle-and-bone arms. He seemed too entranced to realize what Jenks was doing or the extent of the damage he was taking.

With the fourth blow Jenks heard a corresponding crack as bone broke and ligaments snapped. The knee buckled, and his foe toppled to the floor like a felled redwood.

Jenks rolled away and came up with the stick held out protectively before him. His opponent showed no sign of the pain he had to be feeling. He slowly stood, putting all his weight on his good knee, and then tried to take a step toward Jenks. The injured knee wouldn't support

him, and he collapsed on the ground without making a
sound. Doggedly, he got up again, and collapsed again,
as Jenks took a step backward.

"You're a persistent bastard," Jenks told him as he
stood and fell again. "But you're not very smart, are you?
Acting like some brainless zombi . . ."

The significance of Jenks's words struck him.

"No, can't be," he said in horror. "There's no such
damn thing . . ."

But watching the . . . man . . . now crawl doggedly
after him, stony-faced and expressionless, stronger than
any man should be, ignoring a broken leg that would
have any normal man howling in pain, not even breathing, Jenks didn't know what to believe. He only knew
that this creature was not natural.

"What the hell have we gotten into this time?" he
wondered aloud.

He kept backing out of reach of the zombi—or whatever the hell it was—and was almost out of the shrine
when a pungent, rotten odor hit his nose. He took a
deep breath and suddenly realized what it was. Gas.
Natural gas.

He remembered the pipe, now bent and twisted, running through the wall, and he remembered the candles
burning on the altar, falling onto the carpet, starting
small, smoldering fires. A gas leak and fire. Not a good
combination.

"Christ, what next?" he complained.

He slammed the door of the altar room in his foe's
face, and half limped, half ran, from the room, cursing
the pain in his back. He reached the outer door of
Moreau's suite when there was a muted, whooshing roar.
He glanced back and saw that the door to the altar room
had been blown off its hinges by a wall of flame. And
crawling through that wall, leaving a trail of blackening
flesh that was being peeled off him by the fire, was—and
Jenks really believed it now—the zombi watchman.

He slammed the door to the suite as a hot wind blew
against his face, smelling foully of burnt human flesh and
even less pleasant unidentifiable odors. He went down
the hallway to the reception area as fast as he could. He

blew through the lobby and stopped for a moment at the door to the outside, carefully checking that no one was lurking in the parking lot.

His path clear, he sprinted from the building through the parking lot and gate and sought the deep shadows on the other side of the road. He watched for a moment as a huge fountain of flame broke through some windows and flared out into the night. A few more minutes passed, and then a panicked mob came running to the parking lot where they mostly stood gaping at the blaze. Some were running back and forth and issuing orders—Jenks thought he recognized Albert Moreau's huge form among them—but nothing could be done to effectively fight the spectacular blaze that was rapidly engulfing the Lifeline Medical Supply plant.

Jenks slid into the front seat of his Blazer. He fumbled in the brown paper bag on the passenger's seat and came up with the last can of beer. It was warm as piss, but he cracked it anyway and swallowed half of it in a single gulp. It tasted just fine. He started the engine and pulled away with his lights off so he wouldn't attract attention, humming, "There'll be a hot time in the old town tonight."

VI.

PORT-AU-PRINCE, HAITI
30TH SEPTEMBER—11:09 A.M.

Few planes were departing from Haiti International Airport, but even fewer seemed to be arriving. There was no wait, no problem at all for the Lambert International company jet, containing Justice, Jenks, Kim, and Sardi, to get landing clearance.

The airport itself was fairly modern but poorly maintained. It looked as if it had been built sometime within the last twenty-five years and then never even swept out since. It was so dead that the customs agents were playing cards when Justice and his party arrived at the gate. They finished their hand with much argument back and forth, then one agent stood, straightened his tie, put his cap on his head, and went to his window at the counter.

"Yes?" he inquired.

Justice stood at the counter, his lips quirked in a tight, humorless smile. He handed the man his passport.

"Mr. Lambert," the customs agent read. He flipped through the passport. "Are you here on business or pleasure, Mr. Lambert?" His English was good, but heavily accented with French.

"A little of both," Justice replied, switching to French himself. "We're taking some time off for a vacation, but I also hope to find some businesses to invest in."

The customs agent nodded as if he weren't listening to a word of what Justice said.

"Ah, yes." He frowned. "From Haven. I have never heard of such a country." He looked at the other agents, who were sitting and watching. They all shrugged. He looked back at Justice.

Justice smiled a forced smile. "It's a new country. A neighbor of yours, in fact, in the Caribbean."

The agent took out a thick, battered book that was housed in a creased leather binder. He thumbed through the stained pages slowly, licking his thumb elaborately every time he turned a page.

"Haven," he repeated to himself doubtfully. "Haven . . . *hmmmmm* . . . doesn't seem to be here." He closed the volume with a heavy thud and looked at Justice expectantly.

Justice stared back at him. Justice knew what the man wanted, but he was going to make him pay for it. When the man asserted Justice's dominance by breaking eye contact, confused at the harsh expression on Justice's face, Justice reached into his pocket and pulled out a wad of *gourdes*, Haiti's unit of currency. He counted off five hundred-*gourde* notes and handed them to the customs agent.

The man's eyes got big as he stuffed more than a month's wages into his pants pocket.

"Perhaps you'd care to check your book again," Justice suggested.

"Oh, no sir, oh no. Everything is in order, yes sir." He stamped Justice's passport vigorously. "Uh, anything you wish to declare, sir?"

Justice shook his head and stepped aside as the others got similarly expedient service.

By the time they were done with customs, a group of porters were fighting for the right to carry their luggage. When that was all sorted out, Justice and his party were led through the nearly deserted terminal, their footsteps echoing eerily in the vast cavern of concrete and steel. As the only international airport in Haiti, it should have been a busy hub of travel and trade. Instead, Justice noted, it was nearly dead, a sure sign of the rottenness at the heart of Haitian commerce.

"This way, monsieurs and mademoiselle. My cousin has a taxi. He will take you wherever you need to go, at a very cheap price. Very cheap."

There were a score of battered cars, most American, vintage 1970 or earlier, waiting at the curb outside the airport. Their drivers were making enough noise to wake the dead, clamoring for Justice and the others to choose their most excellent vehicle. Their porter ignored them all and marched to a battered station wagon, complete with wood-grain side panels and rusty luggage rack. The driver helped his cousin stow the suitcases.

Justice again dipped into his pocket and pulled out his roll of *gourdes*. He again peeled off five hundred-*gourde* bills and handed them to the porter, who could scarcely believe his eyes.

"Thank you, monsieur, thank you," the man said ecstatically.

Justice nodded as he ducked into the backseat of the station wagon, taking a seat next to Sardi. He had overpaid the porter tremendously—ten *gourdes* would probably have sufficed—but he was damned if he was going to pay an honest workman less than a crooked government official sucking in a bribe. Besides, it was only money, and money was never an end in itself to Justice. He had no desire to accumulate the stuff into bigger and bigger piles. Money was something to spend, to use in the commission of good works. If he had helped the porter put decent food on his table to feed his family, he was more than glad.

As they pulled away from the curb, Justice saw for the first time the huge white banners festooning the terminal's facade. They weren't tied down very tightly, so they were flapping smartly in the brisk wind. Justice could decipher some of what they said about something that sounded like a religious holiday—the Dominican Vespers.

He was going to question their driver about the banners, but immediately upon pulling onto the roadway, they were jolted by a pothole that seemed as deep as a strip mine. It was only the start of a miserably uncomfortable ride.

The road from the airport to the city was bumpy and treacherous. There wasn't much traffic, but what cars there were seemed to be driven by madmen with no regard for the deteriorated state of the road surface or the safety of their fellow travelers. Their driver took it all in good stride and in fact was responsible himself for a few of the closer shaves with oncoming vehicles. He chatted incessantly as he drove with one hand on the wheel, and because his station wagon lacked a rearview mirror, he had the bad habit of turning around to make eye contact while conversing with passengers in the backseat.

"So, this is your first time in my country? How you like it so far?" he asked.

"So far, fine," Jenks said. "I only hope we live to make it to the hotel."

Their driver swerved to miss a monstrous pothole and went right into the path of an oncoming bus painted clashing shades of orange, green, and vermilion. The bus swerved onto the nearly nonexistent shoulder of its side of the road, bumping along and nearly losing half a dozen passengers who were clinging to the top and sides.

"Oh, good," the driver enthused. "I take you to fine hotel, very fine. Hotel Ollofson. Many famous people stay here. Mick Jagger stayed there the last time he visited Haiti."

"If it's so good a hotel," Kim asked, "will they have rooms for us?"

"Oh, sure," the driver said, swerving to pass a donkey cart. He ducked back into his proper lane just in time to miss an oncoming station wagon even more battered than his own. The two drivers blared their horns at each other and waved fists as they passed. "Make room, you lousy driver!" their man shouted, then turned around to look at Kim. "There will be no problem, mademoiselle. You have missed the height of the tourist season."

"Yeah," Jenks said in a low voice. "By about thirty years."

The traffic increased as they neared Port-au-Prince, and the road got marginally better. By the time they reached the outskirts of the city, the roads were clogged with all kinds of vehicles, cars, brightly painted buses, and rattling trucks that looked straight out of *The Grapes of Wrath*. There were also numerous donkey-drawn carts, and even pedestrians encumbered by loads bigger than the men and women carrying them.

Port-au-Prince was a dense city, with old, rickety-looking buildings packed tightly together and sidewalks swarming with pedestrians. Justice remembered reading that Port-au-Prince was designed to house fifty thousand residents but was now teeming with a million, a fifth of whom were homeless.

And it looked as if every homeless person in Port-au-Prince was out on the street. When they spotted the foreign faces in the back of the station wagon, they surrounded it in a teeming mass. Itinerant peddlers poked their wares at Justice and his people, beggars stuck their stick-thin arms at them, hands held out imploringly.

Justice looked out the window stone-faced. They had to follow their driver's instructions and roll up their windows, else everything from sandals made from worn-out tires to live chickens and lobsters would have been thrust into the car.

The wretches who surrounded them were all in dire need. They were not pretending poverty, they were living it. Justice could see it in their emaciated limbs, threadbare clothing, and swollen, starving bellies. But there was nothing he could do to help them. If he ordered the driver to stop the car and he emptied his pockets, throwing all of their money into the crowd, it wouldn't go a tenth of the way toward alleviating the misery that surrounded them.

There was, Justice told himself, staring at the poverty through which they drove, only one thing he could do to help these people. He had to find some way to set the economic system of their country back on its feet again. He had to find some way to enable them all to help themselves. And if, he resolved, that meant cutting the corrupt heart out of every government official that they met, then so be it.

But he wasn't here on some magnanimous crusade. True, he felt a burning desire to help these people, but there was also something that he wanted for himself. He wanted the man who'd helped firebomb his house those ten years ago. He wanted to confront him face-to-face, to see the look in his eyes when he questioned him about the sloppy job he'd done. Sloppy, because he'd left Justice alive and angry and determined to discover who'd been behind the attack.

He wanted the hit man, certainly, but he also wanted the men who'd put the killers on Justice's trail. And the hit man would tell him what he wanted to know. Justice was sure of that.

They finally passed through the poor section of Port-au-Prince into an area where the poverty was less blatant, more genteel. Their driver stopped in front of a gingerbread mansion whose walls were draped in vines of blooming bougainvillea, turned to them, and said, "Hotel Ollofson, eh? What you think?"

"Very nice," Kim said, answering for all of them. Her expectations had been low, particularly since their drive through the Port-au-Prince slum, but this was a beautiful old place.

When they got out and looked closely, they could see

that it was decaying like all of Port-au-Prince, but hard work was keeping the decay at bay. The flowering vines that climbed the walls were beautiful, and the lobby, with its antiquated furniture and slow-moving ceiling fans, had the air of a different era about it. They all felt as if they'd been transported back to a time when things moved slowly and quietly and there was no such thing as desperation, a time when there was hope, when people believed that the future would be better for themselves and their children.

The driver helped the hotel porters bring the suitcases into the lobby. Hat in hand, he stood expectantly before Justice, who dipped into his pocket and paid him off as well as he had the others.

The man smiled widely and bobbed appreciatively several times. "Thank you, monsieur, thank you very kindly. You see that I am a superior driver, eh?" He reached into his back pocket and took out an old battered wallet. He extracted a small, elegantly printed business card from the wallet and handed it over proudly to Justice.

"Lucien Ambroise," he said. "There is my address. I have a telephone," he added proudly. "You can call me anytime you want to go anywhere. I will take you there."

"Thank you, Lucien," Justice said. "I'm sure we'll be needing your services over the next couple of days."

Lucien smiled joyfully and gave a natty bow. "*Au revoir!*" he said, and almost danced from the lobby in his happiness.

Lucien had been right about the availability of rooms. Justice and his team had no problems getting separate rooms grouped together on the second floor of the hotel. After they were shown to their rooms, they unpacked, then met in Justice's room for a war council.

"As I see it," Justice told them, "biggest clue to finding the hit man is Lifeline Medical Supply." He consulted a notebook that he pulled from his briefcase. "We know they have an office downtown, and a plant near the airport with their own shipping facilities in the airport itself."

"Very convenient when a good part of your business is smuggling cocaine," said Jenks.

"Well," Sardi said, "they do import a large volume of legitimate drugs into the country. Though the fact that they have known hit men working for them would seem to emphasize the illegitimate nature of their enterprises."

Justice nodded. He handed out four-by-five-inch copies he'd made of the photos Jenks had taken from the shrine in Gator Grove. "And here's his lovely mug right here. As you may have noted, there aren't a lot of Caucasians on this island. If this scum is still around, he's bound to be very noticeable."

Jenks took the photos from Justice. "Right, Willum. What say you give me a crack at this Lifeline company? After all, I already bombed one of their bases to hell."

Justice smiled. "Okay. See what you can find out at the office first. Try to be a little more subtle this time."

Jenks snorted. "Subtle, hell. That's my middle name." He looked at Kim. "How about being my private secretary?" he leered.

She sighed in her most put-upon manner. "All right, dirty man," she said, "but keep your privates out of it." She fanned herself vigorously with the photos Justice had given her. "Though this tropical heat does make me hot."

"Why am I not surprised?" Justice said.

VII.

PORT-AU-PRINCE, HAITI
30TH SEPTEMBER—3:55 P.M.

Justice figured that the Hotel Ollofson bar was a good enough place to start his and Sardi's half of the quest.

It was a cool, dark place, with the drawn window shades keeping out the afternoon heat. There were half a dozen people drinking in the bar, all obvious foreigners, except a working girl trying to interest a table of three businessmen in her dubious charms.

Justice and Sardi went to the empty bar and sat on neighboring stools. The bartender, an old man with a lined face and steel gray hair, approached immediately.

"What can I do for you gentlemen?" he asked in perfect English with a touch of a French accent.

"I'll try some of your rum," Justice said. "Something with a lot of fruit in it. I missed lunch today."

"Yes, sir. And you, sir?" he asked, turning to Sardi.

Sardi still wore his turban and Nehru jacket, and he still looked impeccable despite the tropic heat. "Fruit juice over ice," he said.

The old man bowed with a quick, birdlike dip of his head, then went down to the other end of the bar to make their drinks. By the time he returned, Justice had taken out the photo of the hit man and his car.

"We're looking for a man," he said. "I wonder if you've seen him around."

The old man looked Justice in the eye for a long moment. It seemed to Justice that he was accustomed to being questioned. If only half of what Justice had read about Haiti under the Duvaliers—Papa Doc and his son

Jean-Claude, who was called Baby Doc—and their successors was true, secret police were everywhere constantly gathering information on everyone.

The old man finally looked up at Justice and shook his head.

"Take the photo, study it," Justice urged, holding it out.

The old man took it reluctantly and looked at it for several seconds before shaking his head and saying, "No, sir, I've never seen the gentleman before."

His words had the ring of truth to them, Justice thought. The old man handed the picture back to Justice. As Justice reached for it, the bartender's gaze fell on the second photo of the hit man, the one in which he looked wasted and ill. Upon seeing that picture the old man's eyes widened, and the hand holding the other photo began to shake.

"What is it?" Justice asked, glancing from the old man to the photo that he still held. He turned it around and held it up for the bartender to see more closely. "Do you recognize him from this photo?"

"No, sir, no," the old man replied. He turned his head and pushed the second photo down on the bar.

Sardi and Justice glanced at each other.

"Have you perhaps seen other people in that same condition?" Sardi asked quietly.

The old man looked at Justice and Sardi, and they could see the fear in his eyes. "I have seen many things," he said in a whisper. "When I was a young man I saw Papa Doc's *tonton macoutes* throw living men, women, and children into a deep trench, then fill the trench to the top with cement, smooth it carefully like they were leveling a section of sidewalk, and walk away laughing. After Papa Doc died, I saw Baby Doc's Leopards drag men screaming from this very bar because they dared write the truth in the newspaper about his sluttish wife. After Baby Doc was deposed, I saw the secret police chop the hands off men and women who were trying to vote." He caught his breath and shuddered. "But this, this is far worse than all of that. This is old—older than even Haiti—old, evil magic." He nodded and drew even closer to Justice and Sardi and whispered in tones so low that they could barely hear. "They say, gentlemen, that the zombis walk again at night, doing the wicked business of the *bokor*."

"*Bokor?*" Justice asked in a low voice.

The bartender looked around the lounge as if afraid that someone had heard Justice's quiet word. "Do not speak of them, sir," he begged, "lest they hear you say their evil name and come. They are the black magicians, the evil sorcerers who serve the *loa* with their left hands."

Justice and Sardi exchanged glances. Justice knew very little about the workings of voudou, but he himself was living proof of the extraordinary power of the human mind. Doctors had given him no chance to walk again after his spine had been severed, and now he ran marathons. He didn't know if there were such things as zombis and *bokors*, but until it was proved one way or the other, he was willing to have an open mind.

"Can you tell us more?" Sardi urged the bartender, but the old man shook his head sharply.

"No," he told them. "Not me. I shall not talk of these things."

"Who will?" Sardi asked.

"Mambo Jennette," he said, after again glancing about the bar furtively.

"How do we find her?" Justice asked.

"She is known. She is very well known."

Justice thanked him, finished his drink, and stood up. He took his standard gratuity from the wad of *gourdes* he carried in his pocket. The old man closed his hand about it quickly and stuffed the bills into his pocket.

"Thank you, sir. May you encounter only beneficent *loas* during your search."

"What other kinds are there?" Justice asked lightly.

The old man shook his head. "You don't want to know."

Justice nodded, and he and Sardi left the lounge. They went into the lobby, and Justice whispered to his companion without moving his lips, "The guy in the sharkskin suit, porkpie hat, and sunglasses." Sardi nodded. "He's following us."

"That's to be expected," Sardi said. "The SD—*Service d'Information* or Haitian Secret Police—are everywhere."

"You keep an eye on our new friend," Justice said. "I'll put in a call to Lucien Ambroise."

Sardi nodded, settled down in one of the lobby's antique overstuffed chairs, and picked up the paper on the small side table. It was a two-week-old copy of *The New York Times*. Sardi pretended interest in the stale newspaper and kept an eye on the Haitian secret policeman while Justice used the lobby's phone. After a few minutes he returned and took a seat next to Sardi.

"Well?" Sardi asked.

Justice shook his head. "I was cut off only three times, but I finally managed to get through to Lucien." Justice glanced at his wristwatch. "He'll get here in fifteen minutes. We're going to meet him in the alley in the back of the hotel."

It was a long fifteen minutes. Justice was used to being watched, but it was difficult not to let on to the man watching them that he'd been made. Justice was incensed by the fact that the secret police were already watching him within an hour of his arrival in their country. The government, he decided, must be truly paranoid. They must see enemies under every bush—or if not enemies, maybe extortion opportunities.

"It's time," Sardi said in a soft whisper.

Justice nodded. "Walk slowly out of the lobby and onto the street. When we reach the corner, run."

Sardi folded the newspaper neatly and returned it to the stand. He stood, stretched, and followed Justice as he sauntered out of the lobby. They both nodded politely to a tableful of people they passed on the veranda, then ambled innocently down the street. Their police tail stepped off the veranda, following after them, just as they reached the corner.

"Now," Justice said, and started running.

It took Justice and Sardi just a few seconds to negotiate the garbage-strewn alley, dodging the starving peasants who were pawing through the hotel's garbage can looking for scraps of food.

They heard an angry voice raised behind them and knew that the policeman was pursuing them and probably shouting for them to stop, but they couldn't make out the words. The scavengers heard the policeman too and panicked, scattering like a flock of pigeons, unwittingly supplying excellent cover for Justice and Sardi.

They easily made it to Lucien's station wagon, which was waiting for them, as per Justice's instructions, with the motor running. Justice and Sardi piled into the backseat, and Justice shouted, "Go!"

Lucien gunned the engine, and Justice twisted around to stare through the dusty rear window. The secret policeman had fought his way through the scattered scavengers and was standing, hands on his hips, staring at the receding taxi. His eyes were hidden behind the dark glasses that he wore, but Justice could see his trembling rage in the way he held his taut, angry body.

"What a swell place," Kim said enthusiastically. "It's got air-conditioning."

"That it does, darlin'," Jenks agreed, wiping the sweat from his forehead with the back of his hand as they were struck by a blast of refrigerated air. They were both happy to get out of the oppressive heat and humidity, though Kim seemed to be suffering less than Jenks.

She looked cool in sandals and a short black dress that exposed plenty of slim, muscular thigh, but then she always looked cool and in control. Jenks was miserable. He'd been forced to abandon his usual style of dress—jeans, western shirt, and comfortable old boots—for a suit coat and tie. Justice had insisted upon the dress-up, since Jenks was playing a Lambert International executive on a business call.

The Lifeline Medical Supply building was one of the few functioning structures located in what was once the heart of Port-au-Prince's business district. Most other buildings were boarded up and looked abandoned, but the three-story Lifeline building loomed like a skyscraper over the bleak skyline of this district. The lobby was similar to the one in their Florida center, with a deep-pile carpet, pictures of other Lifeline holdings on the walls, and decorative furniture. However, this lobby also had a very decorative receptionist who looked up attentively as Jenks and Kim entered.

"Can I help you?" she asked in charming, French-accented English.

"Yes, indeed," Jenks said. "I'm Robert Jenks from Lambert International. This is my confidential secretary, Ms. Bouvier."

The two beautiful women exchanged sizing-up glances, and the receptionist smiled brittlely and nodded. "Oh, yes," she said. She picked up the office phone, spoke into it. "Mr. Jenks is here to see you, Mr. Calloway." She listened for a moment, then hung up. "He said to bring you right in."

The two followed the receptionist down another richly carpeted hallway, Kim poking Jenks in the ribs as he stared fixedly at the revolving figure eights the receptionist's attractive derriere made as she led them down the corridor.

"Keep your mind on business, dirty man," she said in a low voice. "You're an executive now."

"It's not my mind that's wantin' to wander, darlin'," he said back, as the receptionist reached a door and rapped on it smartly. She opened it a crack and stepped aside, smiling at Jenks as he and Kim went by her into the office. She closed the door after them.

Robert Calloway was standing behind his huge desk, smiling, as they entered the office.

"Mr. Jenks. Ms.—Bouvier, is it? I'm glad you could come by."

"Well," Jenks said with what he hoped was sincere heartiness, "I'm glad you could take time from your busy schedule to see us. I know we didn't give you much notice when we phoned from the hotel."

"Nonsense." Calloway bustled out from behind his desk. He was a small, plump black man, dressed in an immaculately tailored suit that would set most Haitians back a year's pay. His hair was short, his face carefully shaved, and he smelled of expensive cologne. The hand that he offered Jenks was small, soft, and well manicured. Jenks disliked him immediately. "I don't get a chance to talk to many Americans out here." His disappointed frown turned into a conspiratorial smile. "But I suppose I shouldn't admit that things have been slow. Drink?"

"Scotch on ice," Jenks said.

"The same," Kim added when Calloway turned to her.

Jenks looked around the room as Calloway puttered at the bar. It was as luxurious and sterile as any office suite of any big-time American corporation. There was no hint that the office was located in Port-au-Prince, Haiti. It could just as easily be in New York, Chicago, or California. The desk—cluttered with papers, unlike Albert Moreau's in Gator Grove—was modern American office fare, the paintings on the wall were all abstract horrors that Jenks wouldn't hang in a barn. The bar, though, was as well stocked as any Jenks had ever seen outside an actual saloon. The Scotch that Calloway handed him, as he went around the desk and motioned Jenks and Kim to sit down, was first-rate.

"Now then, what can Lifeline Medical Supply do for Lambert International?" Calloway asked as he settled down in his comfortably padded chair behind the desk.

Jenks took a sip of Scotch and leaned back in his chair. "As I'm sure you know, we're a large corporation with many areas of interest. On checking import-export registration, we discovered that you're already bringing a lot of medicinals into Haiti. We thought that Lifeline might be interested in a joint venture, with you using your contacts to help us get into the export end of things."

"That certainly sounds feasible," Calloway said, playing with a gold pen from his pen-and-pencil set. "Haiti, of course, is not rich in exportable commodities besides the basic coffee, sugar, and native handiworks markets. Did you have any particular export in mind?"

Jenks nodded. Justice had told him to stir things up, and he was going to do just that. "We certainly did," he said slowly and precisely. "We were thinking about certain distillates of the native herbal medicines. Particularly the compound known locally as 'zombi powder.'"

Calloway was not a good poker player. His eyes widened momentarily, and he dropped the pen he was playing with. He looked at Jenks and Kim for a good five seconds before responding with a brittle, forced laugh. "Zombi powder! Why, surely you're not serious!"

Jenks nodded his head seriously. "We sure are. Tell him, Kimmie, darlin'."

Kim nodded curtly and put on a serious, professorial face. "A recent sample of such zombi powder that came into our hands," she said, consulting her notebook, "was shown to contain a substance known as tetrodotoxin. Our scientists believe such a substance could be very useful in the medical field, for anesthesia, or perhaps treating certain mental illnesses."

"Well," Calloway said, sitting back in his chair. "Well. I'm speechless. I didn't know such a thing was possible. Well."

"Do you think we can cut a deal?" Jenks asked.

"Well. It certainly is an interesting notion. Perhaps if I could get back to my superiors in the States on this?"

"Sure," Jenks said. He drained his drink and stood. "We've got time. We'll be around a coupla days, checking the sights and whatnot. We'll check back with you."

"Yes." Calloway stood also, and Jenks could see him wipe sudden beads of sweat off his forehead. It was difficult to sweat in air-conditioning this low. "I shall call you. You're staying at Hotel Ollofson, is it?"

"That's right." Jenks extended his hand. Calloway's soft palm was also damp with sweat, in contrast to its earlier dryness. "We can find our way out."

Calloway nodded. "Yes. Well, thank you for calling. I'll be in touch."

"Nervous fellow," Jenks commented dryly to Kim once they were out in the hall.

"Yes. He spent most of the time looking at my legs until you mentioned zombi powder. Then he changed from horny man to very nervous man."

Jenks nodded. "Something's up."

The two of them smiled pleasantly at the elegant receptionist who was thumbing through a six-month-old issue of *Cosmopolitan* as they went by her desk. She returned their smiles and called out, "Come see us again."

Jenks stopped by the door and said, "We will, darlin', we will."

He held open the door for the man in the khaki military uniform who was entering the reception area. He was a big man, fat but solid. His chest was full of chicken salad—colorful ribbons and big bronze medals. He was tall, bald, and mean looking, and he wore an eye patch.

He looked directly at Jenks and nodded a precise millimeter of thanks, then swept by commandingly.

"Colonel Moreau!" the receptionist said. "How nice to see you again."

Jenks grabbed Kim by the upper arm and hustled her out the door.

"Hey, what's the matter?" she asked.

"That guy who just came in," Jenks said. "I ran into him in Florida. He's Albert Moreau, head of the Lifeline plant in Gator Grove."

"The drug smuggler?" Kim asked.

"Yeah," Jenks nodded. "Drug smuggler and voudou priest." Jenks shook his head. "But why didn't he recognize *me?*"

Calloway was still shaking when Moreau entered his office.

"They know, Colonel," Calloway said. He gulped his drink, then put the glass down with trembling hands. "They asked about zombis."

Moreau looked at him with disgust. "They know nothing, probably only what you told them."

"But I told them nothing!" Calloway protested. "Nothing at all!"

"You are a weak man," Moreau said contemptuously. "You'd better leave the city before they come back to see you again and you tell them everything."

"But where could I go?" Calloway asked.

Moreau just looked at him, and Calloway shook his head.

"Not there. That place gives me the creeps. There's too many of *them* there!"

Calloway and Moreau both looked at the door that had just opened into another room of the office suite. Standing in the doorway was a tall, thin man with a burned-out stare and a horrid, expressionless face.

"And take your plaything with you," the colonel said.

VIII.

PÉTIONVILLE, HAITI
30TH SEPTEMBER—7:38 P.M.

"There it is, gentlemen. Mambo Jennette's *hounfour*," Lucien said.

Pétionville is a virtual suburb of Port-au-Prince, but it had taken Justice and Sardi some hours to reach it in Lucien's taxi because the roads were so bad. It was a bouncing, jolting ride that made Justice wish they were traveling by something with four-wheel drive and not an ancient station wagon with sprung springs. They drove through Pétionville and stopped in the foothills of the mountains that surrounded it. The *hounfour* was nestled halfway up the side of one of the foothills, deep in the country and far away from any other habitation.

The *hounfour* was a compound of several buildings that could barely be glimpsed behind their protective circle of trees. Things rustled and moved in the branches, and the bleating of goats mixed with the pounding of drums from deep inside the compound. There was the taste of something magic in the air. Justice and Sardi looked at each other. They could both feel the power that permeated the night.

As they got out of the taxi and neared the circle of

trees, they could see skulls stuck in some of the branches, and long flowing ribbons of faded cloth that twisted slowly in the evening breeze. The rustling sounds, they realized, were caused by chickens and pigeons, and nothing of a supernatural nature. The birds looked down at Justice and Sardi with mock seriousness as they approached the only gap in the ring of trees, and the single sentinel who stood before it.

As they neared, the man spoke to them in a language that sounded like French, but which neither Justice nor Sardi could decipher. It was Haitian Creole, the predominant language of the countryside. The words were mostly French, but they were strung together with a West African grammar, and spiced with other words from half a dozen African languages.

Justice and Sardi looked at each other helplessly as the man asked a demanding question. Lucien pushed between them and answered in the same enigmatic tongue. Neither Justice nor Sardi knew what he said, but it must have been acceptable, because the man waved them through.

"What'd you tell him?" Justice asked their driver.

Lucien shrugged. "Just that you are most powerful gentlemen come to see Mambo Jennette on important business. Usually there would be no problem at all in seeing her, but tonight there is a ceremony."

Lucien gestured toward one of the buildings at the rear of the compound. This structure was roofed, but had no walls. The thatched roof was held up by a number of poles, and there was a central, colorfully painted pole in the middle of the structure. A fire burned around the center pole, and about a dozen dancers twirled around it counterclockwise while three drummers kept up a quick, staccato rhythm. An audience of about fifty watched the wild gyrations of the dancers with rapt attention.

Lucien tugged at Justice's sleeve and pointed at a woman in the midst of the revelers. She was dressed in a neat print dress and had an orange madras bandanna tied around her head. She was stoutly built, with a huge bosom and thick, strong-looking arms. There was something to her face and manner, some strength and inner power, that reminded Justice of the Ugandan priestess he had once met.

"That's Mambo Jennette," Lucien said. "I can bring her over to talk, if you want."

Justice nodded. "If we're not interrupting."

Lucien smiled. "Mambo Jennette, if she want to talk, she come. If not, she won't."

Justice nodded again, and Lucien went off on his mission.

"Can you feel it, William?" Sardi asked.

Justice took a deep breath of the fresh Haitian air and nodded.

"I feel it too," Sardi continued. "There is a power to this place, a spiritual energy despite the poverty and corruption that surrounds it."

"Great things can happen here," Justice said, "if the people are only given a chance."

"Great things," Sardi agreed, "or terrible."

He fell silent as Lucien approached with Mambo Jennette at his side. The aura of authority that she radiated was even stronger close up. She looked Justice and Sardi straight in the eye and nodded decisively when they were introduced.

"*Bonsoir, madame,*" Justice began, but Mambo Jennette held up her hand.

"You can speak English," she said. "I learned as a young girl when I worked as a maid in New York."

"We appreciate your seeing us," Justice said.

Mambo Jennette looked at Justice and Sardi both with her dark, piercing eyes. "It is the least I can do. You've come to Haiti," she told Justice, "to find a piece of your past. But you also come with a thought to help. And you," she turned to Sardi, "come for the love of this man, but also because you wish to help."

"How do you know this?" Justice asked.

"I have faithfully served the *loa* for many years. Even as a young girl when I was away from my Haiti, I never forgot the spirits. I prayed and sacrificed to them regularly, and in turn they granted me material success and, more importantly, spiritual favors."

"They made you a *mambo*?" Justice asked.

"They let me work and study long and hard to become one, yes. Voudou," she said, staring hard at Justice, "permeates Haiti. It is in our earth, our water, our air, our very selves. Those fools who live in Port-au-Prince are not the real Haiti. We in the countryside are Haiti. And to understand us, you must understand voudou. To help us, you must believe in voudou."

"We shall try," Justice said. He reached into his jacket pocket and pulled out the two photographs of the hit man. "We're looking for this man," he explained to Mambo Jennette.

He handed the photos to her, and she looked at them and nodded. "Oh yes," she said. "This man has been turned into a zombi."

Justice had had plenty of experience with unusual powers and forces. But there was still something so alien, so distant to the concept of a man being turned into a zombi, that Mambo Jennette saw a flash of disbelief cross his face.

"It is," she told Justice and Sardi, "most unusual for *blancs* to be so afflicted, but it is possible if their belief is great. Belief, monsieurs, is everything. Come, I shall show you."

Mambo Jennette led them to the wall-less hut where the dancing and drumming was still going on. The spectators made room for them uncomplainingly. Justice and Sardi were the only outsiders present. The others were all Haitian peasants from the countryside. Their clothes were old, but clean and neatly mended. Their attitude toward Sardi and Justice was cordial, but proud.

The dancers whirling counterclockwise around the central pole were all amazingly athletic in their agile leaps and rapid pirouettes. Suddenly one dancer broke from the rhythm of the dance and stood in place, her bare feet pawing at the ground as if she were a bull getting ready to charge. She was a young woman, tall and thin, but with lithe, graceful musculature on her legs and arms. Her hair was short and tightly curled, her skin was the color of coffee with plenty of cream. Her face was beautiful, with fine, starkly sculptured features.

One of the drums caught the rhythm of her pawing,

and accompanied her in a wild, staccato burst of energy as her muscles shook and pulsed as if she were in the grip of a great spasm.

She finally started to move again, whirling about rapidly in small circles that brought her closer and closer to the fire that burned at the foot of the hut's central post. Suddenly she bent over and thrust her hands into the fire. Justice made a spasmodic move toward her, with visions of her smooth flesh shriveling and blackening in the heat, but Mambo Jennette laid a hand on his arm and murmured, "Watch. Just watch, and you shall witness the strength a believer has."

No one else seemed overly concerned that the dancer was about to burn herself horribly. She drew two burning branches out of the fire and brandished them over her head, slapping them together to the beat of the drums and ignoring the shower of sparks that sprinkled down on her. She began first to caress, then kiss, their glowing ends.

The heat didn't affect her at all. Finally she bit off the end of one stick and danced around with the glowing ember held between her teeth as Justice and Sardi watched, amazed.

"The *loa*," Mambo Jennette explained, "are strong, and when your belief in them is strong, nothing can harm you. But if you believe in their goodness, you must also believe in the evil that sometimes surrounds them. That is what happened to the man in the photograph."

"Amazing—" Justice began, but turned suddenly at a commotion sounding from the outer edge of the crowd. There was the sound of running feet, then screams and yells, and sudden, hard thuds as if someone were chopping wood.

"What's happening?" Justice asked Mambo Jennette.

She turned eyes full of hate and anger upon him. "*Zobops!*" She spat the word as if it were a curse. "Henchmen of the *bokor* have come to break up our ceremony."

She rushed off into the night, toward one of the other structures in the *hounfour* compound.

"*Bokor?*" Justice asked.

"Evil sorcerer," Sardi reminded him. "A wizard who has twisted voudou for his personal gain."

"We'd better get back to the station wagon," Justice said above the yells and screams, and Sardi nodded.

They headed away from the hut. By now the drumming and dancing had stopped, and everyone was running back and forth in sudden, useless panic. Justice and Sardi made their way through the dark shoulder to shoulder, with Lucien bringing up the rear. They could see figures with machetes racing through the *hounfour*, attacking Mambo Jennette's people, and Justice gritted his teeth, wishing that he had a gun, or a knife, or a weapon of any sort.

Someone, he reasoned, was leading this attack, probably from safety outside of the sanctuary, and getting to the leader might be the fastest way to end it.

They rushed through the break in the tree ring. The guardian of the portal was slumped over, dead at his post, his head and right arm hacked from his body with savage, jagged cuts. The head, eyes open and mouth twisted into a horrible parody of a smile by death-rictus, had been stuck on a low-hanging tree branch. Justice, incensed at the brutality of the man's death, burned with rage. He rushed out into the open night and stopped to stare at a scene right out of hell.

A knot of men stood in a loose circle around Lucien's battered station wagon, most of them bearing torches whose guttering flames lent a flickering unreality to the scene. But the torchbearers were not, strictly speaking, men. Justice realized immediately that these were zombis, like the creature Jenks had battled in Florida.

Jenks had told Justice and the others all about his encounter, and Mambo Jennette had blandly claimed that such creatures existed, but seeing them himself, for the first time, made Justice's stomach turn.

It wasn't fear, exactly, that made Justice queasy, but the undeniable confirmation that such a horrible thing could be done to living, breathing, thinking beings. They had been transformed into will-less automatons, standing stiffly, staring blankly, waiting only to hear, then carry out, the orders of their evil master who stood in their midst.

Justice recognized him immediately. Tall, one-eyed, fat, and mean, it was Colonel Moreau just as Jenks had described him. Only now he was wearing plain fatigues without medals or insignia, as he leaned indolently against the hood of Lucien's battered station wagon.

Moreau looked right at him, the dancing torches casting shifting shadows over his evil face so that he looked like the prince of demons presiding over the courts of hell.

"You have stuck your nose where it doesn't belong, Monsieur Lambert," he told Justice, "and no good will come of it." He shrugged. "Most unlucky of you to be here."

"What are you doing?" Justice demanded. "What do you want?"

"I want these people dead," Moreau informed them blandly. "And since you are with them, I have no choice but to kill you too." He stood up straight and said something in Creole, gesturing at Justice and Sardi, and the squad of zombis began to advance, as slowly and as implacably as death.

"Maybe this will be the place," Kim said, hobbling on her high heels.

"It'd better be, darlin'," Jenks said. "You're getting tipsy."

"You trying to get me drunk or you trying to track down this fellow in the photograph?"

"I know what would be more fun—but why don't we save that for later?"

"Maybe," Kim said, smiling enigmatically, "you'll get your chance."

Jenks smiled back as he held the door open for her. Inside it was like the other high-class Port-au-Prince bars they'd already been to. It was dark and hot and not very crowded. The drinks, Jenks already knew, would be expensive and watered, the bartenders either ignorant of what they needed to know, or afraid to speak to them.

Jenks and Kim went up to the bar—nearly deserted, as usual—and ordered the same drinks—which were watered, as usual. Jenks took a sip and sighed. He put the glass down and motioned to the bartender.

"Looking for a friend of mine," he said, monotony making his story shorter and shorter each time he told it. "Seen him before?"

Jenks showed him the photo and had almost put it back in his pocket before he realized that the bartender was nodding. Kim grabbed his hand and stopped him from putting the photo away. "Then, you *have* seen this man?" she asked.

"Oh, sure," the bartender said. "He used to come in here near every night. Hasn't been in for a while, though."

Jenks and Kim smiled at each other. "Whoo-eeee," Jenks said jubilantly. He pushed his drink away. "Bring us a bottle of the good stuff, and leave the water behind." He handed the bartender a hundred-*gourde* note. The man pocketed the bill and nodded happily.

"Now," Jenks said, when he'd returned with a bottle of Jack Daniels and a couple of glasses. "What about this fellow?" He poured himself a shot, downed it, and looked at the bartender.

"I thought you said he was a friend of yours," the bartender said suspiciously.

"Why, he is," Jenks said. "And so's he." He gave the bartender a peek at another hundred-*gourde* note. "I've got a lot of friends."

The bartender only nodded again, then Jenks poured himself another shot, leaving the bank note uncovered on the bar. When he looked down after drinking the shot, the note was gone and the bartender was studiously polishing a nonexistent spot on the gleaming wood counter.

"He's a tough guy," the bartender said without looking at Jenks or Kim. "And he works for a *really* tough dude. Colonel Moreau."

Kim and Jenks exchanged glances. "Moreau, again," Jenks said. He poured himself another shot and left another bill on the table, and it disappeared again.

"Moreau is one bad fellow. He's head of the SD, the *Service d'Information*."

"Secret police?" Jenks asked.

The bartender nodded again. "And more. People say he deals in drugs."

Jenks snorted. "Tell me something I don't know."

"He's a *bokor*, an evil sorcerer. He has the power to double."

"Double?" Kim asked.

"Be in two places at once," the bartender said seriously, "and he can also turn himself into a big black dog."

Jenks laughed aloud. "Sure. And I can turn into a wolf myself."

He made a grab at Kim, who laughed and slipped backward off her stool. Her giggling stopped, though, when she bumped into something as she backed away from Jenks. She felt behind herself with her hand and quickly realized she was grabbing a man's crotch. She let go and turned to see a man, no taller than herself, dressed in a khaki military uniform with lots of gold braid and chicken salad on his chest. He had a large band-aid on his forehead, apparently covering a recent wound.

Three other men dressed in the informal uniform of sharkskin suit, porkpie hat, stood behind him. All wore big, dark sunglasses, which were weirdly menacing in the dimly lit bar. The sunglasses made them look like soulless automatons without human emotion.

The men weren't looking at her, but were staring—as far as she could tell—at Jenks, who was still sitting on a bar stool.

"So, we meet again," the short man said to Jenks.

Jenks knocked back another shot and shook his head. "Why did I just know you were going to say that?"

Shorty's lips curled slightly. "We are in my country now, and we will do things my way. What did you do with my *cocomacaques*?"

"Your what?"

"My walking stick."

"Oh, that," Jenks said. "Well, I was playing stick-fetch with my dog, and he chewed it all to hell. Too bad too. It was one fine-looking stick."

"This is not the time or place to mock me, *blanc*." Shorty turned his attention to the bartender, who was visibly trembling. "What," he asked the bartender, "did you tell them?"

"Nothing, *mon capiten*, nothing."

"You're lying," Shorty said flatly.

He turned and looked at one of the goons behind him, who suddenly produced a sawed-off shotgun from under his coat, leveled it at the bartender's chest, and without word or change of expression, pulled both triggers.

The dual shotgun blasts sounded like bombs exploding. The bartender was struck in the chest and catapulted backward into the shelves of liquor, shattering the mirror behind the bar and bringing down most of the bottles to smash on the floor.

The rest of the customers ran screaming from the room. Jenks leapt to his feet and shouted, "Someone call the police."

Shorty looked at Jenks expressionlessly and said, "But *monsieur*, we are the police," as one of his goons went around the bar to check the bartender's body.

The man rifled the corpse's pockets, careless of the blood and gore soaking his clothes, and held up the three hundred-*gourde* notes Jenks had given him.

Shorty sniffed. "The man was lying. He was obviously in the pay of foreign agents sent to foment dissension."

The goon came out from behind the bar, stopping first to stuff a few unbroken bottles of liquor into the bulging pockets of his voluminous coat.

"You will come with us," Shorty told Jenks, "where it will be my great pleasure to question you. And you also, mademoiselle," he added, running the back of his hand down Kim's jawline and farther down her neck.

Jenks made an abortive move toward their tormentor, and two double-barreled, sawed-off shotguns swiveled to follow him.

Kim said in a low, urgent voice, "Don't do it. Don't make it worse."

"Excellent advice," Shorty said. "Let us go."

"What kind of place is this?" Jenks ground out through clenched teeth.

Shorty turned and looked at him. "Why, it is my place, where I do whatever I want. For you, *blanc*, I should say that it will be hell."

IX.

Justice and Sardi were outnumbered, outgunned, and nearly surrounded. They did the only thing they could do. They ran.

They turned and ducked back through the break in the tree circle, hoping to find weapons or at least allies in the fight against the zombis. What they found was pandemonium and terror.

Zombis had forced their way through the protective circle of trees, ignoring branches and thorns that ripped their desiccated flesh and tore their ragged clothing. Armed with machetes, they had surrounded the *hounfour*. Mambo Jennette's people were surprised and unarmed. There were quite a number of women among them. Everyone seemed terrified of the emotionless killing machines stalking them in the night, and Justice couldn't blame them.

He suddenly found himself face-to-face with a shirtless man holding a machete. The meat of his left cheek had been torn open from lip to ear, but he showed no sign of awareness of the bloodless wound. He advanced methodically on Justice, his rusted, blood-encrusted machete held high.

"Get out of my way," Justice warned, "or I'll break you."

But talking to the zombi was useless. He either didn't understand or totally disregarded Justice's threat. He kept on coming and, when in range, swung the machete at Justice.

The zombi stood only to the middle of Justice's chest and was thin to the point of frailness. But Justice, as he blocked the blow with his forearm against the creature's wrist, was astonished at its strength. Justice stepped back out of his foe's shorter reach and jabbed a solid right to its jaw, but the zombi didn't go down. It was like punching an unfeeling block of wood.

The zombi raised the machete again, and Justice, desperate for a weapon, grabbed its thin wrist and tried to pry the blade away. They wrestled in the dark. Justice was worried that some of the creature's friends might attack from the side, but it seemed that the zombis, though strong and implacable, were not very intelligent. From what Justice could see of the battles swirling around him, they did not team up on opponents except by sheer chance. Nor did they attempt to attack from an advantageous position, except again by chance. They simply blundered on straight ahead, slashing at anything that moved, sometimes even fellow zombis.

Observing the enemy and formulating tactics was all well and good, Justice told himself, but it wasn't doing anything to get him out of this jam.

The zombi was incredibly stronger than it had any right to be, and Justice realized that grappling it had been a mistake. But there was nothing he could do to remedy that now. They wrestled on, Justice desperately holding its machete wrist. The zombi was pushing him backward toward the wall-less hut where the dancing had taken place. The fire before the central post still burned, casting a fitful light over the pitiful scene.

Nearly a score of bodies, men and women both, lay on the dirt floor of the dancing hut, mutilated and still bleeding from multiple machete slashes. Some of the zombis' victims were moaning and trying to crawl away, but most were dead, hacked beyond recognition by the zombis, who seemed to have a feeble grip on the difference between dead and living foes.

Justice, struggling desperately with his tireless enemy, was beginning to think he might be joining the zombis' other victims himself in a few minutes. He grit his teeth and heaved against his opponent, trying to get leverage with his superior height and weight, but nothing seemed to work.

The zombi's fingers bit into Justice's flesh like claws. Its touch was utterly repugnant. Justice felt as if he were holding hands with a dead thing. He suddenly pulled, rather than pushed, against the strength of the zombi, and for a moment triumph soared through Justice as his foe started to go down.

The triumph, though, was short-lived. The zombi, with the unthinking stubbornness of a dead thing, refused to relinquish its grip, and they both fell heavily to the ground. Justice felt a sudden explosion of pain as he landed on the zombi, and all the air burst from his lungs. Gasping for breath, Justice twisted and drove his knees into the zombi's groin, but still his opponent showed no expression, no sign that it felt pain. The creature rolled atop Justice and pushed down on its machete which hovered above Justice's throat.

Gasping for breath that wouldn't come, Justice thrashed about on the ground, but couldn't break the zombi's supernaturally strong grip. The machete slipped down closer and closer to Justice's throat, until the rusty, blood-clotted blade was only millimeters away.

Justice closed his eyes, mustering strength for a final supreme effort, when suddenly the zombi made a strange, guttural moaning sound and stopped pushing on the blade.

Justice opened his eyes and saw the girl who had danced with the fire sweep by, tossing a handful of white, grainy powder over them. Justice instinctively tried to pull away from it, but it fell over his face and he realized that she was sowing salt, plain simple salt.

The zombi tried to pull away from him, making piteous moaning sounds like an animal in distress. Where the salt had struck its face and bare chest were deep, bloodless holes, as if it had been splashed by a powerful acid.

Justice jerked the machete away, and stared at his foe for a long moment as it pitifully raked its bare flesh with its powerful, bony fingers. Then, moved more by mercy than hate or fear, Justice struck at its neck with the machete. Justice struck again and again with the dull blade, and finally the zombi's head flopped to the ground. Blood oozed sluggishly from the jagged column of its bisected neck.

The rest of the body remained kneeling for a long moment, the hands aimlessly fluttering over the bare chest, while the eyes in the severed head stared and the lips writhed like worms. Justice could swear that the creature was trying to speak.

He wondered if the thing was trying to bless or curse him.

He stood and ran a shaky hand through his hair. Mambo Jennette, also carrying a basket filled with salt, came up to him.

"Not many men," she said, "can boast of having battled a zombi and won."

Justice shook his head. "I wouldn't have won if the girl hadn't poured salt over it."

"She simply aided your fighting spirit. Without it you would have been long dead."

Justice looked around him at the carnage that littered the sacred space of the *hounfour*. "Why the attack?" he asked.

"The Bizango—my secret society—is enemy of the *bokor* Moreau, and his zombi and *zobop* allies. They try to destroy my *hounfour* and crush the spirit of my people, but they shall not succeed!"

Justice nodded wearily. He stared over the battlefield, where Mambo Jennette's people had driven away their enemies with salt and more mundane weapons like picks and shovels and other farm implements. Now they were trying to help the wounded. As Justice looked over the pitiful scene, Lucien rushed up, a stricken look on his face.

"Monsieur Justice, it is terrible, terrible—" he babbled.

"What?" Justice asked.

Lucien took a deep breath. "Monsieur Sardi," he blurted. "The *zobops* have taken him!"

"I'm getting tired of counting the bugs crawling on your wall," Jenks told the man sitting at the desk. But the police clerk remained as silent as he'd been ever since Jenks and Kim had been brought to the station by Captain Shorty and his goon squad.

Jenks and Kim were in what they guessed was a police station somewhere in Port-au-Prince, but they had no idea exactly where. So far they hadn't been badly treated during their ordeal, if you discounted a few pushes and some curses hurled their way. But Jenks was getting tired of the whole thing. As soon as they had arrived at the station, they'd been told to stand and face the wall. It seemed like they'd been staring at the wall forever, but quick glances at his wristwatch told Jenks it was actually only several hours.

Finally, from the edge of his peripheral vision, Jenks saw the man sitting at the desk move. There was a commotion at the door, and the man leapt to his feet with more energy than he'd displayed all the time Kim and Jenks had been shut up in the room with him. Jenks saw him come to rigid attention, and he had the sudden realization that the arrival of these people might not exactly be good news for him and Kim.

And he was right.

He heard someone walk up behind him, but kept staring straight ahead at the wall. Whoever it was stopped behind him and touched him lightly on the shoulder with what felt like the walking stick that some of the Haitians fancied.

"Hello again, Mr. Jenks," a deep, gruff voice said. "You may turn and face me."

Jenks did, and was not happy with what he saw. It was Albert Moreau, eye patch and all, dressed in a khaki military uniform with twice as much chicken salad on his chest as Shorty, who was standing behind him wearing an evil-looking grin. Besides his polished walking stick, Moreau was also holding Jenks's Haven passport.

Moreau reached out again with his walking stick and laid it lightly on Jenks's shoulder. "We have met before, have we not, Mr. Jenks."

"Well," Jenks drawled, "I don't believe we were ever formally introduced."

Moreau's face remained expressionless. "You weren't

so polite the other day in my place of business where you . . . harassed . . . my men."

Jenks shrugged.

"And then later that night the plant belonging to the corporation I work for burned to the ground. Interesting coincidence, wouldn't you say?"

Jenks shrugged again, and Moreau smiled for the first time. Jenks didn't like the looks of that smile. It had nothing of good humor in it. It was pure, obscene evil.

Moreau's eyes flickered over to Kim, who was still facing the wall, and then suddenly and unexpectedly he raised his walking stick and slashed Jenks on the shoulder. Jenks managed to control himself, not even flinching at the sharp pain from the blow.

Moreau's smile only grew wider, and he nodded in approval. "I see that you are what is called a tough guy. I like tough guys. It takes much to make them whimper. Even when they are stone-faced, I know they are hurting, and I like that too."

He raised his stick again, but Jenks put out a large hand and caught the baton before it could smash into his face. The rod made a loud, meaty thunk when he caught it, but the unexpected gasp that rose up among those watching was even louder.

Moreau glared at him with eyes that bugged out of his head. He was so astonished that he made no attempt to pull his stick from Jenks's grasp.

Jenks stared back. "You get one free hit, Porky," he told the colonel. "The rest are gonna cost."

Moreau suddenly came alive. He tried to jerk his baton away from Jenks, but Jenks was ready. He had a firm grip, and he wasn't letting go.

For a moment they stood toe to toe, struggling over the stick. Moreau's face turned even darker, Jenks thought more from anger than exertion. The struggle continued until Moreau gasped, "Henri!" in a strangled voice, and Shorty stepped forward.

Jenks heard the "clack-clack" of a pistol being cocked, and he let go of the rod. Moreau stumbled from the sudden lack of resistance, caught himself, and straightened his uniform coat. He looked at Jenks with eyes that shone with pure anger.

"You are a tough guy," he growled like an aroused animal. "It would be a pleasure to break you, bone by bone by bone until you are howling for mercy that will never come." Jenks met his gaze unflinchingly, and Moreau caught his breath and seemed to bottle his anger. "But there may be a better way," he suddenly said.

He turned to Kim, who'd been watching as best she could from the corner of her eye. He towered over her like a giant. "You travel with a beautiful woman," Moreau said.

He touched the calf of her right leg with his stick and slowly moved the head of it upward in a caressing sweep over her thigh. The tip of the stick disappeared under the hem of her dress, and Moreau forced it up higher, hiking the dress up with it, to the juncture of her thighs.

Kim stiffened under the obscene assault, but neither said anything nor turned around to confront her tormentor.

"A most beautiful woman," Moreau said, and he turned to look at Jenks. He laughed at the look on Jenks's face, a low, rumbling laughter that sounded as if it came from the pits of hell. "You are not so tough, after all," Moreau said. "I just have to know in what manner to strike you."

"You keep that up much longer," Jenks said in an even, conversational tone, "and you'll have to kill the both of us, right here and now. I'm betting you can't do that just yet. I'm betting that right now you've got orders not to mess with the foreigners too badly. You want to call me on that bet?"

While his voice was calm, everyone in the room knew that he was ready to leap among them to certain death. Everyone looked to Moreau for guidance.

He was staring at Jenks. "You would force my hand, wouldn't you?" he asked. "You think you are smart as well as tough?" He stared at Jenks for a moment longer, then pulled his stick away from Kim. The level of tension remained high in the room, but pulled back a little from the brink that it had been ready to tumble over.

Moreau stared at Jenks for a long time, then said unexpectedly, "Why have you come to Haiti?"

"My boss sent me here to stir up a little joint-capital venture with Lambert International."

"I don't believe you," Moreau said. "But there are others who do. Their belief keeps you alive, but I tell you this. Leave Haiti soon, or you will die. Or," he added cryptically, "even worse, you will never die."

He turned suddenly and strode from the room, pausing to fling their passports on the desk in front of the startled police clerk. His entourage followed him, Captain Shorty stopping before Jenks.

"You are in my country now, *mon*. The laws are mine, the guns are mine."

"How about the balls?" Jenks asked him. "Got any of those?"

Shorty laughed. "Joke all you want, *blanc*. I have the feeling that we shall see each other again, quite soon."

"Christ," Jenks rolled his eyes. "I know you're trying to imitate your boss and all by being menacing, but let me tell you. You ain't got the build for it."

Shorty laughed again. "We shall see," he said, and followed the others out of the room.

Jenks immediately went to Kim. "You all right, darlin'?" he asked.

She turned around and nodded defiantly. "Let's get out of here."

"Good idea."

Jenks went to the desk and picked up their passports. The clerk didn't say anything to him and wouldn't meet his eyes.

Outside there was no one on the streets. This part of the city looked dead. Banners proclaiming the remembrance of the upcoming Dominican Vespers hung limply in the still night. It was hot, and so quiet that Jenks could almost hear the sweat rolling down his body.

"Well, I guess we pushed a few buttons," he said.

"You guess!" Kim said in exasperated tones, clinging to him just for the feel of a human touch.

"Good thing someone's keeping Moreau on a short leash, though I wouldn't expect that to last too long." He looked up and down the empty street. "Think we should have asked him for a ride back to the hotel when we had the chance?"

"He would have given us a lift right to the cemetery," Kim said.

"I guess," Jenks replied. He looked around the deserted street. "Well, I think it's a little early to turn in. Want to visit some more Lifeline property?"

"Why not?" Kim said. "We might stir up some real excitement."

X.

PÉTIONVILLE, HAITI
30TH SEPTEMBER—9:35 P.M.

"Did you find him?" Justice asked desperately.

Lucien shook his head. "No, sir, I am sorry. Monsieur Sardi has vanished."

Justice looked out worriedly over the *hounfour* compound. It looked more like a battlefield than an area consecrated for religious services. Mambo Jennette's men had set half a dozen fires in trash cans to light the gory scene while they carried off the dead and tended the wounded. There were few of the latter. Moreau's zombi force had hacked to death most of Mambo Jennette's people who hadn't been able to fight back or escape.

"He has to be around here somewhere," Justice said.

Mambo Jennette, accompanied by two male *houngans*, came up to Justice and shook her head. "The *bokor* must have taken him as a hostage."

"*Bokor?* You mean Colonel Moreau."

Mambo Jennette nodded. "He is a very dangerous man. Very powerful."

"Who is he?" Justice asked.

"In the government at Port-au-Prince he is head of the SD—the *Service d'Information*."

"The secret police?"

"Yes. You see, the government always has an arm to terrorize and control the people. When we had Duvaliers, father and son, there was the *tonton macoute*. Their organization was officially disbanded when General Belloc took over, but many *macoutes* are still powerful men. And the general had his own thugs that he organized into the SD."

"I thought Antoine Voltaire disbanded the SD when he became president," Justice said.

Mambo Jennette sighed. "And General Belloc reinstated them when he deposed President Voltaire. You see, President Voltaire was Belloc's picked man for the sham elections we had last year. Voltaire is a small, nonviolent academician, and Belloc mistook his smallness for weakness, his nonviolence for cowardice. Belloc thought that he would be easy to control. Voltaire, for his part, let the general think what he wanted to think. The professor planned all along to pursue social and economic reform once he was in power long enough, but he made his move too soon. His power base collapsed, he was betrayed by his friends, and General Belloc removed him from office and, for the 'good of the country,' resumed governing Haiti himself."

"What happened to Voltaire?" Justice asked.

"No one knows," Mambo Jennette said, shrugging her massive shoulders. "He supposedly obtained political asylum at the Venezuelan embassy, but the ambassador has denied that he was ever there. Some say," she said, "that Moreau took him for torture and sacrifice."

"Tell me more about Moreau."

One of the *houngans* with Mambo Jennette spit at the sound of his name. "He is lower than a dog."

Mambo Jennette agreed. "He is an evil, evil man. He thinks only of making money. He deals in drugs with the Colombians. He sells tainted blood to hospitals, for which he has earned the nickname the Dracula of the Caribbean. He even steals bodies from funeral homes to sell to foreign medical schools.

"Yet the power of the *loa* runs strongly in him. They say that he can double himself—that he can be in two places at the same time. And also that he can turn into a big black dog who can run unseen through the night."

"Tell me, Mambo Jennette," Justice said, "would your Bizango Society fight him if you could?"

"If we could," she said. "My power is as strong as his, stronger even, for it is rooted in good, not evil. But my people must fight every day for the basic needs of life. We must fight for the clothes on our backs, for decent food to eat, even water to drink. Such a fight wearies my people. They have no strength to draw on, except for their faith. And faith is useless against automatic weapons when all you have to back it up are a few shotguns and hunting rifles. And his zombis! You yourself have seen firsthand what potent soldiers they make."

"Was what you told me earlier a sham?" Justice asked quietly.

"A sham?"

"You told me that I needed faith to understand and believe in you. That your people have faith so strong that they can dance in fire and kiss burning coals without harm. Does your faith serve you any less against the *bokor* and his zombis?"

"My faith is great," Mambo Jennette said. "But I know also that it is not wise to goad the *loa* to perform impossibilities. Some of my people may well believe that the *loa* can shield them from bullets. I would not lead such faithful hearts hopelessly to their deaths."

Justice smiled grimly. "I can supply you with hope, in the form of all the weapons and ammunition you need. If you promise to help me find Sardi, I can give you whatever you need to defeat the *bokor*."

Mambo Jennette's eyes gleamed. "If you promise to do that, Monsieur Justice, not only will the Bizango find your friend, we will also wipe the evil of the *bokor* from the face of the earth. This I swear."

Justice nodded. He believed her because her words rang with sincerity and simple truth. And he had to believe her, because it was only with her help that he had a hope of finding Sardi.

He thought about it all the way back to Port-au-Prince, castigating himself for allowing Sardi and the others to accompany him on what was essentially a personal mission.

If Sardi had been hurt—or worse, killed—that was one more price the man he hunted would have to pay. And, human, zombi, or whatever, Justice would make him pay.

"Keep an eye out for the watch-zombis," Jenks warned Kim. "They can be real nasty buggers."

"Not half as nasty as you," Kim said as she ducked through the hole in the fence.

This Lifeline facility was different from the one in Florida and the office center in Port-au-Prince. Located on the outskirts of town, it stood fenced off among a group of fallen-down warehouses. It was a vast expanse of naked, level asphalt, broken and cratered and scarred by weeds punching up through its surface, with a trio of ancient Quonset huts surrounded by nearly a score of railroad cars.

A single yellowish light burned feebly above the door of the middle hut. The rest of the facility was draped in darkness, though the moon cast a glimmering, silvery light when it wasn't obscured by the drifting clouds.

As Kim and Jenks approached the cluster of huts and railroad cars, they could hear the hum of electrical generators hulking in the darkness next to the huts. Cables ran from the generators to the railroad cars. They were opening the door of the nearest car, when the zombi guard stepped out of the shadows that surrounded it and stalked toward them with steady, measured steps.

Kim made a face. "Ugh. Ugly mothers, aren't they."

"This'n seems no worse than most," Jenks said.

He and Kim stood next to each other, about two feet apart. As the zombi approached, his head swiveled so that his empty eyes stared first at Jenks, then at Kim.

"We've got him confused, darlin'," Jenks said. "He doesn't know which one of us to go after."

"Let's move apart," Kim suggested, and they separated a few more feet.

This seemed to trigger the dull mental processes that

flickered in the zombi's brain. He looked at them both again, then started to move after Kim, who kept backing away at the same pace. After a moment, all of the creature's attention was focused on her, and Jenks had sneaked up behind him.

"Like shooting fish in a barrel," he muttered, drawing his boot knife (the only weapon he'd been able to bring in through Haitian customs) and slipping it into the back of the zombi's neck, severing its spinal cord.

The creature managed another step before it realized what had happened, then it went down like a puppet whose strings had been cut. It collapsed in a heap on the asphalt and feebly attempted to move, though all it could manage were spastic contortions of its torso, which soon ceased.

Jenks slipped the knife back into its sheath, and Kim sidled around the creature, who followed her every movement with its staring eyes until she was out of range.

"It's not dead yet," she said, and Jenks shook his head.

"I don't know about that. It was prob'ly dead when we first laid eyes on it. Come on, let's check out these railroad cars."

The sliding door of the first car was pulled shut, but it wasn't locked. Jenks slid the door open on its tracks, and a blast of cold air struck them, billowing out of the railroad car like a fresh arctic blast.

Jenks got out his pocket flashlight and thumbed it on. The car was packed with tall plastic bags, dangling from rods set in the ceiling. They went into the car to get a better look, and Jenks shone his flashlight directly on one of the bags.

A dead face with vacant, open eyes stared back at them.

"Jesus," Jenks said. "Frozen stiffs. Must be a hundred of them."

"And there's at least twenty of these cars."

"Two thousand bodies on this lot," Jenks calculated, "if all the cars are as full as this one. This must be where they keep the bodies before shipping them to Florida. The ones they use to smuggle cocaine."

"I wonder where they get all the bodies," Kim said.

"Don't ask."

They stopped to stash the zombi in the back of the refrigerated railroad car before breaking into the Quonset huts. The zombi watched them with wide-open, rolling eyes as they dragged it into the corner of the car and left it lying in a heap. Jenks felt a stab of pity as its unblinking eyes stared at him.

"It's like leaving a wounded deer suffering," he told Kim.

She nodded. "Isn't there anything you can do?"

Jenks shrugged. "I don't know. Let's see."

He hunkered down before the creature and slipped his knife from its ankle sheath. The zombi stared at him emotionlessly as Jenks slipped the knife between its ribs and into its heart.

Jenks pulled the knife from the wound, cleaned a minute amount of blood off the blade, and put it away. The zombi stared at Jenks for what seemed a long time, then its gaze lengthened, turned even glassier. Jenks stood.

"Well," Jenks said, "at least we know these babies can die."

Kim nodded and rubbed her arms vigorously. "I'm getting goose bumps, and it's not just from the cold. Let's get out of here."

The Quonset huts were all empty. One was set up as a rest place, with a couple of cots, some broken-up furniture, and a grimy coffeepot. Another had a pile of coffins stacked haphazardly in it. The coffins ranged from fancy jobs to plain pine boxes, and some of them were no bigger than orange crates. They were all empty.

The hut in the middle was an office. It lacked the luxury of the other Lifeline offices Jenks had been in, but to make up for that it had a lot more paper lying around in disorganized piles.

Jenks glanced through some of the papers and scratched his head. "I'm afraid that my French isn't up to this. What're they saying here?"

Kim took them from Jenks. "Bills of sale and lading, mostly. For bodies. It looks like they buy them from hospitals." She scanned through them rapidly. "But not in the number they have stashed here."

She sat down at the desk and rifled through the drawers until she found an ancient, battered account book. She shook her head as she flipped through the pages. "What ghouls," she said, suppressing a shudder.

"What is it?"

"Here," she said, slapping the account book, "are their full body accounts. Not only do they buy them from hospitals, but it seems that they go to morgues, funeral homes, and even police stations on a regular route. They've bribed attendants and officials to look the other way while they pick up bodies and bring them here."

"You mean someone could be at the funeral home ready to send off Uncle Charlie, and when they open the casket, he's not there?"

Kim nodded.

Jenks shook his head. "That's cold. That's really cold. Stealing corpses."

Kim flipped through more papers. "Apparently they send the bodies to the airport—"

"Where they most likely add the cocaine," Jenks added.

"—then ship them to the Lifeline plant in Florida, where they retail them to medical schools and universities all over the world."

"First taking out the cocaine."

Kim nodded. "I don't imagine bodies from Haiti get a very close look going through customs nowadays."

"Well, we've got this part of the operation nailed down. Tomorrow we'll visit the airport and scope out the rest of it." He leered at Kim. "Want someone to protect you from the zombis tonight?"

"I think I could use a whole squad of zombis to protect me from you, dirty man."

As they left the Quonset hut there was a commotion at the front gate.

"What is it?" Kim hissed.

"A bunch of vans," Jenks said. "They're stopping at the gate. Shit! They're coming in. It looks like a big delivery."

"We've got to hide," Kim said.

They looked around desperately, and at the same time both had the same thought.

"In a railroad car," they said together.

"Good idea," Jenks said. "Which one?"

"A full one," Kim said. "And a nearby one," she added as the vans approached with their headlights pushing back the night.

The first one they checked was almost full of corpses.

"This'll do," Jenks grunted.

"It'll have to, they're almost here," Kim said, pushing him inside.

They pulled the door closed after them. It was black as an underground cave at midnight, smelly as an embalming room, and cold as an ice-cube tray.

Jenks flicked on his flashlight. "Over there," he pointed. "Get in the corner so no one will see us."

Kim nodded and followed Jenks into the far dark corner of the railroad car. Jenks sat down with his back against the wall, and she joined him, nestling in the crook of his arm. Jenks turned off his pocket flashlight, and it was totally dark.

They sat huddled together for what seemed an eternity, then the door to the car was flung open from the outside. They heard numerous jabbering voices, and then the unloading of bodies.

They pushed as far into the darkness as they could and no one seemed to notice them. After a burst of activity the door slammed shut again.

Jenks and Kim sat silently in the darkness for another eternity, then Kim said, "Do you think they're gone?"

"I don't know, Kimmie darlin'. They're probably screwing around with the other cars."

"I'm cold," she said after another moment.

"Me too," Jenks said.

He heard the rustling of clothes, then Kim pressed against him.

"Warm me," she said.

He reached out in the darkness and touched a soft, firm, naked breast, its nipple stiffened by the cold.

Jenks groaned. "Kimmie, darlin', this isn't the place."

"We must warm each other," she said. "I am cold, so cold."

"You feel hot to me," Jenks muttered, but her fingers unbuttoning his shirt did feel chilled, and when she pressed her bare chest to his, her skin was as cold as ice.

He slipped his shirt around her bare shoulders as her mouth sought his. Her tongue was warm and moist as it probed his mouth.

"Warm me," she moaned again into his mouth, and Jenks did the best he could.

XI.

SOMEWHERE IN THE HAITIAN
COUNTRYSIDE
1ST OCTOBER—12:17 A.M.

Sardi awoke to a steady, pounding rhythm and an aching head. At first he thought the thumping was in his head; then he realized that it was simply the continual jolting of the vehicle in which he was stretched out on the backseat. They were clearly riding on a very bad road.

He touched the side of his head carefully and winced. His fingers came away with dried blood, and he suddenly remembered the fight at the *hounfour* and the empty-eyed zombi that had struck him with the flat of his machete blade. For such a wasted-looking specimen he'd struck a hard blow, and it was probably only the mass of hair under the now-missing turban that had saved Sardi's life by cushioning the machete stroke.

Now that he was awake, he wanted to know exactly where he was. He sat up, which was a mistake. An attack of vertigo seized him, as if he had a mild concussion. He squinted at the passing countryside, but could see little because it was dark.

He looked inside the vehicle and shrank back against the door when he realized that he was sharing the backseat with a zombi. A tremor of fear and outrage went through him again. The creature sitting next to him could have been a young man, but the peculiar hardness of the zombi had been stamped on his face. He seemed to have no interest in Sardi, but stared straight ahead with unblinking, seemingly unseeing eyes.

Sardi considered hurling himself out the door against which he was leaning, but his feeble hope of escape was dashed by a voice from the front seat.

"I warn you not to attempt flight," the sardonic voice said. "We are traveling on steep mountain roads at a high rate of speed, and I'm afraid you'd only hurt yourself and delay us as we stop to pick you up."

Sardi blinked blearily against the pain in his head and concentrated on the speaker. It was Moreau, grinning evilly in the darkness.

"You may try to escape," he said, "but I promise you that such an attempt will only lead to further pain. But don't take my word for it. Try. Go ahead. Try."

It was Moreau's obvious glee that convinced Sardi that an escape would be impossible. He settled back on the seat, deciding to save his strength for a more realistic escape attempt.

"Why did you kidnap me?" Sardi asked.

"Kidnap?" Moreau asked, then laughed. His laughter was unlike anything Sardi had ever heard before. It was like an animal growling deep in its throat. There was no humor in it, and Sardi could never imagine Moreau laughing at anything genuinely funny. The colonel, Sardi felt, would only laugh at something that caused someone else pain.

"We haven't kidnaped you," Moreau continued, as if he were correcting a fundamental misconception on the part of a very small child. "Not at all. In fact, we rescued you from the midst of a very dangerous leftist terrorist group. No telling what might have happened to you if we hadn't come along."

Sardi, gently probing the sore spot on the side of his head, winced. "No telling," he repeated.

"In fact," Moreau went on, "you should be quite honored by what is about to befall you. We are about to show you something no foreigner has ever seen before. It is an experimental agricultural station made possible by the farsighted leadership of our glorious leader, General Jean-Jacques Belloc."

"Agricultural station?" Sardi asked. He looked at the zombi sharing the backseat with him. The zombi had still shown no interest at all in the conversation. He just sat silent and unmoving. Sardi had a sudden sinking feeling. He thought he knew what made up the work force of this experimental agricultural station.

Moreau, though, talked on, ignoring the sudden look of horror that had spread over Sardi's face. "As you know, monsieur, we are a poor country. When Jean-Claude Duvalier and his slut of a wife departed our shores, they took much that was of value with them. They left no money to run the government. And the United States, which had been such a generous patron to the Duvaliers, has cut their foreign aid from a mighty river to a sputtering trickle that cannot begin to provide for everyone. We need to pull ourselves out of the depths with an economic revolution."

"On the backs of those?" Sardi asked, gesturing at the zombi with disgust.

Colonel Moreau shrugged. "We are a poor people. We must use what resources we have. Our soil is eroded. Our water is dirty. Our crops are thin. All we have is our people." Moreau smiled into the face of the unseeing zombi, and Sardi had the impression that he would have patted the creature on the head like a dog if it had been within reach. "Our peasants are hard workers, but not even they could perform the herculean tasks necessary to bring about this economic miracle. Not unless they were . . . changed."

"Is that what you call it?" Sardi asked. "Changed?"

Moreau shrugged again. "It is not so bad. They do not feel the heat of the sun or the bite of hunger. Their labors do not tire them. They work all day long and take their ease when the sun goes down. They neither complain about the work they did this day nor the work they have to do the next."

Sardi could not express his horror. "It is monstrous," he whispered, just as the driver started to slow down.

"Well," Moreau said, "now you'll be able to judge firsthand."

The driver slowed as they approached a thrown-together checkpoint by the side of the road. The checkpoint consisted of a tall, narrow guardstand that looked like a poorly built coffin standing on its end, and a guard sleeping curled up on the ground next to it, clutching his rifle as if it were a voluptuous woman.

"Stop," Moreau said to the driver, and the Blazer braked to a halt not five feet from the head of the sleeping guard, who slumbered on.

Moreau got out of the vehicle, his movements surprisingly graceful for a man his size, and walked around the front of the Blazer. He stood with hands on his hips watching the still-sleeping sentinel. Then, without a warning, he lashed out with his heavily booted foot and caught the guard in the ribs.

The guard finally woke. He rolled over twice and tried to bring his rifle up, but his arms got tangled in the strap. He tried to bring his rifle up just to protect himself, but Moreau, shouting in Haitian Creole, loomed over him and stamped down with all the power of his massive leg. Sardi heard ribs snap in the guard's chest as he screamed. Moreau continued to curse and stomp as Sardi watched in fascinated horror, and soon the guardsman stopped screaming. Soon after that he stopped moving.

Moreau stood over the body for a moment, his back to the Blazer. When he turned around again, he looked perfectly composed, though in the clear moonlight Sardi could see that his face was covered by a sheen of sweat.

He looked at the driver, who was watching the colonel in what seemed to be a state of rigid terror. "When we reach the compound, have another guard sent down to relieve this man."

"Yes, sir," the driver managed with a tremor of fear in

his voice as Moreau marched precisely around the front
of the vehicle and took his place in the front seat. The
driver started off, and Moreau looked to the front as if
nothing unusual had happened.

Sardi leaned against the backseat, half convinced that
the stories about Moreau were true. Even if he had no
special voudou powers, he was an evil man who killed on
a whim. He had obviously enjoyed the killing, but it also
seemed as if it were nothing special to him. He killed
like someone with a sweet tooth would eat a bowl of ice
cream. It was enjoyable enough, but once it was over,
well, it was no big deal.

He was, Sardi thought, a man to truly fear. A monster
who had to be removed from power as soon as possible.

At first, as they drove past the now-guardless checkpoint, Sardi noticed nothing different about the countryside; then he realized that for the first time while in
Haiti he was actually seeing cultivated fields. It was
difficult to tell from a moving car at night, but it seemed
as if the crops were thick and healthy.

They passed what looked like fields of sugarcane moving like a rippling sea in the gentle night breeze, and
other fields planted with subsistence crops like maize
and wheat.

It was almost enough to make Sardi believe in the
reality of Moreau's economic miracle, but then he glanced
at the emaciated wreck of a man sitting stiffly on the seat
with him, and Sardi knew that even if the miracle had
worked, it had come at too stiff a price.

They saw no one else until the jeep pulled up before a
group of buildings clustered together beyond the fields.
The buildings were nestled at the base of the foothills of
a tall mountain ridge. The ridge loomed darkly in the
night, blocking the stars of a great slice of the sky, and
somehow to Sardi it seemed ominous and threatening. It
seemed, even from this far away, that terrible things had
been done on its slopes, and that its crest held memories
of uncountable atrocities.

There was not much more to see. The buildings were
all dark except one, before which a light still burned. A
man sat smoking in a chair in front of it. He jumped up

as the Blazer pulled in front of the building and the driver killed the ignition.

Moreau turned to the driver and said, "Do as I've ordered. I'll see to the zombi."

The driver nodded and went off toward one of the dark buildings.

Moreau turned to Sardi. "All right, *monsieur*, time to get out. Do not have any illusions of running, my friend." Moreau slapped the pistol holstered on his thigh. "I am a fine shot."

Sardi got out of the vehicle and stood cautiously. His head wound made him still feel woozy, and he had no intentions of running anywhere. He leaned on the side of the vehicle for support as Moreau got out, leaned over, and opened the door by which the zombi sat.

"Out," Moreau said, and the zombi stood and climbed clumsily from the car. "Wait," he added, and the zombi stood its ground with the infinite patience of its kind.

The man who had been waiting before the building came up to Moreau. He was a black man, dressed in an immaculate linen suit.

"Well, what happened?" he asked in a voice that revealed a tense nervousness. "How did it go?"

"It went fine, my friend," Moreau growled in his unfriendly manner.

The man looked at the zombi. "Where are the others?"

"We lost many of them," Moreau said casually. "But what does that matter? There is an almost limitless supply. The Bizango cannot say the same for themselves."

"Who's that?" the man asked, glancing at Sardi.

"Ah. Our prize of the evening. He is Lambert's man."

"Lambert will come looking for him—"

"Let him," Moreau said. "Then he will be doing nothing important, eh, to interfere with our commemoration of the Vespers."

"If he finds this place—"

"You worry too much, Calloway," Moreau said in a voice that was even harder than usual. "If he finds this place, he finds it. He will never leave it alive."

Calloway, heeding Moreau's warning, clammed up.

He puffed nervously on his cigarette and watched Sardi narrowly as Moreau turned to the zombi.

"Come," he said.

The zombi started to follow him with a slow, measured tread.

"You too," he said to Sardi.

Moreau strode imperiously through the night, not looking back, Sardi and the zombi at his heels.

It burned Sardi that Moreau treated him as contemptuously as the poor, unfortunate creature he walked beside. But there was nothing he could do at this time. He could only bide his time, get stronger, and find out what he could about this horrible place, for one thing Moreau had said was true.

William Justice would come, and he would not be so easy to handle as Moreau assumed. Moreau was used to dealing with his own people, cowed by centuries of repressive totalitarian government. But Justice could not be frightened by a stern word or terrorized by a show of force. When aroused, he was an elemental force of nature unstoppable by anything human.

He would come, Sardi silently promised the stricken creature shambling by his side, and when he did, Moreau would pay.

The colonel led them to the farthest of the buildings, a large, open-sided barn with a ceiling of corrugated tin. Two armed guards patrolled the perimeter of the structure. The one walking the near side snapped a smart salute as they approached.

Moreau turned to the zombi. "Stop," he said. "Any trouble tonight?" Moreau asked the sentinel in a tone that indicated that there better not have been.

The guard shook his head. *"Non, mon colonel,"* he said.

"I want to show our workers to our guest." He turned again to the zombi. "Come."

Both the zombi and Sardi followed him to the structure. Sardi caught his breath at the sight of several hundred zombis sleeping, or resting at any rate, on orderly rows of thin rush pallets. They made no sounds in their sleep, nor did they twist or turn on their uncomfortable-looking beds. Sardi watched one for a long time before he saw it take a single, long, even breath, then lapse into perfect stillness again. They were all thin to the point of emaciation. All were dressed in rags. Some were nearly naked. Most were men, but there were some women among the zombis, their breasts shrunken to nothing, their arms and legs as thin as sticks.

Moreau pointed to an empty pallet and said to the zombi, "Sleep there," and the creature obeyed instantaneously, folding his gaunt, wasted limbs with slow precision, and closing his eyes as his head hit the thin mat.

Moreau and Sardi watched them for a moment, then Sardi looked up at the colonel. "What," he asked Moreau, "do you suppose they dream about?"

For a second Moreau looked startled at the thought, but only for a second. He shrugged and said, "The true death, perhaps? I don't know." He looked down at the zombis again for a moment, then back at Sardi. "But come. Your night's accommodations await you."

Sardi followed him to a peculiar structure that stood next to the zombi barn. Its roof and sides were tin. It had a single door, but no windows, and was as wide and deep as an outhouse, but not as tall.

The door had a padlock on it. Moreau took a large key chain out of his pocket and opened it. He pulled open the door and gestured for Sardi to enter. When Sardi got close, he was struck with a noxious stench that was almost as strong as a slap in the face. It was the smell of sweat and fear combined with excrement ripening in a hot sun.

"I regret to say that the previous occupant was not a neat man," Moreau said, "but this is the best we can do for you on such short notice." He laughed again, and his hideous gaiety sent another wave of nausea rippling through Sardi's stomach.

Sardi hesitated at the threshold, until Moreau put a heavy hand on his shoulder and forced him down on his knees and into the tiny room. It was perhaps three feet to a side and five and a half feet high. There was no way Sardi could stand upright in it, and there was barely room enough to sit. The floor was covered with human excrement and urine stains. The smell was overpowering. Sardi could taste it on his tongue. He turned and faced the door, where Moreau was smiling at him.

"I suggest you get some sleep while it is cool. The sun makes sleeping in the daytime rather difficult." Moreau started to close the door, stopped, and said, "Pleasant dreams."

For a moment Sardi stared at him, with his eyes wide and mind radiating the hypnotic power that he possessed. But either the poor light prevented it from having any effect, or Moreau was one of those strong-willed people immune to such an attack. Whatever the reason, Sardi's hypnotic powers were useless against him.

Sardi could hear Moreau's horrible laughter as he slammed the door and rammed the padlock shut.

XII.

PORT-AU-PRINCE, HAITI
1ST OCTOBER—6:03 A.M.

Justice woke up even though the man coming into his hotel room through the window was very quiet. He lay in bed wishing he had a weapon. Right now there wasn't anything more lethal in the room than the water pitcher by his bedside. Though, come to think of it, the pitcher was big and heavy and could do a fair amount of damage to an intruder's skull if placed against it with the proper amount of force. At any rate, Justice thought, it would have to do.

Justice watched through slit eyes as the man slithered through the window and crept silently to the foot of the bed. He didn't appear to be carrying any weapons, but it was difficult to tell in the predawn gloom.

Justice tensed himself to make a move for the pitcher when the man made a low, insistent hissing sound from the foot of the bed. Justice immediately revised his plans.

Burglars and assassins don't usually try to wake their victims.

"What is it?" Justice asked in a low voice without moving or opening his eyes.

"Ah, you are a quick one," the man said in English, in a very feminine voice. "Mambo Jennette was right."

"Did she send you?"

The figure scuttled around the side of the bed to its head. "Yes. We must be quiet. The walls are thin, and the government has placed men in the room next to yours."

Justice turned to face the intruder and opened his eyes. "I'm not surprised," he said.

But he was surprised to see that he was talking to a woman and not a man. Like many Haitians, Justice's intruder was rail thin, but there seemed to be more strength and resilience to this youngster than most. Her dark green eyes were full of energy and life.

"Why did you come?"

"To bring you news of your friend—and an offer from Mambo Jennette."

"What is it?"

The intruder shook her head. "Not here. Let's go outside where there are no ears."

"Okay." Justice started to slip out of bed, then stopped. "I sleep nude, you know."

The intruder giggled. "I have seen men before," she said in sophisticated tones, "but I will turn my back if it makes you feel better."

She suppressed a giggle as she turned her back, and Justice had to fight down the sudden urge to brain her with the water pitcher anyway. He slipped into the clothes lying on the chair by the bed and whispered, "All right, let's go."

The girl threw him a backward glance and gestured toward the window. She went through it confidently, and when Justice looked out, she was shinnying up the drainage pipe that ran up the wall an arm's length from the window.

Justice glanced downward to the cobbled street barely discernible below. They were on the top floor of the

hotel, three stories up, so it was a potentially killing fall
to the street. Justice watched her go up to the roof, then
look down and gesture to him, her head silhouetted
against the early morning sky.

Justice took a deep breath and reached out for the
pipe. It wasn't that he doubted his climbing ability. The
problem was that he had little faith in Haitian construc-
tion skills, especially turn-of-the-century Haitian con-
struction skills. The pipe had held the girl, but she
couldn't weigh a hundred pounds soaking wet. Justice
weight more than twice that.

She gestured at him again, impatiently, and he realized there was no halfway to this. It was all or nothing.
He swung out of the window, putting all of his weight on
the pipe. He held his breath as it buckled outward and
groaned somewhere above him. But the pipe held.

The essence of this climb, Justice decided, was speed.

He pulled himself up hand over hand as fast as he
could and tried to take as much weight off the pipe as
possible by pushing off the wall with his toes. He grabbed
the edge of the slanting roof just as the top of the
drainpipe pulled away from its uppermost brackets.

He grabbed the roof edge with his other hand, hauled
himself over the lip, and lay against the sloping roof. The
girl next to him was giggling again.

"You moved very fast, Monsieur Lambert, like a mon-
key up a banana tree."

"A tree that was ready to fall down at any moment,"
Justice said. "If Mambo Jennette really sent you, then
you'd know my true name, which I told her last night."

The girl nodded. "I shall call you Justice, then."

"Fine." Justice looked around. "This isn't exactly the
place I had in mind for a meeting."

The girl shook her head. "We shall go over the roofs.
Follow me."

Justice did. She moved with tremendous confidence
and grace, not once looking down. She was barefoot, and
her jeans were short and ragged, exposing long, lithely
muscled, dark-skinned legs. Her short-sleeved shirt was
clean and carefully mended. Her arms were as well

muscled as those of an athletic boy. In fact, she could almost pass for a boy but for the curving hips filling her jeans and her small, pointed breasts, which pushed against the thin fabric of her shirt with every step she took.

Watching her graceful stride suddenly reminded Justice where he had seen her before. She was the girl who had danced with fire at the *hounfour*, the girl who had saved his life when the zombi had him ready for the killing. He had wondered last night if he would ever get to see her again.

She led Justice across the roof of the Ollofson and over a long, narrow plank she'd placed between it and the adjacent structure. The plank bulged dangerously when Justice went over it, but held. She pulled it up after them and placed it out of sight on the roof. This building had a rickety fire escape that looked about as trustworthy as a strung-out hooker. The first landing was ten feet below roof level. The girl simply hung off the roof feet first, and dropped to the landing. It shook, but held. She motioned to Justice, and he followed, hitting the landing beside her just as the sun edged over the sea to the west.

She looked at the sun happily and smiled. "Ah, we are just in time for breakfast." She looked at Justice. "Are you buying?"

Her eyes, he saw in the light of dawn, were green. Her hair was short and worn natural. Her face was lean and aristocratic. In almost any other country, he thought, she'd be a fashion model. In Haiti she's apparently some kind of voudou revolutionary given to dancing with the gods and running about hotel roofs at dawn while cadging breakfast from strangers.

"It's the least I can do considering you saved my life last night," Justice said. "One thing, though. I never buy breakfast for anyone whose name I don't know."

"In that case," she said, smiling, "let me introduce myself. I am Marie Salomon." She dropped a graceful curtsy after saying her name.

"Charmed," Justice said, bowing himself. "Now, about breakfast."

There was a small café down the street that was just opening as Justice and Marie approached. They took chairs at an outdoor table and gave orders for coffee and croissants to the sleepy-eyed waiter.

"This must be a very popular religious holiday coming up," Justice remarked conversationally as they were waiting for their food and drink.

"Pardon?" Marie asked.

Justice gestured at the banners hanging from the buildings across the street. "The Dominican Vespers," he said. "I've seen signs about them all over the city, ever since we arrived."

Marie nodded seriously. "Oh. I see. I suppose it is a holiday of sorts, a holiday commemorating the most terrible days of this century."

"What happened?" Justice asked with a frown.

"In the past," Marie told him, "many Haitian peasants traveled all over the Caribbean to work on the sugar plantations. Dictator Rafael Trujillo of the Dominican Republic hated and despised Haitians, particularly those of dark skin. He was afraid that too many poor Haitians were coming to live in the Dominican, so he ordered them killed."

"Just like that?" Justice asked incredulously.

"Just like that," Marie replied. "The Dominican army rounded up the Haitian sugarcane workers, then, not wanting to waste bullets, clubbed and bayoneted them. In the end they herded them into the sea to feed the sharks. The Dominican Vespers, as the massacre became known, started October second. In three days thirty thousand Haitians were killed. The Haitian government did nothing about it. It is a period of great shame in Haitian history that is rarely acknowledged publicly."

Justice shook his head. The waiter arrived with their order, but somehow the steaming, rich coffee tasted like sludge, the hot, flaky croissants were like sawdust.

"Why do you suppose the government is making such a fuss about the Vespers this year?" Justice asked.

Marie put down her cup and shook her head. "I don't know. General Belloc is a beast. The people are angry. Perhaps he is trying to divert attention from himself and give the people a focus for their anger. He has been talking about the Vespers for weeks now on the radio. Perhaps they plan an anti-Dominican parade."

"Would this be enough to divert the attention of the people?"

Marie shrugged. "Perhaps. For a while. The people have a great anger that is building, building, until it must burst. The general must sense this and hope that he can turn their anger against the Dominicans for this ancient wrong, rather than him for his daily depredations."

"Clever move, if he can pull it off."

"Clever," she agreed. "But we have more important things to talk about." She put the last bit of croissant in her mouth and daintily licked the fresh fruit jam off her fingertips. "Tell me, Monsieur Justice. What do you see when you look at me?"

"A very young, very beautiful girl."

Marie flushed. "Well. That is not exactly what I meant, but it will do for a start. Mambo Jennette has told you that you must understand—and believe in—voudou if you are to understand Haiti."

"That's right," Justice agreed.

"I will be your guide to the world of the *loas*," Marie said, "and this is the first lesson. This," and she touched herself on the breast with a graceful, long-fingered hand, "is the *corps cadavre*, my body, flesh, blood, and bone. But it is only part of me, if you follow?"

"Certainly," Justice said. "There is also the mind. The soul."

She nodded. "Yes. This soul, as you call it, has four parts. The *n'ame* is the spirit that allows the body to function. This is an energy, a gift from God. When the *corps cadavre* dies, this energy passes slowly to the organisms of the soil as the *corps* gradually decomposes. The *z'etoile* is the part of the soul that resides in the heavens. It is the star of destiny, the blueprint for the soul's next life. The final parts of the soul are the *ti bon ange* and *gros bon ange*."

"Little good angel and big good angel," Justice murmured.

"Yes, that is right. The *gros bon ange* is the life force that everyone shares. It enters one at conception and keeps the body alive. At death it returns to God and becomes part of the great ocean of energy that supports all life. The *ti bon ange* is the essence of the individual. It is the source of everyone's personality and character."

"What has this got to do with voudou?" Justice asked.

"Very much," Marie told him. "It is the removal of the *ti bon ange* that makes one a zombi."

"And how is that done?"

"Through powders and prayers that I can show you. If," she challenged, "you are brave enough."

Justice drained his coffee cup and placed it carefully on his saucer. He looked at Marie seriously. "Show me," he said.

Marie nodded. "Very good. The lessons begin today."

"Fine," Justice said. He was eager to know the heart of this land and trusted Mambo Jennette enough to follow the path she decreed. "First, though," he added, motioning to the waiter, "I have to make a phone call."

The waiter approached, poured more coffee, and waited expectantly.

"Can you bring me a telephone?" Justice asked, and the waiter nodded and went off.

Justice and Marie waited. This part of Port-au-Prince, so early in a fresh, new day, seemed almost hopeful. The streets were still nearly deserted. They seemed clean. The buildings sparkled brightly with dew as the newly risen sun shone benignly over their heads.

Even the few people on the streets looked more alive and vibrant than usual. The young man walking toward them now was even wearing a Walkman and gliding gracefully to the inner music playing in his brain.

Justice took a sip of coffee and glanced at Marie. She met his eyes and smiled. She was a beautiful girl, very self-assured for one so young. Perhaps, Justice thought, when one danced with the gods, it brought about a certain inner calmness and maturity. He put his coffee cup down, and the sugar bowl behind him exploded with a terrifying loudness and unexpectedness.

Justice reacted instantly. He hooked Marie's chair with his foot and flipped it over, sending her spilling onto the patio floor. That same moment he dived off his own chair as another bullet smacked into it, blowing its back out and toppling it over.

Justice had a quick glimpse of the street, all but one of the few pedestrians on it scattering like frightened birds. The young man with the Walkman stood not ten feet away, feet braced and both hands gripping a monstrous old pistol whose barrel was aimed at Justice.

Justice rolled away as the assassin squeezed off another shot that ricocheted off the patio flooring. Justice scooped up a chair from the next table and threw it with all his strength at the assassin. The man didn't even flinch as the chair hit him high on the chest, pushing his arms up and out of line.

Justice grabbed the round metal table that had been paired with the chair he'd thrown and charged the assassin at full speed, adrenaline and anger pushing his reactions to their maximum.

The man brought the gun down and squeezed off another shot. Justice felt the bullet smash the table which he was holding out like a shield. It whined off at an angle, and then he was on his assailant.

He used the table like a battering ram and smashed his foe like a berserk fullback plowing for the goal line. The man went down, and Justice tossed aside the table and landed on him, in no mood for mercy or kindness. He grabbed the gun his assailant was trying to turn on him and twisted savagely. His massive hand closed on the grip, and he yanked at the trigger. It blasted three times before the pin clicked on an empty chamber, and Justice's unknown assailant jerked three times as he took three bullets in the upper chest.

Justice let him go. To his astonishment he saw him half rise from the pavement, point the gun at him, and uselessly pull the trigger four times. Justice looked at his face and saw the staring eyes and wooden expression.

"Zombi," he said, as his foe collapsed on the pavement, a trickle of blood seeping from the holes blown in his chest by the ancient revolver.

In sudden inspiration he plucked the headphones from the sidewalk where they'd fallen. A voice said, "Kill the *blanc*, kill the *blanc*," and then suddenly terminated.

He turned back to the patio café. Marie was looking at him worriedly, though her expression changed to jubilance

when she saw that he was all right. The waiter standing
next to her had a telephone dangling from his hand and a
look of sheer terror on his face.

Justice went up to him and took the phone. He dialed
the operator. The adrenaline had washed out of his system, but the anger was still there.

"Hello, operator?" he said. "I'd like to place an international call. Yes. To Haven. Hurry. I can't wait."

Sometime toward morning Kim and Jenks somehow
managed to fall asleep. The sound of the railroad car
sliding back on its hinges awakened them, and they
huddled together in the dark corner under their pile of
clothes.

A workman shouted to someone outside, "Load the
ones on this rack after you get the other car finished,"
and jumped back out, closing the door behind him.

Jenks looked at Kim. "You thinking what I'm thinking?" he asked.

Kim reached down and grasped his crotch. "I don't
think so," she said disappointedly.

"Stop that," Jenks ordered. "You'll get your chance
later." He looked at her near-naked form as she pulled
away from him and slipped into her black dress, the
nipples on her small, pointed breasts still erect from the
cold. Or perhaps it was the enforced closeness they
endured all night. "Right now we got to think of survival."

Jenks dressed quickly, wondering why the timing between the two of them never worked out. He knew,
though Kim had never told him, about her feelings
toward Justice, and he suspected that Justice would never
be able to reciprocate them. He didn't know exactly how
he felt toward Kim, other than that she was a fine,
beautiful woman and he'd be happy to take her mind off
Justice. Only it never seemed to work between them.
Something always came in the way, like a railroad car full
of bodies.

They didn't know how much time they had before the
workman returned, so they had to move fast. They chose
body bags near the middle of the rack. It took a few
moments to unzip them and remove the frozen corpses,

then stow the bodies in other bags toward the rear of the car.

Kim climbed into the first empty bag. "It's cold," she complained. "And it smells terrible in here."

"I know," Jenks said. On impulse he leaned forward and gave her a deep, probing kiss like the ones that had kept them warm and awake all night. He pulled away and zipped the bag up, leaving a few inches undone to allow fresh air inside. "Pretend to be stiff," he said before leaving Kim hanging in her bag.

She shook her head. "That one's too easy. I'm not saying anything."

Jenks got into the bag behind her just as he heard the door slide open. He zipped it as best he could from the inside as he heard footsteps stalk across the floor of the car. He held his breath, half in fear of being discovered, half because Kim was absolutely correct. These bags stunk like hell. Besides the stench of dead flesh, the smell of powerful chemicals, preservatives, and disinfectants predominated, chief among them a sickening, lemony rest-room odor. Great, Jenks thought, just great. When he got out of this thing, he'd smell like a damn toilet.

He tried to peer through the translucent plastic of the bag, wondering if they'd been spotted. Fighting inside a plastic baggie could prove difficult, he thought, but a couple of minutes went by without an alarm being raised, and he knew they were safe. So far.

They could hear banging and feel the overhead rack vibrate as workmen pulled the bags from the railroad car and carried them outside. When his turn came, he kept himself as rigid as possible, hoping the difference between a frozen corpse and a warm, living body wouldn't be too obvious.

It was difficult to see through the translucent material of the body bag, but Jenks suddenly realized why the man carrying him couldn't tell the difference between the living and the dead. His handler, it turned out, wasn't a man after all, but a zombi.

Five of them were doing the heavy carrying under the watchful direction of a single human supervisor. Jenks's zombi lifted him without effort, and carried him into a waiting van. The zombi laid him atop the pile of bodies they'd already stowed.

Jenks had a bad moment when they laid another bag atop him. He hated the thought of ending his career by being smothered by a bunch of stiffs. But after loading a last body into the van, the supervisor slammed the door, and the van took off. Jenks scrunched and unzipped the bag a little, and peeked out.

Fortunately he was facing toward the front. The driver was alone. He was singing loudly and off-key in accompaniment to the transistor radio that was hanging from the rearview mirror and blaring a loud, obnoxious, rap song.

Jenks took a chance and whispered, very quietly, "Kim? Kim, are you here?"

"Yes," came a hiss from below. "I'm being squashed," she said. "It's terrible."

"All right. I'm right here. Hang tight, darlin'."

"I'm not going anywhere."

They passed the rest of the trip in silence. Fortunately, it was a short one. Within half an hour the van pulled through a double gate leading to the freight section of the airport. The driver, still whistling and singing, headed directly toward a warehouse sitting by itself in one section of the terminal complex.

Jenks unzipped his bag and slowly and silently crawled out of it as the driver waved at the guard at the warehouse door and pulled the van inside.

It was a large building, full of tarp-covered piles of boxes and crates. The driver pulled over and parked next to a refrigerated locker at the rear of the building. He turned the key off and reached up to take his radio down from the rearview mirror. Just then he heard a small noise and glanced in the mirror. His eyes widened in shock and fright, and he opened his mouth to scream just as Jenks's forearm crushed against his throat.

He dropped the radio, grabbed Jenks's arm, and tried to pull it from his throat, but he might as well have tried to bend a solid-steel bar. Jenks grabbed the side of his head with his other hand and twisted savagely. There was a loud crack, and the driver jerked like a man with a live wire attached to his private parts, then was still.

Jenks pulled him out of the driver's seat and onto the pile of corpses.

"Come on out, darlin'," he called quietly. "Help me put this guy away."

Kim came out of her bag and helped Jenks with the awkward job of putting the new corpse into the bag Jenks had just vacated. Then they climbed out of the front of the van, first checking to make sure they were in the clear, dragging Kim's now-empty bag with them. They stashed it behind a stack of aluminum tins and looked around the gloomy building.

"What now?" Kim asked.

"This has to be where they store the cocaine and stuff it in the bodies before they're loaded on planes for America."

Kim nodded in agreement. "Do we try to find the dust?" she asked.

"Might as well," Jenks said, "since we're here and all. We'd better be careful, though, there's at least one guard at the front door."

"Human?" Kim asked.

Jenks shrugged. "Maybe."

They kept close as they searched through vast piles of junk, from pallets of paint to cases of medicine and crates of Uzis.

"Too bad we can't get these to Justice," Jenks murmured when they'd found them, but quickly realizing it didn't matter too much. There were plenty of guns, but not a single round of ammunition to be found.

They had searched the back half of the warehouse quietly and without interruption and were debating the wisdom of searching the half near the entrance, when the squeal of tires on the concrete warehouse floor put an end to their debate. They huddled together behind a huge crate stenciled "Farm Implements, Compliments of the People of the United States and President Eisenhower," while a huge, black limo pulled to a halt in the middle of the cleared space in the center of the warehouse.

The rear door slung open and Colonel Moreau stepped

out, nattily dressed in a business suit that had gone out of style sometime in the 1960s. Shorty was with him, dressed in his *capiten* uniform complete with his bullshit medals.

"I leave things in your hands," Moreau told Shorty, who nodded smartly. "Timing is all important, if our little commemoration of the Vespers is to go off correctly."

Shorty nodded again, and Moreau was interrupted by the arrival of a canvas-sided troop transport. They watched the troops disembark from the troop carrier. The soldiers were dressed in clean, well-pressed civilian clothes, and, oddly enough, all wore Walkmans. Jenks, staring at their jerky, not-quite-human movements, was horrified by a sudden realization.

"They're all goddamned zombis," he whispered to Kim.

For the first time they noticed a handler talking quietly into a walkie-talkie, directing them as they formed into ragged but serviceable ranks. Jenks counted quickly and tallied fifty of the creatures.

Moreau beamed at them like a proud father. "Look at them," he told Shorty. "The perfect soldiers! The perfect assassins who will kill without remorse or hesitation. The elite of my zombi force!"

"Very impressive," Shorty murmured.

"Of course they are. Have the plane brought around and start loading them in their boxes." Moreau checked his wristwatch. "I have dinner reservations in New York, but that's not until six o'clock. I think I'll have a bite to eat before boarding."

Shorty nodded smartly, and Moreau got back into his limousine, which pulled away with a squeal of tires.

Jenks tugged on Kim's sleeve and motioned for her to follow him back to the dark half of the warehouse.

"This is incredible," he said. "What do you think he's going to do with those creatures?"

"He's not taking them to New York to see the Statue of Liberty."

"We've got to get word to Willum about this," Jenks said grimly.

"Right. Let's get out of here now—"

"No time," Jenks said. "There's no time." He took

Kim by the shoulders. "You've got to get through to
Willum. I'm going to follow this . . . this zombi goon
squad to New York. I can get help there." He groaned
and shook his head. "If I can get anyone to believe me."

"I want to go with you," Kim said, but Jenks shook his
head.

"No. As much as I hate to say this, we've got to split
up and attack this problem from two fronts. That way
we'll double our chances of stopping this horror."

Kim nodded. As much as she wanted to stick with
him, she saw the wisdom of his argument.

"All right," she said. She suddenly flung herself against
Jenks, threw her arms around his neck, and pulled him
close to her. She gave him the kiss of a lifetime, her
tongue darting into his mouth, twisting and probing frantically, her firm body pressed up against his as if she
were trying to push herself through his chest.

It went on until Jenks had to pull away, gasping for
breath. "What was that for?"

"It was just to make sure you'll be careful, so you can
come back for more."

"Sounds good to me," Jenks said, reaching for her.

But Kim was already gone, fading back into the shadows, on her way to Justice.

XIII.

SOMEWHERE IN THE HAITIAN
COUNTRYSIDE
1ST OCTOBER—NOON

Sardi sat by himself in the stinking darkness. It was
bad during the night, but it got worse as soon as light
started to filter through the cracks around the door of the
poorly constructed cell.

It got hot fast on the Haitian plains, and Sardi's cell was designed to catch, hold, and magnify that heat. By early morning the temperature inside the cell was well over a hundred degrees. Sardi had thought upon entering the cell that it smelled worse than anything in the world, but he soon found out how wrong he was. Under the baking sun the odor intensified into a palpable force that seemed powerful enough to kill.

Sardi knew that he had only one defense against his cruel confinement. He settled himself cross-legged on the floor of his cell despite the filth and lack of space, smoothly pulled his legs into the lotus position, and set his mind to the task of survival. His mouth had gone absolutely dry, and every cell of his body was crying out for water, but he refused to hear that call. He breathed in the stinking odor of rotting feces with every breath, but told himself he was breathing the finest perfume. His stomach grumbled with hunger, but he told himself that he had just consumed the finest meal he had ever eaten.

It almost worked.

His powerful mind at least made tolerable an imprisonment that would have broken most men, but it was still with an overwhelming sensation of relief that he heard footsteps outside his prison, and the sound of the lock being removed. Light poured in with a blinding force as the door opened. Sardi tried to blink away his blindness, but the dancing spots remained.

"Well, come on," a voice said testily. "We haven't got all day."

Sardi rose easily out of the lotus position, his muscles still limber and flexible thanks to years of training. His vision cleared enough so he recognized the man standing before him as the one who'd been waiting for Moreau the night before. Today he was wearing white shoes, white pants, and a white shirt already stained around the armpits by perspiration. His panama hat was also white, as was the handkerchief he was holding up to his mouth.

"Christ, you stink," he said through the handkerchief.

"I do," Sardi said, "though it is not precisely my fault."

There was another man standing behind the black, but no matter how Sardi blinked or tried to shade his eyes, he could make out only that the other was a Caucasian.

"True," the black agreed. "Listen, Colonel Moreau can be pretty harsh sometimes—you know how it is in these third-world cesspools when you give a man of strictly limited mentality some power."

"I am just finding out," Sardi said with sardonicism that appeared to be lost on the other.

"Sure. Listen. I'm Robert Calloway, Lifeline Medical Supply." He held out a hand, then when he saw the filth smeared on Sardi's palms, drew it back quickly. "I'd like to make up for the rough treatment of last night. If you'll just follow me . . ."

Sardi nodded. "I would love to, but I'm afraid that I wouldn't get very far without a drink of water."

"Of course. Certainly." Calloway turned to the other man and said very distinctly, "Bring water."

Sardi's vision was clearing, and he was able to make out a young, wasted white man with the blank and terrible eyes of the zombi. The man looked familiar. Sardi's mind was still sluggish from the punishment he'd absorbed over the last twelve hours, but as the zombi shuffled away, Sardi suddenly realized who he was.

He was the man in the photo. The man they'd come to Haiti to find.

"Something wrong?" Calloway asked him. "You look like you'd just seen a ghost."

Sardi shook his head and gestured vaguely at the retreating zombi.

Calloway nodded. "Oh yes. Ghastly creatures, aren't they? Take a bit of getting used to. They're not very bright, of course, and they can be very clumsy sometimes, but still they're profitable. And the applications are nearly endless."

Sardi was aghast. Calloway might not be as thuggish as Moreau, but he was every bit as evil. The zombis he'd seen so far defined human misery, and all Calloway talked about was their profitability.

The ex-hit-man zombi came shuffling back with a rusted metal bucket and a dipper. He stopped before Sardi, who took up a cupful of water. It was hot, and particles of dirt, rust, and less identifiable things were floating in it, but Sardi knew he had to take a chance on infection. He had to get water into his dehydrated body. He drank several dipperfuls, then used the rest to wash away as much of the filth as possible.

"All better, then? Good. We have a bit of a hike ahead of us."

Calloway took the lead, staying upwind from Sardi. The zombi brought up the rear, and Sardi could feel his expressionless gaze bore into him as they passed the empty zombi barn.

"Where is everyone?" Sardi asked.

"Working," Calloway replied. "We'll go by the fields. It's really quite interesting."

The fields, as Calloway had promised, were crawling with zombis. They seemed quite capable of performing simple agricultural tasks with minimal supervision, so there was no more than a single overseer for every twenty or twenty-five zombis. They also seemed capable of nearly unceasing labor. Not once did Sardi observe one stop for even a sip of water.

"Amazing, aren't they?" Calloway asked as they passed the fields. "Tireless workers, and they require very little food. They don't even have to stop for a midday meal, though we do give them water then."

"Generous," Sardi murmured.

Calloway shrugged. "We are, really. These people are the hope of an entire country—"

"I heard Colonel Moreau's speech last night," Sardi interrupted, "and I didn't very much like it then. Those are indeed people out there in the field and not chattel animals."

"Slip of the tongue," Calloway said, correcting himself. "They're not people anymore. Not really. According to Moreau their souls have been removed. It's fantastic, I know, but who am I to argue with hundreds of years of tradition? We didn't invent the zombi, you know, but we are trying to show Moreau how to use them in a cost-efficient manner."

Sardi shook his head. There was no use in arguing

with Calloway, but there was still plenty of information to be gotten from him. "Where are you taking me?"

"Headquarters," Calloway said. He pointed to the mountain looming before them. There, far atop the mountain peak, Sardi could see the remains of majestic stone towers and turrets of a great fortress. "We can take a jeep partway up, but I'm afraid the road peters out half a mile from the top. We'll have to hike the last part."

"What is that?" Sardi asked, suddenly realizing that the towers must be huge to be visible from this distance.

Calloway stopped at the jeep parked in front of the barracks where he'd been sitting the night before. He motioned Sardi into the front passenger seat and ordered the zombi to climb into the backseat.

"It's the Citadelle La Ferriere. It was built by Christophe, Haiti's mad emperor, when was it? About 1800. He was afraid the Europeans were going to come back and kick his ass, so he had his people build this fortress. Took two hundred thousand men more than ten years— and it's said that over twenty thousand of them died in the effort. Towers are one hundred and forty feet high and walls are fourteen feet thick. Damn impregnable then. And today."

"What happened to Christophe?" Sardi asked as Calloway put the jeep in gear and started up the trail to the citadel.

"Oh, the Europeans never came. His people got sick and tired of him, and he shot himself before they could tear him to pieces. It's said they threw his body in a lime pit and then buried what was left in the middle of the citadel's parade ground."

"There's a lesson in that," Sardi murmured quietly.

The jeep labored up the mountainside, straining and shuddering against the steep grade on the poor road, which stopped a distressingly short distance up the slope. Calloway pulled the jeep over onto a small level space by the end of the road and killed the engine.

"Normally," he said, "we could take horses up to the top. There's a bunch of them corralled by the barracks. But I'm afraid that animals, particularly horses, don't react well to the presence of our chum, here." He nodded at the white zombi. "Something about zombis bothers them. We'll have to walk the rest of the way."

"Walk?" Sardi asked. It was at least half a mile to the citadel, and the path was steep enough to daunt a mountain goat.

Calloway nodded glumly, and they took off. It wasn't long before Calloway was huffing and puffing with every step. The man was in terrible physical condition. Sardi, who'd just spent a horrendous night without water and food in a cramped, stinking prison, was confident that he could take off down the mountainside and lose Calloway in about three minutes. If it wasn't for the zombi, that is.

The remorseless creature paced at Sardi's heels like a monstrous windup toy with a perpetual spring. Its pace never varied, but was a steady, relentless stride that Sardi doubted an Olympic runner could outstrip.

Besides, Sardi was unsure that he *should* escape even if he had the opportunity. There was a lot more to learn about Calloway, Moreau, and their zombis. Moreau had proven immune to Sardi's hypnotic abilities, but he had yet to try Calloway, who seemed to be of definitely lesser will than the colonel.

For Sardi the hike was almost pleasant. Hot and hungry as he was, it was uplifting to be out of his little cell and in the fresh, clear air. The mountainside scenery was also exhilarating, and if it wasn't for the horrors that Sardi knew lurked on the plain below and the uncertainty of what he would face above, he actually would have been enjoying himself.

It took a little less than an hour to reach the gates of the citadel, but only because Calloway was so woefully out of condition. He was wheezing as if he'd just run a mile under four minutes, and his shirt was totally soaked with sweat.

"Imagine," he puffed, waving at the guard who let them through the portal without a challenge, "hauling every stone that went into this place up that slope. No wonder the workers dropped like flies."

No wonder, indeed, Sardi thought, gazing about himself in awe. The towers of the outer defenses soared fourteen stories into the pristine Haitian skies. The walls through which the portal was cut were thicker than two men lying head to toe.

Once through the portal Sardi and Calloway gazed down upon the open inner ward of the citadel, a vast, flat open expanse several football fields in extent. And it wasn't empty.

Sardi stared in astonishment at ranks upon ranks of men drilling in the vast open area surrounded by the high fortress walls. They all wore the khaki uniforms of the Haitian military, and, oddly enough, all were wearing Walkman headsets. There were no drill sergeants in evidence. Though several soldiers stood watching in relaxed postures, no one was shouting orders at the assembled company. Yet they moved in time, albeit stiffly, and executed drilling orders, a little clumsily and slightly out of step, like a company of new, slightly inept recruits.

Sardi watched them drill for several moments before he was struck by the awful truth. He wasn't watching raw recruits, inept or otherwise. He was watching a company of zombis.

The thought of a zombi army chilled Sardi to the bone. They would be the perfect soldiers, uncaring of whom they killed, unfeeling of pain inflicted upon them, all but unstoppable except for direct hits. In the hands of Moreau and his conscienceless superiors they would be an unstoppable force that could ravage any foe.

"This way," Calloway was saying, "are our quarters. They're not much, but at least they're better than the beastly barracks down on the plain. We have much to talk over that could be advantageous to us both."

"Certainly," Sardi said, "but first I'd be interested in knowing what's going on down there."

Calloway glanced down at the marching zombis and dismissed them with a wave of his hand. "Oh, that. It's nothing, really. Nothing at all."

Sardi fixed Calloway with his steady gaze and continued to speak in his soft, smooth, persuasive voice. "I think it's very interesting," he said. "Very interesting and very important. Don't you think so? Don't you think what's happening down there on the drill grounds is important?"

Calloway's eyes became glassy, his stare fixed on Sardi. "Yes," he said in a soft, heavy voice. "Yes. You are right. It is very important."

"Why?" Sardi urged gently. "Why is it important?"

"They are training zombis as soldiers and assassins."

"Why?" Sardi prompted again.

Calloway continued to stare at him, a line of spittle drooling down his chin. "To invade."

"Invade? Invade what country?" Sardi asked. It was like prompting a recalcitrant child who had important information but didn't realize what it was.

"The Dominican Republic. To avenge the Vespers, the massacre of Haitian peasants by the Dominican army."

Sardi fell silent, thinking furiously. Vishnu preserve us, he thought. The banners all over the city proclaimed the Vespers to start on October second. Tomorrow! Sardi knew now that he had to escape and bring this information to Justice. There was no time to waste.

"Will these zombi assassins be sent elsewhere?" he asked.

"Oh yes," Calloway said dreamily. "To prevent others from causing trouble when the invasion starts, assassins are already in place—"

"You fool!" a deep, gruff voice roared behind Sardi, waking Calloway from his hypnotic stupor.

Sardi whirled to see Moreau standing behind him, glaring like a mad animal. A squad of soldiers armed with automatic weapons stood behind Moreau, their guns up and ready. Sardi's heart sank. He'd waited too long. There was one thing he could try. He fixed his gaze on Moreau, but the giant Haitian simply glared at him.

"You idiot! You tried that once before!" He slashed out with his walking stick, but Sardi ducked the blow. "I am too strong for your stupid tricks. Ogoun, *loa* of war, has given me strength which your pathetic magic cannot overcome."

Moreau gestured at the squad of soldiers, and two came forward and grabbed Sardi firmly by the arms. Sardi knew that he could break free of them, but where could he run?

Moreau turned his attention to Calloway. "And you, what were you doing with my prisoner?"

Calloway was not a good liar. He stuttered and tried to avoid Moreau's eyes, but the power in them drew his frightened gaze like a snake enticing a baby bird to its death. "Nothing, Colonel, nothing. I thought that I would simply discuss certain affairs with him. Business affairs. Perhaps try to cut a deal that would make Lambert leave—"

"Liar!" Moreau roared. "You were trying to make a deal to save your own black ass in case things went wrong. Liar and coward!"

Having worked himself into a titanic rage, Moreau lifted his stick to strike Calloway, who flinched backward and put up his arms to protect his face. Moreau caught his breath and seemed to think better of it, and instead merely poked Calloway lightly on the chest.

"No, you are a cowardly flea, but you are my flea. Listen, flea, and believe. Your masters sent you here to work with me, but you are theirs no longer. You know too much now about our plans, so you belong to us to crush to powder or to reward handsomely as we see fit. From now on be a true and loyal flea, or," he nodded at the zombis stumbling through their paces below, "there is always room in the ranks."

Calloway bobbed his head nervously and nodded.

Moreau turned toward Sardi. "To the dungeons," he said softly.

The soldiers hustled him away. Sardi followed meekly, because there was no point in kicking and screaming. He would have to wait, and his chance would come. He hoped it wouldn't take too long.

They led him past the marching zombis tirelessly drilling in the hot afternoon sun, to a stone stairway that spiraled downward into the bowels of the fortress. The light was dim in the staircase, and it was pleasantly cool, but as they continued downward, the mild coolness became distinctly, wetly chilly. The light was poor, provided only by guttering torches set in rusted wall sconces.

They reached the basement after following the staircase through several spiraling downward loops and stopped

before a block of small rooms with windowless doors.
The soldiers shoved Sardi into one of the cells, slammed
the door behind him, and rammed the bolt home. He
could faintly hear them through the door as they marched
away. The cell was utterly dark. At first Sardi thought it
was better than the baking prison in which he'd been
recently confined. It was bigger for one thing, long enough
to allow him to stretch out. And it was cool and moist
enough so that he could get some water by licking the
perspiring stone walls.

At first he thought that he was in a much better
situation than before, but then he heard the rats.

The beach was deserted except for Justice and Marie,
who stood ankle deep in the rising surf. The shoreline
was rocky but clean, the water was clear and warm. The
sun was shining brightly through banks of thick, drifting
clouds. It was a beautiful day.

"This voudou business doesn't seem too terrifying so
far," Justice said. "In fact, it's rather like having a picnic."

Marie smiled, showing her beautifully even, dazzlingly
white teeth. "It may seem so now, but wait, the dark
time shall come."

With that cryptic comment she boldly stripped off her
shirt and laid it on top of a convenient rock, then, to
Justice's further astonishment, unbuttoned and stepped
out of her cutoff jeans.

She was naked, her smooth skin gleaming like rich,
milky coffee in the sun. Her legs were long and leanly
muscled. Her thighs looked strong and inviting. Her
hips were slim, her breasts small and conical with large,
dark nipples. She flashed Justice another smile.

"Now follow me if you dare," she said, and ran off into
the surf, muscles playing in her thighs and buttocks with
smooth, easy grace.

Justice wondered if this was some obscure test or the
whim of a playful girl. Either way, he couldn't afford to
let her out of his sight. He quickly stripped out of his
clothes and followed her out into the bay.

The water had the warmth and clarity of a carefully
tended swimming pool, but none of the chemical bite.

He followed Marie's smoothly kicking legs as she swam gracefully as a seal, poking through the rocky crevices along the shoreline.

"What are we looking for?" he asked.

She treaded water easily, her breasts bobbing gently on the surface, their nipples becoming enlarged by the coolness of the water.

"A fish," she said, "and a toad, and a snake. I shall point them out, we shall catch them." She passed Justice one of the netbags that had been floating from her left wrist. She took a deep breath and dived again.

Justice followed her. This time they scared up a large toad from among the rocks. Justice recognized it from his diving sessions around Haven as a sea toad, common around the Caribbean, but which he usually avoided because it had protective glands that secreted a number of potent poisons. The poisons weren't strong enough to kill a healthy man, but they could make you sick as a dog for several days.

The toad tried to make its escape, but Marie was on it in a flash. She was quick and graceful in the water as a seal. She snared the amphibian in her net and transferred it to one of the bags attached to her wrist. They broke the surface again, and Marie threw back her head, exultant.

"We have one ingredient," she said, and before Justice could reply, she suddenly reached out and put her arms around his neck. Clinging to him from shoulders to ankles, she kissed him suddenly and deeply, her legs clinching around his waist as he trod water. Surprised, he found himself returning the kiss automatically. Her tongue was a warm, living thing in his mouth, hot as the coals he had seen her kiss the night before. Her mouth was sweet and wet, her hard little breasts ground into his chest. Warmth radiated from the juncture of her thighs, which was straining against her lower abdomen.

He felt himself rising to meet her, then she pushed away, laughing, and kicked down into the water again. By the time he caught up with her, she'd collected a second specimen, a long, slim snakelike creature that he recognized as a species of sea worm. She slipped it into a

second collecting bag and pointed excitedly at a small
fish that was swimming about, minding its own business
as it nosed along looking for food.

It was an innocuous-looking fish, no more than six
inches long, and rather plainly colored so that it blended
in almost perfectly with the sandy ocean bottom. But as
it became aware of Justice and Marie, it blew up like a
balloon, and dozens of sharp little spikes became erect
all over its body.

There was no mistaking this species. It was, as Justice
recognized immediately, a puffer fish. Harmless, meek,
and mild, it depended on its protective coloring for
survival. When that failed, it had its spikes. When the
spikes failed, there was the deadly poison it carried in its
internal organs. The poison wouldn't help a puffer fish
eaten by a predator, but it would ensure that the predator wouldn't eat any more of its species. The poison
it carried was so deadly that one fish could easily kill
half a dozen men.

The little fish darted about the ocean floor quickly, but
Marie was an expert with her net. Within moments she'd
snapped it up and motioned to Justice, who held out the
bag that she'd given him at the start of their expedition.
She transferred the fish from her capture net to Justice's
bag, then gave a thumbs-up motion to the surface.

They went up to the surface side by side and leisurely
swam in toward the shore, Justice admiring her lithe
muscularity as she matched him stroke for stroke. Marie
took the wrist bag from Justice when they reached the
rock formation where they'd stashed their clothes. She
slung all three nets up on the rock and looked at Justice
seriously.

"There are the first ingredients of the zombi powder,"
she said.

Justice nodded and reached for his pants. "Do we get
the rest at the corner grocery?" he asked.

She grabbed his wrist with one hand. With the other
she reached out and grasped his cock. It instantly sprang
to life at her touch.

"You want me," she said in a low, silky voice. "And I
want you."

She released his cock for a moment and put his free hand on the juncture of her thighs. The warmth and wetness that was there didn't come from the sea.

"Tell me," she said. "Tell me that you want me."

Marie looked up at him with her great green eyes. Her hand rested on his, holding it still at the juncture of her thighs. She nodded and smiled at him. "You do not have to tell me of your need with words," she said. "I can read it on your face, feel it on your body. Lie down, my sweet *blanc*, and give yourself to Haiti."

Without really knowing how, Justice was suddenly on his back on the soft sand, the surf surging gently around him. Marie lowered herself on him with a soft moan of pleasure and began to ride him as if she were dancing for the *loas* again.

Justice couldn't take his eyes off her fine, taut body as she pumped and swiveled on his erect cock, her eyes closed, her nipples stiffened like smooth, dark figs. She crooned a tuneless song of pleasure as she rode him, building an intense, quickening rhythm like the beating of Haitian drums. She moved with the pulse of the surging surf, and for a moment Justice felt as if he were somehow being swept away to sea where he would drift forever in a lost haze of sexual heat.

When climax came, it was explosive. Justice lifted off the sand, thrusting into her, as she ground down into him. She bent down and laid her head on his chest, and he pulled her to him and kissed her lips. They tasted salty.

Above them on the rock formation, the sea toad let loose a plaintive croak from his netbag, and Marie opened her eyes. They were clouded and dreamy, but she became all business again as she disengaged from Justice.

"We must go now," she said, reaching for her clothes. "We have much to do yet, and the day is half-over."

Marie gave no acknowledgment of their new intimacy as they dressed and went up to Lucien's battered station wagon that Justice had hired for the day. It was as if they'd merely exchanged kisses. Justice wondered if this too was part of a test. He decided to follow her lead. As with everything else between them, it wasn't as if he really had a choice.

Once they reached the car, Marie took out a cardboard box she had placed on the rear seat. The box had some old jars in it. She put the puffer fish in one jar and the toad and the sea worm, or snake, as she'd called it, into another. She shook the jar with the toad and worm. The toad tried frantically to scrabble out. The worm coiled around its leg and hung on.

"See the toad," she said, holding the jar before Justice's face and giving it another shake. "Placing it in the same jar with his enemy, the snake, enrages it. It makes his poison all the stronger."

She stashed the jars back in the box.

"Where to now?" Justice asked.

"We return to the *hounfour* to gather the rest of the ingredients—and to prepare for tonight."

"What's happening tonight?"

"Tonight," she said, "is your real test. This," she gestured out toward the sea, "was only a romp. A chance to get to know one another."

"So do we know one another yet?"

Marie shook her head. "Not entirely. After tonight we shall."

They got into the car, Marie driving. As they pulled away from the deserted beach, Justice turned to her. "Can we stop at the hotel first?" he asked. "I'd like to check on the rest of the team."

"Certainly," Marie said. "We shall even have plenty of time for you to buy me lunch." She flashed another dazzling smile at Justice. "Breakfast, after all, was so interesting."

XIV.

SOMEWHERE IN THE AIR
1ST OCTOBER—1:38 P.M.

Jenks had been in tight places before, but this had to be one of the worst.

He was stuck in a plain, pinewood coffin with a zombi. Fortunately, the carpenters hadn't been concerned with well-fitting joints, so enough light and air seeped into the box to allow Jenks to see and them both to breathe. It was claustrophobic, though. Despite the fact that Jenks had sneaked into the box with the smallest zombi, there was barely room for the two of them. Fortunately, his companion wasn't the fidgety type. Didn't move at all, in fact.

Jenks found out why when he removed his traveling companion's headphones and heard a continual, soft murmuring of "*Dormir . . . dormir . . . dormir . . .*"

Jenks's French wasn't all that good, but he knew that meant "sleep." He debated trying to wake the creature to question it. They seemed pretty docile unless one gave them specific orders, and maybe the zombi knew what was going on. Jenks certainly didn't.

"Wake up," he said in French. He wasn't exactly proficient in the language, but Haven had been a French colony, and Jenks had picked up a smattering of the language after living on the island for several years.

When the zombi's eyes opened, Jenks found himself eyeball to eyeball with the thing. It was spooky, but actually more pathetic than frightening. Though Jenks had fought zombis, he also pitied them. It had once been a man, but now it'd been robbed of something. It'd been turned into some kind of machine. Jenks knew that he'd have to face the things in combat again, maybe even this one, but right now he felt more sorry for it than anything else.

"Are you awake?" he asked.

"Yes." The zombi's voice was soft, but deep and toneless, as if it were a computer simulation that was almost human, but not quite.

"What's your name?"

There was a long silence, then, "Don't know."

All right, Jenks thought. So much for trying to get chummy. Question two on *Stump the Zombi*. "Okay, pal, what's your mission?"

The silence was shorter this time, but the answer was the same.

"Don't know."

Jenks had figured that these clucks wouldn't have been told any details ahead of time, but he had to ask, just in case.

"How'd you get this way?"

The silence dragged on until Jenks thought that he had totally stumped the mental processes of his roommate, but then the zombi spoke again, haltingly, almost humanly.

"A . . . writer. A newspaper writer . : . yes . . . wrote for a newspaper . . . newspaper." There were long pauses between words as if the creature were dredging them up from what was left of its soul. "Wrote about Colonel . . . Moreau . . . bad . . . bad . . . hurt . . . beaten . . . killed . . . buried . . . awoke . . . awoke again . . ."

The last word was an anguished gargle. Hearing such emotion from the zombi was almost unbearable.

A dry, hacking sob heaved up from the zombi's chest, but no tears could come.

"Sleep," Jenks said softly. "Sleep, sleep again."

He slipped the Walkman back over the creature's ears, and its eyes closed immediately. Son of a bitch Moreau has a lot to pay for, Jenks thought. And I'll be more than happy to cash his check.

The rest of the flight passed in uncomfortable solitude. They hit turbulence a few times, and the boxes, not stowed down too tightly, bounced and rattled, but Jenks got through it with no more than a few bruises. The landing was a real treat too as most of the boxes shifted, sliding forward as the DC-10 touched down and hit its brakes.

Jenks was out of the box even before the plane stopped taxiing, looking for another place to hide. He found a storage compartment full of poorly packed, moth-eaten parachutes and squirmed in among them. He had another tedious wait, then the freight bay doors opened, and the baggage handlers wheeled a conveyer belt up to the compartment and started to unload the boxes.

Jenks could hear snatches of their conversation above the rumble of the conveyer belt as they slid the coffins from the plane to a waiting van.

"Bodies, manifest said, for the Haitian consular building? What the hell?"

"Hey, we just gotta unload 'em."

"Shit, I don't want to touch 'em. They came from Haiti . . . yeah, place with all the AIDS."

"Jeez . . . let the guys in customs handle 'em. They give me the creeps."

What was Moreau's plan? Jenks wondered. The accents of the baggage handlers verified that they'd landed in New York City. Why? He certainly wasn't using live zombis to smuggle in cocaine. Jenks twisted around silently in the storage compartment, trying to get away from whatever it was that was poking him in the back. He finally reached back and shoved at the annoying thing. It was, he discovered, a crate.

He squirmed around until he could see it, wondering if he'd found an extra, unused zombi crate. But it was much too small for that. He lifted the lid a fraction and stuck his hand in, hoping to God the Haitians weren't also smuggling poisonous reptiles into the country.

But his hand didn't touch something hot, squirming, and deadly. It was something hard and cold, but just as damn deadly. He didn't have to see what it was. He could tell by feel.

It was a crate full of Uzis.

Jenks clamped his jaw together, too stunned to swear.

Zombis, he thought. Zombis and Uzis. Christ, what a combination.

Kim was waiting for Justice when he and Marie walked into the Ollofson's lobby. She was obviously tense and worried, but when she saw Marie, a new light came into her eyes.

Somehow, Justice thought, she knew, with that strange feminine sixth sense, that Justice and Marie had been intimate. Justice knew Kim had strong feelings toward him. So strong, in fact, that she'd offered herself to him several times. But he had turned her away because he knew it couldn't just be sex between himself and Kim. There had to be more, but he had nothing more to give.

Kim and Marie sized each other up. Justice, not tuned to their feminine wavelength, couldn't tell what they saw in each other, but he recognized grudging respect in their eyes—despite the fact that Marie had just had the man whom Kim desperately wanted.

He introduced them quickly, then asked, "Where's Jenks?"

Kim sighed. "There is a story to tell," she said.

Justice glanced around the room, not lingering on the ever-present goon in the porkpie hat and dark glasses pretending to be reading an upside-down newspaper in a corner of the lobby.

"Let's go take some air on the veranda," Justice said. "There's a table near the end where we won't be overheard if we speak quietly."

They exited the room and settled themselves in the rattan chairs around a table overlooking the hotel's garden. It was a tranquil, lovely setting, the perfect anodyne for all the horror Justice had uncovered on this strange and fearful island. But Kim shattered the mood of idyllic peacefulness as she told Justice and Marie in a low, shuddering voice what had happened to her and Jenks over the last twenty-four hours.

"They all had Walkmans?" Justice said thoughtfully as she recounted the mustering of the zombi troop.

Kim nodded.

Justice looked at Marie. "Just like the zombi assassin

who tried to gun us down this morning." He turned to Kim. "Did you get any clue as to where they were going?"

"Only that they were flying off the island on a big plane. A DC-10. And they were probably headed for New York."

"New York?" Justice asked. "Colonel Moreau and a planeload of zombi assassins?"

"Zombis are the perfect assassins," Marie said grimly, "because they have lost their souls. They will commit any heinous crime and will never betray the ones who gave them their orders. They have lost their past and cannot even comprehend their present."

"Can they be brought back to humanity?" Justice asked. He thought of the man he was searching for and the questions he wanted to ask once he found him. He had to be able to delve into his past in order to put the next piece of the puzzle into place. Otherwise, all this would have been in vain, and the empty, aching void inside himself would remain unfilled.

Marie looked at him peculiarly, as if she sensed the urgency of his question. "Sometimes," she said, "though no zombi has ever totally returned to the way it used to be. Often something as simple as a matter of diet can do the trick. Feed zombis meat or fish, or salt in the proper amounts, and they will begin to regain their selves."

Justice nodded. A fire burned in his eyes that Marie had never seen before. It made Kim weak, as if she wanted to mother him and make fierce love to him both at the same time.

"I'm tired of operating in the dark," Justice said in a low, savage voice. He stared straight at the SD man who had followed them onto the veranda but was forced to sit at a discreet distance because of the configuration of the tables. Justice felt like grabbing the man by the shirt and pounding the hell out of him, but, temporarily satisfying as that might prove, it would do no real good. But Justice suddenly smiled, and at the sight of it the SD man backed away into the lobby.

Kim grabbed Justice's forearm. "You have an idea?"

"Yes," Justice said shortly. He glanced at his wrist-watch. The timing was perfect. "An idea to kill two birds with one stone."

Kim was a magnet for what seemed like every beggar in Port-au-Prince. Well dressed, an obvious foreigner and a woman alone, every time she took a step, she was besieged by a horde of beggars and street merchants importuning her for money. She ignored them as she entered the Iron Market.

The March de Fer, a huge market hall erected in the 1880s, was the heart of Port-au-Prince's commercial district. It was said that anything that could be purchased in Haiti could be found at the market, and Kim had a very specific idea of what she was looking for.

She passed the stalls where all the varied Haitian food-stuffs could be found—colorful maize, rice, beans, man-ioc, yams, pineapples, mangoes, coconuts, and all the other tropical fruits of bewildering sizes, textures, and colors. She passed the meat stalls where stock both live and already butchered could be purchased, and the fish market where all the provenance of the sea could be found.

She slowed down a little in the native handicraft section, glancing over the wood carvings and colorful paintings, and finally stopped to browse more closely in the metalwork area. Still, it seemed that she couldn't find what she was looking for, so she stopped to ask, "*Fusil?*"

The owner of the stall shook his head and put away the pots and pans he was showing her. Kim smiled to herself. She knew that she was on the right track.

She got the same reception at the next few stalls. Eager interest, then sudden dismay when she told the stall owners what she was looking for. After a few more moments of this, she heard a familiar voice speak to her from behind.

"You must think we are very, very stupid, m'mselle." She turned to face a grinning Captain Shorty. "Where are your brains, eh?"

She looked blankly at him. "What do you mean?" she asked innocently. "I was only shopping for souvenirs."

Shorty roared with laughter. The three soldiers behind him smirked. "Souvenirs! Hah, that's funny, m'mselle. Since when are guns souvenirs?"

A look of terror crossed Kim's face, and she glanced through the crowd as if searching for a way of escape. Captain Shorty gestured, and two of his men came forward and grabbed her firmly by the arms.

"I told you that we would be keeping a close eye on you. Did you not believe us?" he asked rhetorically, and then gestured at the men holding her. "Take her to the jeep. We'll take her to headquarters and . . . question her . . . thoroughly."

Kim struggled and kicked, but it was no use. They had her firmly in their grasp and weren't about to let go. They weren't gentle about dragging her along, nor were they careful about where they grabbed her. They copped feels and grabbed at her derriere as they dragged her through the crowd that magically melted away before them.

They'd parked their jeep in a side alley since it had been impossible to follow her in it through the crowds of the Marche de Fer. There was no one near as they dragged Kim up to it. Beggars knew better than to cluster around a government vehicle and ask for alms, and no thief in his right mind would touch it.

Captain Shorty grabbed her by the hair and jerked her head around, smiling sweetly at her. "What's the matter, m'mselle. Are you so shy that you're afraid to be questioned by several men at once?" As he spoke, he caressed her breasts with his free hand.

Kim smiled savagely back at him. "I might be excited by the thought if you were real men and not *cochons*."

Shorty drew back his hand to strike her, and she spit right in his face. The globule struck him between the eyes and started slowly to run down the side of his nose. He froze, in shocked astonishment, and the tableau held for a second as Kim's laughter rang out.

"For that," Shorty growled, letting go of her hair to wipe away the spittle, "we take you here and now, we screw you until you can no longer beg for mercy, then we kill you slowly and sweetly."

Kim laughed again and kneed him in the groin.

It was hard to say what dominated Shorty's face, pain or surprise. He gabbled something indistinguishable as he closed up over his throbbing privates, and then Kim stamped down heavily with a spiked heel on the instep of one of the two men holding her arms.

Bones crunched, and he let go, yowling and hopping around on his good foot. She whirled and smashed the other man in the nose with the palm of her hand. He didn't have a chance to make a sound, but died instantly as she drove cartilage and bone into his brain.

The other soldier was bringing up his rifle, savage hate on his face, when Justice took him from behind, slipping a strand of wire around his neck and twisting, hard and savage. The man dropped his rifle, gurgled as his throat crushed inward, and jerked for a few seconds. Justice eased him to the ground, then turned to the soldier who was hopping around them like a barefoot man dancing on hot coals.

"Nighty-night," Justice said, and swung from the heels. The soldier took it on the chin and went out like a blown light bulb.

Kim squatted before Shorty, who was hunched over, kneeling on the pavement, still moaning in pain. "You still feel hot for me?" she asked, and reached out and grabbed his crotch.

Shorty opened his mouth for a scream, but Justice closed his huge hand over it, muffling all sound, as Kim squeezed. Tears ran from Shorty's eyes even after she let go.

"Quite a grip you got there," Justice said as he took a roll of duct tape from his pocket and circled Shorty's mouth and eyes a few times, then taped his wrists and ankles.

Kim sniffed. "I tell you, there wasn't much to grab."

Justice looked back toward the main street. A few Haitians had been watching surreptitiously, but they knew through long experience never to interfere with anything to do with soldiers.

"Let's roll," Justice said.

They all piled into the jeep. Justice grabbed Shorty by the belt and tossed him on the floor in front of the rear seat, where Kim used him as a footstool. Marie swung into the back next to Kim, and they took off.

Justice drove. Marie gave directions, leading them through unpeopled back streets out of town. Within half an hour they were out of Port-au-Prince and in a deserted cove overlooking the ocean.

"All out," Justice called as he braked to a halt, sending sand spraying.

Justice dragged Shorty out of the back of the jeep and dumped him unceremoniously onto the sand where he wriggled like a worm on a hook until he managed to jerk himself up into a kneeling position. Muffled but angry-sounding noises came from his taped mouth.

"Let's hear what he's got to say," Justice said.

Marie bent down to remove the tape, but Kim said, "Please, let me."

Kim grabbed the tape and yanked it away with a vicious tug that tore hairs out of Shorty's mustache and skin off his lips. The first sound out of him was a yelp of pain followed by a string of profanity in French and English that would have made any longshoreman proud.

"You will pay for this!" he sputtered.

Kim shook her head. "Shorty gets all his dialogue from old movies."

"My name is not Shorty, it is Captain Henri Michelle!" he said savagely. "And I shall see you all flayed alive and every bone broken in your miserable bodies—"

Justice hunkered down on the sand in front of Michelle, and the look in his eyes silenced the captain's tirade.

"I'm afraid that you don't understand your position," Justice said in a quiet, yet dangerous, voice. "Look around you. There is nothing but the sand, the sea, and three people who would like to see you dead. You are far from any help, and no one will ever know what happened on this beach except us."

"You, you would not dare to harm me."

"Why not?" Justice asked.

Michelle had no answer.

"We don't want to hurt you," Justice continued in his same, earnest voice. "Unlike you, we don't get any enjoyment out of hurting people. But we can if we have to. If you don't talk."

"Talk about what?" Michelle asked sullenly.

"First, what are the connections between Moreau, Lifeline Medical Supply, and cocaine?"

Michelle shook his head. "I don't know anything about that."

"Oh, come on," Kim said, squatting down next to Justice. "You were there in Gator Grove. You have to know all about the operation."

Michelle shook his head stubbornly.

Kim looked at Justice. "Let me take an ear off. Or how about an eye?" She flashed a rusty, dull-looking knife. "Maybe I should cut off his peanut-sized balls," she suggested. "I know that the knife isn't very sharp, but I'd be able to get them off eventually."

"All right," Justice said to Michelle's horror, "but first let me open his channels for pain reception, so he'll feel it even more."

Justice knew they had to break Michelle down totally, but he was philosophically opposed to the use of torture. The threat of torture, however, was a different thing. His own experience with building himself up after the failed attempt on his life had given him intimate knowledge of the human body, some of which he was about to share with Michelle.

He reached out and probed at the nerve mass at the base of Michelle's neck with his steellike fingers. Michelle screamed at the savage thrust of pain that ran up his head and down his shoulder to his fingertips.

"There," Justice said with false satisfaction in his voice. "Everything will feel ten times as painful now." That wasn't true, but Michelle didn't know that. He turned to Kim. "Get cutting," he ordered.

Justice stood up, dusting the sand from his hands. Marie grabbed Michelle by the ankle and pulled him down flat on the ground. Michelle screamed as if he'd been dumped on a bed of hot coals and tried to wriggle away.

Justice reached out and grabbed his other ankle. "Hold still," he admonished Michelle, "or I'll rip your ears off."

Michelle was blubbering now. Marie unbuttoned his khaki overalls and pulled them and his shorts down to his knees. Kim loomed over him with her rusty knife, a look of awful savagery on her face. She lifted the knife.

"Wait, wait, wait!" Michelle screamed. "Wait, I will tell you!"

Justice suppressed a smile. "All right," he said to Kim. "Put the knife away." He turned to Michelle. "Talk."

"It began with Robert Calloway," he whimpered. "The colonel got to know him several years ago when Lifeline was shipping donated medicine into Haiti. Calloway had the shipments delivered to the colonel, who sold them, and they split the profits. He used Lifeline's connections to help the colonel set up a blood-bank business, and also a body-selling business."

"Body selling?" Justice asked.

"Oh yes," Michelle said. "Very profitable. The colonel collects bodies from morgues and police stations and through Lifeline sells them to many foreign universities for students to cut. But the AIDS epidemic has slowed down business considerably. People are afraid to buy bodies from Haiti." Nationalistic pride asserted itself as Michelle sounded insulted by the notion that Haitian body parts were thought inferior.

"Moreau's profits were shrinking?" Justice prompted.

"That's right. That's when he decided to go into the drug business by acting as middleman for Colombian cocaine cartels."

"They ship the stuff in here wholesale," Justice said, "then you break it down into manageable lots, which are—were—shipped to the Lifeline plant in Florida, where they were sent all up and down the East Coast."

Michelle nodded eagerly. "Yes, that's it. That's it exactly."

"Well," Justice said thoughtfully. "Jenks burning down their plant will put an end to that business for a while."

"Getting rid of Moreau and Calloway would put an end to it forever," Kim said.

Justice nodded. "On to other business," he said. "What do you know about zombis? One took a shot at me this morning. I didn't like it one bit."

Michelle's eyes grew wide, and a look of true fear came into them. "Zombis? Nothing! I swear, nothing!"

Justice nodded at Kim. She took a step forward brandishing her knife, and Michelle curled into a fetal ball.

"Really, I have never worked with them. They are out of my line. I have seen them, but that is all."

Justice sighed. "You're lying. You helped your colonel load a bunch of them on a plane this afternoon."

"Yes, that's true, but the colonel doesn't tell me his plans."

"Do you at least know where he was going?"

"America. Someplace important. That's all I know."

"Not what they're going to do when they get to their destination?"

Michelle shrugged. It was an awkward gesture while lying on his back with his pants pulled down around his knees, but he managed. "They are his elite zombis. The ones whose brains weren't damaged too badly when they were . . . changed. They are still in his total control. They still obey all his orders to the letter. But they are smarter than the others. They need less direction."

"They're more deadly," Kim said.

Michelle nodded vigorously. "You can guess as well as I what he intends to do with them."

"Multiple assassinations," Justice said lowly.

"They have to be stopped," Kim said.

"It's up to Jenks for now. Unless we can get more information."

Kim grabbed Michelle's shriveled cock and laid the blade of her knife against it. "Maybe I can cut some out of him."

Michelle screeched, imploring mercy, and Justice shook his head. "He's probably telling the truth about not being the colonel's confidant. He's nothing but cheap muscle, anyway."

Kim looked up, disappointed. Whatever Justice's views on torture, she didn't share them. At least in regard to Henri Michelle.

"Does that mean I don't get to cut him?" she asked, disappointed.

"Not just yet," Justice said.

"What are we going to do with him?" Marie asked. "We can't keep him in your hotel room. We certainly can't turn him loose. Maybe we should just drop him in the ocean."

"That's a thought," Justice said, "but I don't think we'll have to get that drastic."

He checked his wristwatch, and just on cue there was a great bubbling a hundred meters out in the deserted bay.

Michelle, totally unhinged by his experience, started screaming, "Agwe, Agwe-taroyo is coming!" until Kim slapped him silent.

When the bubbling stopped, a dark tower was pointing up from out of the sea, and a huge, fat man with a cigar stuck in his mouth was waving and calling out from it, "Ahoy, ahoy!"

It was the Haven nuclear-powered submarine fleet, and its admiral, Jake Ousteoputcha. Joachim One Eagle popped up in the conning tower next to him and also waved at the shore.

"Right on time," Justice said with satisfaction. "Right on time."

XV.

CHRISTOPHE'S CITADEL
1ST OCTOBER—5:00 P.M.

The prisoners locked up in the dungeons of Christophe's citadel were fed once a day. Promptly at five P.M. a trio of soldiers wheeled a huge pot of cornmeal gruel down the corridor of cells, ladling out a bare cupful to each unfortunate prisoner.

They were especially careful when they got to Sardi's

cell. First one of them filled a rusty, leaking cup that was held together mainly by the caked remnants of previous servings. Another soldier announced their presence by banging on the door and then opened it, while the third pointed his rifle into the cell in case Sardi was planning a desperate escape attempt.

They should have saved themselves the effort, for all their caution proved to be in vain.

No sound came from the cell when they'd banged on the door, but when the door slowly swung open, casting a glimmer of dim light into the solid blackness of the cell, the guards froze in sudden terror. Sardi was calmly sitting on the floor in the lotus position with his eyes closed, and on him and all around him were hundreds of pairs of red, shining eyes.

Rats by the score sat patiently on his shoulders and lap and legs, and even perched unmoving on the top of his head. They sat all around him on the floor, noses quivering, eyes blinking in the sudden dim patch of light.

Sardi suddenly opened his eyes, brought up his right arm, and pointed it straight at the guards. "There," he said clearly, "there is the food that I promised you."

The rat perched on his right shoulder, a huge gray monster that must have weighed six pounds, ran lightly down Sardi's arm. When he reached Sardi's hand, he leapt off onto the floor and ran out into the corridor toward the guards.

That seemed to signal the rest of the rats. Almost as if they had one mind, they bolted into the corridor in a streaming, unstoppable mass, and the guards panicked.

The one holding the cup of gruel dropped it and ran. The one pointing the rifle screamed, dropped it, and also ran. The third followed his companions while a few of the rats gave halfhearted chase for a few steps, then settled down to lap up the spilled gruel puddled on the damp dungeon floor.

Sardi stood up easily, despite the hours he had just spent in the same position, and laughed despite his still-desperate situation. He hadn't had any mystical control over the rats. Like most animals they simply reacted to the emotional aura that Sardi displayed. Like dogs who will attack if fear is shown, or who will cower if confidence and strength are emitted, the rats responded to Sardi's aura of peace, tranquillity, and absolute confidence and mastery.

It being their habit to gather around mealtime each day and fight over the scraps of food left behind by the prisoners, Sardi easily attracted a few extra rats into his cell with his unmoving stoicism. They in turn attracted more and more of their fellows until he had a veritable horde of rodents waiting with him for feeding time.

The scent of the food was all it took to set them off to charge the corridor. The guards thought they were attacking, but the rats just wanted to get at the food.

Sardi stepped into the corridor, careful not to tread on any of his furry allies. They were skittish now that he was moving about them. Many ran back into the cell and disappeared, a few scattered to the dark sides of the corridor where the light from the torches failed to penetrate.

"No need to be afraid of me, my little friends," he said. "Here, this is the least I can do for you." He tipped over the pot of gruel, and a few of the bolder rodents came out into the light, cautiously sniffing, then enthusiastically feasting.

Sardi looked up and down the corridors. "I know there are more prisoners here," he said aloud. "I know also that you can't hear me, but I'm making a promise anyway to return and free you all. Please just try to hang on. I promise that I'll be back."

He stepped over the abandoned rifle, not even for a moment considering taking it. He was a nonviolent man. He met force with nonresistance or redirection. He had lived his entire life without firing a gun, and he wasn't going to break that pattern now.

He hustled down the corridor, as swiftly and silently as he could. The guardroom at the end of it was abandoned. He briefly considered searching for keys to the other cells, but rejected the idea. One man could possibly make it out of the citadel. A group of men, some probably severely crippled by the rigors of their imprisonment, had no chance to escape without being seen.

He went up the spiral staircase as fast as he could and barely managed to duck into a dark alcove as the mess party came back with an officer in tow. He could hear bits of their conversation from his hiding place.

". . . a sorcerer, I tell you," one of the soldiers was saying.

"Yes," another chipped in excitedly. "He was sitting among a thousand great rats, all big as dogs, and he pointed, and the rats came out after us and chased us."

"He led them," the third said. "He is a *bokor*. He changed into a giant rat himself. . . ."

The officer was looking dubious, but not entirely eager to proceed farther. He stopped at the entrance of the spiral staircase and said, "Perhaps we should get some reinforcements. . . ."

The mess crew was nodding eagerly as Sardi slipped away with a smile.

The citadel had been only half rescued from decay and was only partially inhabited. There was plenty of cover, which Sardi used to his advantage as he passed through the fortress. He was most exposed as he dashed through the portal, but no one challenged him as he went flying down the mountainside into the woods.

Once in deep cover Sardi flung himself to the ground and took several deep breaths to calm his racing heart. It felt good to be outdoors again. He had lost all sense of time during his imprisonment. He glanced at the sky, but couldn't judge the time of day because the sun was blocked by scudding mountains of dark, menacing clouds. A cold wind was blowing, and the scent of rain was in the air.

Sardi smiled. A thunderstorm would provide perfect cover for the second part of his escape. All he had to do was make it to the agricultural station at the base of the mountain, steal a vehicle, and race off to Port-au-Prince. Of course, he suddenly realized, he had no idea where Port-au-Prince was in relation to his current position. He shrugged. That he could worry about later. Getting cleanly away was his first priority.

He stayed off the trail on his way down the mountain, though he saw no one else either coming up or going down. He hoped fervently that someone had left a jeep at the end of the road like Calloway had when they'd first come up to the citadel.

That hope, though, proved to be in vain, and Sardi continued making his way by foot as the sky grew darker and the clouds more menacing. By the time he'd reached the outskirts of the agricultural station, it was raining big, cold drops, and he took a few moments to hold his face to the sky and at least wet his tongue with the first water he'd had since being released from his tin cell earlier that day.

It tasted sweeter than the finest wine, but it was like trying to quench a daylong thirst by drinking from a thimble. After a few moments he lowered his head and plodded on.

The station looked deserted, and Sardi couldn't believe his luck when he saw Moreau's Blazer parked where they had left it the night before. Now if only the key was still in the ignition!

Sardi headed straight for the vehicle, but all his hopes were dashed when he heard a voice call out, "Hey! Stop! What are you doing there?"

Sardi froze, almost overcome by the agonizing frustration of coming so close to escape, then failing at the last moment. He heard footsteps behind him and someone angrily saying, "How'd you wander off? Why aren't you with the others?"

Hope returned to Sardi like a ray of sunlight bursting through a cloud bank. The guard had mistaken him for a zombi! He did his best to put on an utterly wooden expression and blank all emotion from his eyes as he turned around slowly as the guard approached.

"Come on, come on," the man was saying. "You zombis are worse than little children! This way, come on."

The guard waved exasperatedly with his rifle, and Sardi shuffled off in the direction he indicated. The guard continued to grumble, looking up in the sky. "It's going to really piss on us soon." He snapped his fingers as if sudden inspiration struck him. "I could just take you to the zombis' shed. Yeah, that's it. Found you wandering around, didn't know where you came from . . . that'll be a good excuse. All right, to the shed. You know where it is."

Sardi did indeed. He went toward it on a straight, though slow, path, the guard behind him bitching to himself and dragging his rifle on the ground butt-first.

When they arrived at the structure where the zombis lived when not laboring in the fields, Sardi could see that something was going on inside. There were four guardsmen, smoking and standing in a loose group. One waved and called out.

"Hey, Pierre, come out of the rain. What you got there?"

"A stray," Sardi's captor announced. "I caught him wandering around. Christ knows where he's supposed to be. Got any hot coffee?"

"Got something better," the soldier replied. "Come on over and look."

They did. As they approached, Sardi saw to his disgust a woman lying on one of the sleeping mats. Her face was utterly expressionless and her eyes were blank. She was naked, and one of the guards was between her legs with his pants pulled down around his knees, pounding away.

"Got a new batch this afternoon," the guard who had called out to Pierre said. "Some of them even have some meat on them."

Pierre smiled broadly. "Hey, let me in."

"Wait your turn," one of the other guards said.

The man who was with the zombi finally finished. He grunted as he achieved release, then stood up, pulling his pants up. The female zombi just lay there, her face blank and legs open.

"Who's next?" Sardi's captor said, and there was a brief, heated argument that took a moment to resolve.

Sardi stood over in the corner, fighting to keep the revulsion off his face. His disgust was so great that he considered for a moment grabbing one of the rifles that the guards had left lying around and finishing off these men who were worse than necrophiliacs. He considered it, but he couldn't ignore his lifelong discipline of nonvi-olence. He set his face away from the horrid sight, comforted at least by the fact that the zombi didn't realize what was happening to her. He resolved once again to bring an end to this atrocity as soon as possible.

The fat raindrops made loud, splattering sounds as they pelted down on the tin roof. The sounds quickly became louder and Sardi realized it was hailing. Drops of ice ranging from marble to golf-ball size pounded off the roof. This was, Sardi thought, a sign that the coming storm would be a big one.

The sky darkened further, though it was still daytime. After fifteen minutes of hail, a lightning bolt hit in the fields not far from the shed, thunder cracked like an artillery volley, and the sky opened.

Rain came down in sheets, thundering on the tin roof as loud as if a truckful of bowling balls had been dumped on it. It was an awesome display of primitive nature unleashed. Sardi was glad that he wasn't outside and wondered about the poor zombi workers who were.

It wasn't long before they came straggling in. Their human overseers came running in first, staggering from the pounding power of the deluge that was engulfing them. The zombis started to trickle in after them. It took a long time for all of them to make it out of the storm. Some were battered to their hands and knees from the force of the rain, and they came in crawling, inch by inch, and collapsed in grotesque, deathlike poses as they made their way under the roof, seeking shelter from the storm.

"Someone should go get their food," one of the soldiers suggested.

"Not me! I don't want to get wet."

"Wait until it stops raining," another said.

"That could take hours," the first soldier suggested.

"So? You so anxious to see them fed, you go get the food."

The first soldier looked out at the rain. "Well, I guess it wouldn't hurt—"

He never finished his sentence.

There was a crash like a bomb exploding on the shed's metal roof. Sardi was flung to the ground. As he went down he saw lightning chain from the sky and shoot through a score of bodies, soldiers and zombis alike, burning and sparking like a pinwheel gone mad. Sardi smelled ozone and burnt flesh, and then there was a great, ear-shattering clap of thunder, and he felt as if he were struck by a hammer of the gods.

And then there was nothing.

"I assure you," Jenks said with a calmness he didn't feel, "the ambassador is a personal friend of mine."

The man at the door of the Haven consulate looked down his long, patrician nose. Jenks knew that he was dirty, his clothes were filthy, and he hadn't shaved in what felt like a week. In other circumstances he would have found his situation funny, but he knew that there wasn't any time for slapstick. A company of killer zombis was about to be unleashed on New York City, and this geek in a butler's costume was keeping him from reporting it.

The butler apparently made up his mind. "I'm afraid, sir, that I'll have to insist on seeing your invitation."

Jenks stared at him. "I didn't travel a thousand miles in a coffin with a living dead man, sneak through customs, then make my way across town with nothing but my good looks and a pocketful of *gourdes* to be stopped now." He put his hand on the butler's chest and shoved. "Out of the way, Jeeves," he said, and stalked into the consulate's antechamber.

Sounds of merriment were coming from the large reception area off to the right. Jenks followed the noise, and the butler followed him, expostulating noisily and angrily. Jenks ignored him and upon reaching the reception area scanned the sea of tuxedos and evening gowns for Jorge Vanderhoff, Haven ambassador to the United Nations.

He was easy to spot. He was the only one in the crowd whose eye patch matched his crushed-velvet tuxedo. Jenks put his fingers in his mouth and blew a shrill, blasting whistle. Every head in the room turned to Jenks and the embarrassed butler who was trying, and failing, to drag him away by his left arm.

Jenks waved the right one in Vanderhoff's direction, beckoning him. Vanderhoff sighed in a put-upon way, excused himself from the glacial Scandinavian beauty in a very low-cut designer gown whom he was chatting up, and headed Jenks's way.

"That will be all, Ferguson," Vanderhoff said to the butler, who was still trying to physically remove Jenks from the scene.

The butler let go of Jenks's arm, straightened his vest, and bowed. "Very good, sir," he said huffily, and went off searching for a tray of canapés to circulate.

Vanderhoff regarded Jenks sardonically with his one good eye. He was a tall, slim man who carried himself with impeccable grace, despite the fact that he was missing his left eye and had an artificial left hand that he habitually covered with a black glove. Once he had been one of Justice's best field operatives, but the massive injuries he'd sustained in Panama forced him to retire from active duty. He still served Justice and Haven as Haven's ambassador to the United Nations.

He shook his head at Jenks. "Well, you certainly know how to make an entrance," he said.

"We don't have time for your fancy words, Jorge," Jenks said bluntly. The two were old comrades in the field, but they didn't always see eye to eye on things. "We got us a crisis on our hands."

Vanderhoff realized that Jenks was dead serious, so he refrained from making any comments about the ex-lawman's wardrobe. "What is it?"

Jenks opened his mouth, then shut it again. He shook his head at Vanderhoff. "All right. I'm going to give it to you straight, though I reckon that it'll be hard to believe." He took a deep breath. "A company of zombi assassins have just been smuggled into New York by the Haitian special envoy to the United Nations."

Vanderhoff didn't even blink. "Are you drunk, my friend? I know that you look like you're coming off a week-long bender—"

"Dammit, Jorge, do you think I'd make up something this stupid?"

Vanderhoff spread his arms in a mystified shrug. "I don't know—"

"Look, we shouldn't be jawing like this in the open. Let's go to your office and talk things over."

"That would be wise," Vanderhoff said. "This way."

"Wait a sec." Jenks had recognized Ferguson the butler, who was circulating a tray of finger food along the outer edge of the crowd. "Ferguson!"

The butler pretended not to hear, but Jenks called again, louder, and gestured for him to come over.

"Sir!" Ferguson said, bowing and offering Jenks his tray.

"Thanks." Jenks took the tray from Ferguson and popped a pâté-smeared cracker into his mouth. "Food service was lousy on the flight up from Haiti," he told the astonished butler. "Bring me a couple of cold beers too, would ya?" he asked as he followed Vanderhoff while wolfing down tidbits from the tray.

Vanderhoff's office, like the man himself, was rather elegant and refined. Jenks didn't spare any attention to the decor. He demolished the tray of hors d'oeuvres, washing them down with the bottles of cold St. Pauli Girl that Ferguson had brought for him, while Vanderhoff spoke at length on the phone.

Vanderhoff finally put down the telephone and turned in his swivel chair to face Jenks as he swilled down the last bottle of beer.

"Well?" Jenks asked.

"Well . . . Justice and Sardi and Kim are somewhere in the wilds of Haiti. Justice has ordered Jake Ousteoputcha and the submarine to Haiti for unknown reasons. Also Joachim One Eagle and a detachment of Haven commandos. Jake has made contact and is awaiting further orders, though Justice and the others seem to be incommunicado for now."

"So you believe me?"

Vanderhoff nodded. "It's a most amazing story, but I'm sure that I have to believe you. If what you say is correct, we don't seem to have much time." He paused thoughtfully. "If I'm to help you with this, I'll have to delegate some authority if Haven's preparations for the worldwide economic summit are to be completed in time."

"What summit?" Jenks asked. "You're privy to all this political bullshit, but I don't know squat about it."

"You would be if you paid more attention at Haven board meetings. Let's see . . ." Vanderhoff stared at the ceiling as he gathered his thoughts. "Many of the heads of state have already arrived. . . . The first official meeting will be tomorrow morning. Bush will be there, and Thatcher and Gorbachev. Mulrooney from Canada. Walesa from Poland. Mitterand, whoever's in charge of Japan now—they change so fast I can't remember—and half a dozen others. Tomorrow night there'll be a gathering in the square before the United Nations building, where Bush will address—"

"That's it!" Jenks said excitedly, pointing his beer bottle at Vanderhoff. "That's when it'll take place!"

"This zombi attack?" Vanderhoff said with a frown.

"Sure! We know they're going after a big target here in New York City. What could be bigger than the heads of state of the dozen greatest nations of the world?"

"But why?" Vanderhoff asked.

Jenks shook his head. "I don't know. Not just yet. But I've got the feeling that this is really only the tip of the iceberg as far as Moreau's plans are concerned. Almost, maybe, even a feint . . ."

"Assassinating the heads of a dozen powerful nations—and no telling how many others in the crowd—only a feint?"

"You don't know the man," Jenks said. "I do. I've seen him in operation up front and personal. The guy's evil. That's the only word for it. He'd torture a child to death just to wile away some time on a slow afternoon. The man would do anything."

Vanderhoff nodded, impressed by Jenks's earnestness. "I believe you. But what can we do? How can we stop him?"

Jenks looked Vanderhoff in the eye. His jaw was set grimly, his pale blue eyes shone with a determined light. "There's only one thing we can do," he said. "We take down the Haitian consulate. Tonight."

Vanderhoff stared. "That's against international law!" he said.

"So's turning people into zombis and setting them loose with Uzis and a microphone blaring 'Kill! Kill!' in their ears." He leaned forward intently. "Don't you see? Our only chance to stop them is while they're holed up in the consulate like rats. Once they're dispersed around the city, there's no way we can get them all. It's gotta be tonight!"

Jenks and Vanderhoff stared at each other for a long, long time, then Vanderhoff nodded. "I hope to Christ that you're right about this."

Jenks leaned back in his chair and shook his head. "Don't matter if I'm right or not. Either way our asses are gonna be cooked. Either the zombis'll get us, or the international diplomatic community will."

Vanderhoff smiled. "Well, I was getting a little weary of this job, anyway."

XVI.

SOMEWHERE IN THE HAITIAN COUNTRYSIDE
1ST OCTOBER—9:07 P.M.

The rain had slowed to a misting drizzle, but lightning still rent the sky with stunning regularity, and thunder burst upon Justice's ears like a never-ending cannonade. The air smelled crisp and fresh. The breeze was cool and cleansing. Justice looked around the graveyard, shovel in hand, waiting for Marie to make her selection.

"This one," she finally said, pointing at a grave that had bare earth piled upon it. A pathetic, sun-bleached wreath of plastic flowers was stuck on its apex. "Dig here."

Justice shoved his shovel into the dirt. It was hard and claylike, scarcely moistened by the tumultuous rain that had struck its surface and run off without sinking very deep. The digging was hard work, not helped by the fact that Justice had mixed emotions about being here. He had no strong religious feelings that could be tied to any particular church, but he felt that they were disturbing something that after a weary, spirit-crushing life, at least deserved an unbroken rest.

He hadn't gone down more than three feet before his shovel struck something with a different feel. Marie held up the lantern, and its light showed a mat woven of reeds. Justice cleared the dirt away from its surface, then at Marie's nod dug through it, exposing several layers of cloth. Under that was the wooden casket.

"Pull it out," Marie ordered, and Justice bent down and grabbed the corners. He heaved and the casket came reluctantly from its resting place. It was only about three feet long.

"That's for a child," Justice said, and Marie nodded.

"Child's bones are best for the zombi dust. They are sweet and innocent, yet full of bitter energy at a life cut too short."

As she spoke she smiled, her eyes wide and full of a dark knowledge. Cloaked against the cool wind, her haunting eyes shining in the lantern light, Marie was a different woman from the so very human female who had taken Justice's love that afternoon on the beach. She was a different person now, whom Justice did not like very much.

"Break into the casket to make sure there's a body," Marie ordered.

Justice looked at her for a long moment, then complied, smashing in the wooden front with the blade of his shovel. They both peered down to look in it, Justice with a grimace of distaste, Marie with a wide smile.

"Oh, yes," she crooned. "A perfect specimen. Perfect."

It couldn't have been in the ground very long, no more than a month or two, because most of its flesh, though gray and claylike, still clung to the bones of its

face. Its eyes were sunken, its lips shriveled away from
its small, drooping mouth. It was the body of a little boy
who looked as if he'd lived sixty years of misery instead
of just six.

"Take the entire coffin."

As she stood, turning to go,' Justice grabbed her arm.
"Doesn't this bother you?"

She seemed surprised at his question. "Why should
it?"

Justice shook his head. "It seems like a desecration—"

"It is," she said calmly. "Remember what I asked you
earlier? Do you have the courage to know voudou? It can
sometimes be a very difficult thing."

Justice only nodded.

"Very well then. As I said. Take the coffin."

Justice slipped the coffin into the large burlap sack
Marie handed him and slung it over his shoulder. She
led the way out of the cemetery, holding the lantern
high. Justice followed and couldn't help but think that
the misting rain was weeping for a child forced into a life
of poverty and need, then deprived of the only rest it
knew.

The sentinel on guard at the entrance back at the
hounfour carried an ancient shotgun that looked more
suitable for knocking pigeons off a branch than protection
against enemy soldiers. He nodded grimly at Marie and
Justice as they passed into the *hounfour* compound.

Mambo Jennette met them before her hut. She embraced Marie, and Justice was struck by a sudden realization upon seeing the two women together for the first
time. Their faces were the faces of mother and daughter.
True, Mambo Jennette's was round and jowly, but carve
away the fat, and there were the same high planes and
fine bone structure that made Marie's face a fashion
photographer's dream. There was no doubt about it.
Marie was the Mambo's child.

Mambo Jennette looked at Justice and smiled a quirky
smile. "You don't believe," she said, almost as if she
could read his mind, "that a fat old woman could have
such a daughter?"

Justice shook his head. "I'm sure you weren't always a fat old woman."

"Once I was young and slim and danced for the spirits," Mambo Jennette said. "As Marie now does." She put an affectionate arm around her daughter and looked at Justice's pack. "Your journey to the cemetery was not in vain, I see."

Marie shook her head. "Your prayers to Baron Samedi pleased him. He allowed us to pass unmolested with just what we needed for the powder."

"Bring it inside," Mambo Jennette said. "The brazier has been lit. The other ingredients have been gathered."

Justice followed them into the spacious hut that Mambo Jennette had indicated. Inside, it was well lit by several lanterns. A charcoal brazier was burning in the center of the room. Various objects were laid out on the table beside it.

"Now," Mambo Jennette said, "we begin."

Justice set his burden down and watched as she turned to a shallow bowl sitting on the table next to the brazier. She lit a match and dropped it into the clear liquid in the bowl, which immediately flamed up. She dipped her hands into the flame, and it leapt and danced on her skin as she made vigorous washing motions, almost as if she were a surgeon scrubbing up before an operation. She gestured to Marie, who approached and held out her arms.

Mambo Jennette passed the flame on to her, rubbing the flesh of her hands and arms vigorously. Then she turned and gestured to Justice. He looked at her for a moment, then stepped forward.

She slapped fire onto the palms of his hands. It didn't burn. It felt warm, then cool as she rubbed the flame all over his arms. It was somehow cleansing, as if all his humanity were burning away, leaving something distant, unattached, somehow godlike.

After Mambo Jennette finished washing him with flame, Marie approached and rubbed his arms, hands, face, and neck with an oily, aromatic liquid. It felt like suntan lotion and smelled of lemon, lime, and a multitude of tropical fruits.

"What's this?" Justice asked.

"Protection from the powder," Marie said, rubbing all her own exposed skin with the oil. She gave him a red satin scarf and took a similar one and tied it around her face, as if she were preparing to rob a stagecoach. "And this is to keep us from inhaling any."

Justice followed suit. Mambo Jennette was already similarly attired. She went to the coffin and removed the broken wooden lid. A single yank of her powerful-looking hands pulled the head off the tiny corpse. She squeezed the skull, crushing it. It collapsed inward like a wooden sculpture with dry rot, releasing a repulsive odor that Justice could smell despite the scarf protecting his nose.

Mambo Jennette put the skull on the grill, covering it with a battered copper pot, and then turned to the table, picking up a jar that Justice recognized from their fishing expedition earlier in the day. The toad was still in it, now lying dead on its back with the sea worm lying curled up around it. Mambo Jennette took the toad out of the jar and laid it on the grill next to the skull. She spread out all its legs to dry the corpse of the unfortunate amphibian over the fire.

While she was doing this, Marie had gone back to the coffin and pulled away another part of the tiny body. It was the left tibia, the large leg bone. This she proceeded to grind against a metal file, letting the powder sift down into a mortar made from a block of wood. As she ground, she sang a song in Haitian Creole, using the rasping, grinding sound of metal on bone as the rhythm line. Mambo Jennette took up the song as she placed the body of the puffer fish that they'd captured that morning on the grill next to the toad.

Marie, without breaking the cadence of her song, caught Justice's attention by kicking him and nodded toward another bottle on the table. As he retrieved it for her he glanced into it. It contained half a dozen dead tarantulas and an equal number of curled-up millipedes. At Marie's instruction Justice dumped them all into the mortar in which Marie was grinding the child's bone.

"That's fine," Marie said, as she dropped the last fragments of bone into the mortar. "Now those leaves—don't touch them with your bare skin. They have hairs on them that get into your flesh and make you feel as if you have slivers of glass under your skin."

Justice handled them gingerly, using an ancient pair of tongs that was on the table. He dropped them into the mortar with the other ingredients.

For a fleeting moment he thought of saying, What, no eye of newt? but he didn't. This was deadly serious. He could tell from the looks of absolute concentration on the women's faces.

Mambo Jennette added the now-dried bodies of toad and puffer fish to the mortar, and Marie took up the foot-long carved wooden pestle that looked more than vaguely penislike and began to grind everything together.

"There is more than one kind of zombi powder," she told Justice as she ground the ingredients down with even, measured strokes. "Depending on the proportion, and strength, and freshness of the ingredients you put in, some powders can cause instant death, some can cause the skin to rot on contact, others can make the victim waste away slowly."

"What about this one?" Justice asked.

He saw her smile under her satin scarf. Her hand gripped the pestle just under its swollen head as she caressingly drove down on the shaft. "Here," she said, "we're aiming for instant death."

A noxious yellow smoke was rising from the brazier. Mambo Jennette took the cover from the child's crushed skull. The bones had practically turned to charcoal. She handled them carefully with the tongs that Justice had used earlier and added them to the mess in the mortar.

"That is it," she said to Justice. "The final ingredient of the zombi powder." She watched Marie grind away with the pestle for several moments, then nodded approvingly. "That is perfect. I will take over now."

She moved in behind her daughter, and they exchanged the pestle like relay runners exchanging a baton without breaking rhythm or speed.

"Come," Marie said to Justice. She led him out of the hut's rear door, out into the Haitian night. The rain had stopped, the breeze had turned from cool to warm.

"We have to change our clothes," she told Justice, "in case some of the powder was blown on them."

Justice followed her as she went through the compound with her lithe, sinuous walk. They went past the huts, then an open field, and to a bubbling spring screened from the compound by a shield of trees. Marie stripped off her clothes, carefully and slowly, as Justice watched. He wondered how much of this was necessity, how much show.

"Do we really have to do this?" he asked.

"Absolutely."

She came to Justice and slowly unbuttoned his shirt, and then carefully pulled it away from him without letting it touch any part of his skin. Then she kneeled before him and unsnapped his trousers and pulled down his zipper. With excruciating care she peeled down his pants to his ankles. He stepped out of them.

"Now a good wash," she said.

"Is this also necessary?" Justice asked.

She shrugged, her breasts bouncing in the moonlight. "It is better to be careful than sorry."

She walked gracefully into the small spring-fed pool, glancing coyly back over her shoulder at Justice. After a moment he followed her.

The water was cool and sweet. Her flesh was hot and demanding.

Sardi came to with the smell of sizzling human flesh in his nostrils and wails of pain and fear ringing in his ears.

The storm had slowed to a major downpour. Lightning and thunder were still crackling and growling overhead, but at a distance, receding over the mountains.

It looked as if half the zombis were missing from the shed. Sardi could see them roaming about aimlessly in the compound, some even heading back to the fields. Sardi couldn't tell if they were searching for food or enjoying a newfound freedom caused by the wild tumultuousness of the storm.

Some of those still under the sheltering roof were burned by lightning. Sardi stared at a zombi whose entire right side was still smoking. It looked blankly around out of its left eye while its right ran like scalded jelly down the side of its blackened right cheek.

Some of the guards had also been hit by the bolt that had bounced back and forth through the shed like a deadly pinball. The injured guards were moaning while some of their fellows tried to help them, and others were attempting the near-hopeless task of rounding up a couple of hundred aimlessly wandering zombis.

It was time to go, Sardi thought. He'd never have a better chance.

He simply walked by the guards, out into the rain. The Blazer was still parked before the barracks, keys in the ignition. Who, after all, was going to steal Moreau's Blazer? One of the soldiers? One of the zombis?

Sardi got in and sat behind the wheel, dripping all over the upholstery. He flicked on the dome light and rummaged through the glove compartment. To his delight he found a much-folded, multiply stained road map. He studied its tattered but still readable surface and discovered that he was approximately one hundred and eighty miles due north of Port-au-Prince. In any normal country that was about a three-hour trip. Double that, Sardi decided, for Haiti. At least.

Sardi folded up the map and dropped it onto the passenger's seat. He started the Blazer, backed up, and took off. He passed one of the soldiers and waved. The soldier stared at him for a long moment, utterly nonplussed by the sight of a zombi driving off in the colonel's car. By the time he thought to take a shot at him, Sardi had already disappeared around a long, steep curve of the road, heading south to Port-au-Prince and freedom.

XVII.

HAVEN CONSULATE, NEW YORK CITY
1ST OCTOBER—MIDNIGHT

"Have you gone mad?" Charlie Mandrake demanded. "Do you want to end up back in federal prison?"

Jenks looked at Mandrake seriously and shook his head. Mandrake worked for the State Department. He was someone Justice and his people could always count on for support, and Vanderhoff had insisted that Mandrake be informed of events. When Jenks told him that he intended to crash the Haitian consulate, Mandrake seemed ready to draw the line.

"That's sovereign Haitian territory you're talking about," Mandrake expostulated. "Why, it'd be like invading Haiti itself!"

"Haiti's already invaded the United States," Jenks said.

Mandrake shook his head vigorously. "Yeah, you told me. With a force of zombis. Christ, man, you've been watching too many horror movies lately." He turned to Vanderhoff, the only other person present in Vanderhoff's office. "Can't you talk some sense into him?"

"He *knows* I'm not bullshitting, Charlie," Jenks said. "And you should too." He stood up and paced before the desk. "As nutty as it sounds, I've seen the damn things. I've fought 'em. Christ, I even shared a fucking pine box with one all the way here from Haiti." He stopped pacing in front of Mandrake's chair and leaned down on its arms, his face six inches from Mandrake's. "They're *real*, my friend, real as death and taxes, and if you don't believe me by this time tomorrow morning you're going to be up to your ass in death. Take it to the bank."

Mandrake was flustered, but still not convinced. "Can't we talk to Justice about this?"

Jenks slammed his palms down hard on the chair's armrests and jerked away in frustration.

"Justice," Vanderhoff reminded Mandrake, "is off somewhere in Haiti. I've left a message for him at his hotel room to call us, but," Vanderhoff shrugged, "there's been no reply yet."

"And there's no friggin' time to waste," Jenks said heatedly. "We've dicked around too much as it is. We've got to move while those zombis are all in one place, otherwise they'll be damn near unstoppable tomorrow."

"Zombis," Mandrake groaned, holding his head in his hands. He looked up and waved off Jenks's coming protest. "All right, all right. Let's say you've experienced *something* during your visit to Haiti. Call them zombis. Call them terrorists. Call them whatever you want. You claim they've been smuggled into the country, and that complaint is serious enough to warrant an investigation." He stood up decisively. "Let's go."

Jenks shook his head. "Ohhh, no. You're just a desk jockey—"

"Who's coming along for the ride." He held up his hands and shook his head. "No arguments here. You want to do this insane thing, you're going to have company. You need someone to talk you out of prison when you get caught," Mandrake added in a mutter.

Jenks and Vanderhoff exchanged glances.

"All right," Jenks said. "But try to stay out of the way."

"I'll do my best," Mandrake said sardonically. "Where is this consulate, anyway?"

Vanderhoff took a diplomatic directory off the shelf behind his desk and flipped through it. "Here it is," he announced after a few moments of searching. "The Haitian consulate is located in a suite on East Forty-second Street." He looked up at Jenks. "Doesn't seem a likely place to keep fifty zombis."

"At least it's a place to start looking."

Jenks, Mandrake, and Vanderhoff rendezvoused in the parking garage where Vanderhoff kept his Volvo. The

Haven consulate was on East Forty-second Street, but considerably closer to the United Nations complex than to Haiti's consulate, which was less than a block east of Fifth Avenue.

Mandrake looked at Jenks and frowned. "Isn't it a little warm to be wearing an overcoat?" he asked.

Jenks shrugged. "I hear they're fairly common on Forty-second Street any time of year. I got more to hide than most of the others running around with overcoats, though."

He flashed it open, and Mandrake stared at the sleek plastic-and-steel weapon that looked like a refugee from a futuristic war movie. "What the hell is that?" he asked.

"Combat shotgun," Jenks explained. "Called the Jackhammer."

He held it out for close inspection. All visible parts were shiny black plastic but for the barrel, muzzle compensator, and flash eliminator. A cylindrical rotary magazine sat behind the pistol-grip handle, right in front of the fore end of the stock. The sights were set in a channel on the assembly atop the barrel, which also was a carrying handle that ran almost the entire thirty-inch length of the weapon. Jenks had the shotgun strapped into the inside of his coat through the handle. He pointed at the magazine.

"Ten-round ammo cassette," he explained. "Spent cartridges stay inside the cylinder. The whole thing drops out when it's empty." He opened the other side of his coat where nearly a dozen cassettes were attached to the lining. "On full automatic a ten-round cassette can be emptied in two point three seconds."

"What are you planning on taking on," Mandrake asked, "tanks?"

Jenks shook his head. "Something worse," he said softly. "Dead men. Very, very tough dead men."

Mandrake shook his head in disbelief and started to get into the driver's side of the Volvo. Jenks grabbed his arm and shook his head. "Shotgun," he called, and Mandrake sighed and got into the backseat.

Vanderhoff drove skillfully with his one hand, clutching the wheel with his prosthesis when he had to shift. Traffic was still rather heavy despite the fact that it was midnight, and when they reached the Haitian consulate building, there were no nearby parking places.

"Pull over into the closest side street," Jenks suggested.

Vanderhoff stashed the car behind a dumpster behind a building away from the structure that housed the consulate. "What now?"

"One of us should stay with the car," Jenks said. "We might have to make a quick getaway."

They both turned to look at Mandrake, who shook his head. "I'd love to stay behind, fellows, but I can't."

"Why not?" Jenks asked.

"I can't drive a standard."

"Combat veteran," Jenks muttered. He turned to Vanderhoff, who sighed and nodded reluctantly.

"I guess I'm elected, although I'd really like to get in on the action. There's not much opportunity for gunplay when you spend most of your time on the floor as a UN delegate," Vanderhoff said dryly. "Though at times that wouldn't be a bad idea."

Jenks clapped him on the shoulder. "Stay alert. I have the feeling that we're going to need the cavalry before this is all over. And you're it."

The building housing the Haitian consulate was locked up tight for the night.

"Shit," Jenks complained. "There's enough electronic circuitry wired into this door to build a computer. We can smash our way in, but the cops will be all over our asses real fast."

"This is New York," Mandrake reminded him. "It'll probably take half an hour for them to get here. But that still doesn't give us enough time. We're going to have to try something you're not very familiar with—subtlety. Follow me."

Mandrake led Jenks around to the front of the building and rapped loudly on the glass doors opening into the front lobby. Within a few moments a gray-uniformed security guard was staring out at them through the glass. "Yeah?" he asked. "What do you want?" His words were all but indistinguishable through the thick glass.

Mandrake held up his identification. "Justice Department," he said.

The guard unlocked the door and let them in. "What's going on?" He was a young guy, black, who regarded them with suspicion. The name tag over his breast pocket said "Fred."

"Sting operation, Fred," Mandrake told him in his most official voice. "We've got to set up a listening post in one of the suites upstairs."

The guard scratched his head. "I wasn't told nothing about any sting operation."

"Of course not." Mandrake rolled his eyes as he glanced at Jenks. "It's secret. We're notifying you now."

Fred wasn't totally mollified. "But my boss never told me—"

"Of course he didn't," Mandrake said in a confidential tone. "He's one of the major targets of the probe. What was the name?" he asked, looking at Jenks with an impatient expression.

"Uhhh—" Jenks began.

"Mr. Sinclair?" Fred asked unbelievingly.

"Yeah, that's it. Sinclair."

"What's he supposed to be doing?"

"Helping drug smugglers," Jenks suggested.

"The bastard," Fred said. "How're they doing it?"

Jenks looked at Mandrake.

"In bodies," Mandrake said. "Dead bodies flown into the country packed with cocaine. Seen any being delivered here lately?"

"Jeez," Fred shuddered. "That's creepy." He pulled at his lower lip reflectively. "I don't remember anything. Let's check the visitors' log."

Fred led them over to his small desk against the far wall of the lobby and pulled out a battered ledger, running his finger over the night's entries and "hmmmming" to himself.

"Well," Fred finally said, "there was a delivery truck here, came by, what, about eight o'clock. I remember, I seen 'em carry some big cases up there. Coffin-sized, I'd say." He frowned suddenly. "That's funny."

"What?" Mandrake and Jenks said at the same time.

"Some Colonel Albert Moreau signed in, he never

signed out." He looked up at Jenks and Mandrake. "He must still be up there."

"Tall, fat, black?" Jenks asked. "Mean looking with an eye patch."

"That's him," Fred said.

Jenks and Mandrake looked at each other. "He's our man," Jenks said.

"We have to go check it out," Mandrake agreed.

"What do you want me to do?" Fred asked.

"Wait here," Mandrake suggested. He looked at his watch. "If we're not down in twenty minutes, call in an alarm."

Fred nodded decisively. "Okay. Good luck."

Jenks glanced at Mandrake while they were in the elevator going up.

"You took quite a chance back there."

Mandrake shrugged. "Not really. Knowing how to handle people is my job. I just had to get the guard involved, get him on our side, and everything was all right."

"Yeah," Jenks said, "but showing him your ID was pretty ballsy."

Mandrake shook his head and took his ID wallet out of his pocket. "Hey," he said, "I may work for the government, but I'm not stupid." He flashed the ID at Jenks. Pinned into the wallet was a school crossing-guard badge. "I've had that since the sixth grade. First time I ever used it."

Jenks shook his head. "You're not as square as I thought."

"I've been working with you guys for too long," Mandrake said.

They got out of the elevator on the floor that contained the Haitian consulate. The corridor was dark and quiet, and it looked as if everyone had long gone home. But Jenks knew that wasn't true. Moreau was there somewhere, surrounded by a squadron of his undead assassins. He hoped that the zombis hadn't been armed yet. Otherwise the odds were going to be mighty steep.

"I'll go first," Jenks whispered. "You watch my back."

Mandrake nodded and drew his snub-nosed .38 from where it had been clipped to his waist.

Jenks shook his head. "You're going to need more stopping power than that."

"You do things your way," Mandrake said, "and I'll do them mine. I'm getting really sick and tired—" he began, then Jenks shoved him and yelled, "Get down!"

A tall, dark, lean figure had appeared in the mouth of the corridor not twenty paces in front of them and cut loose with a burst of gunfire that ripped across Jenks's chest and flung him to the floor.

Mandrake glanced back at him, then at the steadily approaching figure who was goose-stepping forward inexorably while ejecting his used clip and fumbling for another to ram home into his Uzi.

Mandrake blanked his mind. There was no time to worry about Jenks now. He rose to one knee and extended his pistol in a two-handed firing stance. Taking careful aim, he squeezed off a shot. The .38 bucked in his hand, and his shot struck home high on his target's chest. The target stumbled, then continued to come down the hall toward him.

Mandrake stared. The lighting in the hall was dim, but he could see the entrance hole his bullet had torn through his target's shirt—right over the heart. But still the man came on.

Mandrake quickly aimed and squeezed off two more shots, one right after the other. The man jerked twice at the impact of Mandrake's bullets ripping through his upper chest but still came on.

"Sweet Jesus in heaven," Mandrake mumbled. He could see the man's face now, and it wasn't human. The eyes were blank and staring, the other features totally wooden and immobile. It didn't even seem to breathe as it finally rammed home the clip with its fumbling fingers and pointed the Uzi one-handed right at Mandrake. Mandrake gaped at it helplessly, and suddenly there was an explosion from behind him, and the assassin disintegrated—that's what you had to call it—disintegrated right in front of Mandrake's eyes.

The thing's torso disappeared in a storm of shot that juiced its chest and stomach to bits of indistinguishable flesh. Its limbs were blown away, looking as if they'd been half devoured by a storm of invisible locusts. Only through a trick of chance did the head survive relatively untouched. It was blown back with the rest of the corpse, which splattered against the corridor wall and left a dripping Rorschach pattern of vibrantly gruesome hues.

Mandrake swiveled around to see Jenks standing behind him, a savage, determined look on his face, his feet spread wide and his automatic shotgun up from under his long coat. He ejected the ammunition cassette and slammed another one home.

"We better move," Jenks said. "We can safely assume the others now know we're here."

"I thought you were dead," Mandrake babbled. "Dead or hurt bad."

Jenks tapped his chest. "I'm not stupid," he said. "Kevlar."

"You still gotta be hurting."

Jenks coughed. "Tell me about it. I'll have time to piss and moan later, when this is all over. Right now we've gotta move."

He yanked Mandrake to his feet, and they both ran down the corridor in the direction the assassin had come from, avoiding the disarticulated limbs and gory ooze that was all that remained of the killer.

The door to the consulate suite was closed.

"Fuck it," Jenks said, "enough subtlety," and swept right to left across the door and nearby walls, emptying another ammunition cassette on full automatic. Jenks charged after the fusillade, smashing through the door that was dangling from its upper hinge.

Two more zombi assassins had been standing in ambush on either side of the door. They were both down, mangled by blasts from the Jackhammer, but were still crawling for the Uzis that had been blown out of their grasp by the impact of the shotgun pellets.

"Head shots!" Jenks ordered as Mandrake followed him into the wreckage of the reception room.

Mandrake looked at one of the zombis still struggling to reach its weapon despite its massive wounds. "My God," he said. "How can anything live with such injuries?"

"I told you!" Jenks said with exasperation. "They're

not alive. Not exactly, anyway. Finish them off so we can move on."

Mandrake did so, distastefully, putting two shots in the head of one of the zombis, three in the head of the other, before it finally stopped moving.

"Believe me now?" Jenks asked.

Mandrake only nodded.

"In there," Jenks said, pointing into the interior offices.

They penetrated the suite, moving fast and low and taking advantage of all available cover, but it was no use. It was deserted. A back door, still open, showed how the others had made their escape.

"I'd better call Fred," Mandrake suddenly said, "and tell him to lay the hell low. He'd be no match for this bunch."

"And it'd be nice to have a live witness to tell us where they headed."

Mandrake got to Fred just in time. When they reached the lobby, he was crouched behind the railing of the candy counter in the corner of the room. He jumped up when Mandrake and Jenks approached, Jenks still moving gingerly and favoring his right shoulder. The kevlar had stopped the Uzi from turning him into swiss cheese, but he'd still been bruised and battered by the impact of the half-dozen slugs that had stitched across his upper chest and shoulder.

"Who were those guys?" Fred asked with wide eyes.

"Exactly what did you see?" Jenks asked.

"The big guy," Fred said, "the guy you described before, surrounded by maybe half a dozen guys toting Uzis, I mean just holding them out for all the world to see—"

"How long ago?" Jenks burst out.

"About a minute—" Fred said, and they ran for the door.

Mandrake glanced over his shoulder and yelled back, "Call the police!" as they reached the glass door and hit the street.

It was late, but traffic was still running on Forty-second Street, and there were still a fair number of pedestrians heading for subway stops or looking for taxis after the late shows of the nearby Times Square movie houses. As Mandrake and Jenks frantically looked up and down the street, they saw a tight cluster of men walking west. The big guy in the lead was trying to flag down a taxi but was having no success as they reached the corner of Forty-second and Fifth Avenue.

"Get Vanderhoff," Jenks told Mandrake. "We may need the car to keep up with them. I'll follow on foot."

Mandrake nodded and took off while Jenks, his Jackhammer secure under his coat, sauntered down the street after Moreau and his zombis, trying to look as inconspicuous as possible. He got halfway down the block when a taxi stopped to pick up Moreau and his party. Mandrake and Vanderhoff were nowhere in sight.

"Hey!" Jenks shouted, breaking into a shuffling run. "Stop, hey!"

No one was paying him the slightest attention. There was a way to deal with that. He swung the Jackhammer out from under his coat and let loose a single blast into the air. There was a moment of stunned silence as pedestrians stopped and drivers out on Forty-second Street slowed to peer at what was happening.

Jenks yelled "Hey!" again and pointed his shotgun at the cab, a hundred feet down the street. "Stop!"

Of course, he didn't.

Moreau was half in the cab. Jenks couldn't hear what he told the driver, who immediately hit the gas as Moreau hung precariously in the doorway, one foot in, one dragging on the pavement. He couldn't hear what the colonel had said to the zombis, either, but they reacted in a predictable manner.

Before Jenks could say or do anything, they all had their Uzis out and blasting. Some were more precise in their aim than others. Some shot toward Jenks, others aimed in a more-or-less random fashion, blasting away at the sky, or at the unfortunate pedestrians caught between them and Jenks.

Half a dozen New Yorkers went down, clipped by the Haitian assassins. Jenks threw himself into the gutter and emptied a cassette, trying to attract attention to himself so the zombis would stop firing at innocent pedestrians.

He looked up to see the taxi, which had Moreau half hanging out of the rear seat, heading right toward him.

Jenks tensed to roll back onto the sidewalk, and then Vanderhoff's Volvo appeared from nowhere, crossed lanes, and skidded in front of the taxi.

The taxi slammed into the passenger side of Vanderhoff's car, flinging Moreau free. He got up immediately and staggered back to the cab, where he yanked the driver out and flung him on the pavement. Moreau jumped back into the taxi as Jenks got to his feet and, zigzagging through the ragged fire from the zombis, headed toward the scene of the collision.

Moreau settled behind the wheel, dropped the cab into reverse, and stomped the accelerator. Displaying great skill and cool nerve, he swerved around the few cars still traveling east on Forty-second Street.

Moreau jammed on the brakes as he reached his band of zombis and shouted at them to get into the taxi. As they reacted with their usual slowness, Jenks threw himself up against the driver side of the Volvo, where Vanderhoff was groggily trying to shake off the effects of the collision with the taxi.

"After them!" Jenks screamed as he pulled open the driver-side rear door and flung himself into the seat.

Vanderhoff mumbled something under his breath and wiped away the blood streaming from a cut on his forehead. Mandrake fumbled on the floor for his pistol, and Vanderhoff engaged the gears and roared out after Moreau and his taxi full of zombis.

All but two of the creatures had piled into the cab.

"Kill them!" Moreau screamed at the two zombis, pointing at Jenks, who had just thrown himself into Vanderhoff's car. He stomped down on the accelerator again, backing up. To go forward, he would have to drive right into the teeth of Jenks, who was hanging out the Volvo's driver-side rear window, bringing the Jackhammer into line.

Moreau burned rubber as the cab screamed away in reverse, but he quickly realized that Fifth Avenue was blocked by a phalanx of cars whose drivers had stopped to avoid the firefight. There was nowhere for him to go.

Except up the stairs of the public library building.

Moreau clenched his teeth and kept his foot mashed onto the accelerator.

"Look at that crazy bastard!" Jenks yelled, his eyes squinting, his hair blowing back in the wind as he leaned out of the car window.

"Never mind him!" Vanderhoff shouted in reply. "Look out for those!"

The two zombis left behind stood beside each other, about ten feet apart. They brought their Uzis up simultaneously and blasted withering fire that shattered the Volvo's windshield.

Just before the bullets stitched through the glass, Vanderhoff slid under the seat, driving by sheer instinct. Mandrake joined him on the floor, as Jenks aimed at the zombi on the left.

It was kind of like shooting clay pigeons in reverse. The target was just sitting there while the shooter was moving like a bat out of hell.

Jenks felt slugs from the zombi's Uzi tear through his coat and screech and ping on the car door all around him. He squeezed off a double blast from the Jackhammer, and the zombi's head blew up much more messily than any clay pigeon Jenks had ever shot.

The zombi's body stood pointing the Uzi for a moment longer, then realizing that it was finally, irrevocably dead, it collapsed like a marionette with its strings cut as Vanderhoff smashed the second assassin full on the front grille of his car. For a moment it clung to the hood like some kind of ghastly ornament, then slipped down on the pavement. There was a double bump and bounce, then they were by the second zombi.

It tried to crawl after them, but most of the bones in its body had been pulverized, so after a while it gave up and finally died.

"What do we do now?" Vanderhoff screamed into the wind gusting into the car through the hole where the windshield used to be. He squinted against the breeze and shook his head vigorously, shedding most of the glass that was caught in his hair.

"Follow the bastard!" Jenks ordered, so Vanderhoff

did, right up the broad marble stairs of the public library building.

Moreau had left the taxi halfway up the stairs. It was sitting there, all its doors hanging open, looking like a toy abandoned by a careless giant. Vanderhoff bumped and clattered up to it, swearing every time his Volvo's undercarriage banged on the marble stairs.

"My insurance agent will never understand this!" he howled as he slammed on the brakes right next to the abandoned taxi.

"Act of God," Mandrake suggested, as a zombi who had been lying low on the seat popped up, aiming his Uzi. Thanks to the creature's slow reaction time, Mandrake was able to whirl his gun around and plant a slug right between its eyes before it could fire its own weapon.

The zombi stared at Mandrake for a long moment, blinking slowly and laboriously. It looked as if it wanted to say something, but simply slipped down and sprawled bonelessly over the taxi's seat.

"Watch it," Jenks warned. "This looks like a good place for an—"

And two pairs of zombis popped up from their hiding places behind the pillars that flanked the library's central door and opened fire.

"—ambush."

Jenks and Vanderhoff returned fire at the ones on the left, while Mandrake fired at the ones on the right, just as they heard an amplified voice screech over the battle scene, "This is the police speaking! Everyone put your weapons down! I repeat, this is the police! Put your weapons down!"

"Great," Jenks groaned aloud. "Just fucking great!"

"My car has diplomatic plates," Vanderhoff said.

"I don't think they'll do us much good just now," Jenks said, jamming in another ammo cassette.

The zombis continued to fire, even when, turtlelike, their opponents had pulled their heads inside their Volvo shell.

"Put your weapons down immediately!" the policeman on the loudspeaker boomed at them, and when they didn't, he called in the tear-gas strike.

"Let's get out of here!" Jenks shouted, and Vanderhoff put the Volvo in reverse. It slid down the stairs, bumping hideously as they dropped down every riser.

"Justice Department!" Mandrake shouted at the top of his lungs, waving his *real* ID, as they finally shuddered to a stop on the bottom of the landing.

They were passed by a squad of cops in gas masks charging up the stairs, but there was still half a dozen standing behind the open doors of their cars, guns drawn and aimed at the Volvo.

"What's going on?" the cop in charge blared through his bullhorn.

Jenks thought fast. The zombi story wouldn't do. They'd all end up in backward coats in Bellevue. "Drug dealers," he yelled out, hitting upon something the cops were familiar with. "Drug-crazed Rastas! Watch out, they're weirded out on something, makes 'em feel no pain."

"That's crazy!" the guy on the bullhorn shouted, just as the zombis, unaffected by the tear gas, opened fire on the cops charging up the steps. They cut them down to a man, then patiently fell silent, waiting for other targets to come charging through the billowing clouds of gas.

"Let's let the cops deal with these bozos," Jenks said in a low voice to Vanderhoff and Mandrake. "I have the feeling that Moreau's not hanging around here. I want to go after him."

Mandrake nodded. The three men got out of the car and let Mandrake, the only one with legitimate ID, do the talking. The cops momentarily seemed satisfied with his story and were really more concerned with getting the killers who'd gunned down their men on the library steps.

"I'll try to flank them," Jenks offered, and before the officer in charge could accept or decline his offer, he was gone.

He circled around the public library and came upon Bryant Park, which abutted it on the west side of the building. The park was dark and as inviting as any New York City park at night. It would, Jenks figured, offer a perfect refuge for Moreau to hide out and regroup.

Jenks pulled out his pocket flashlight, and swept the ground back and forth next to the library building. After a few moments he found what he'd been hoping for. A trail of fresh blood splatters ran from the library building directly into the park.

It had to be Moreau, a wounded Moreau, running to ground in the park. Jenks hooded his flashlight as best he could and followed the trail of blood.

It was almost like the old days when he was a sheriff back in Kansas running hoodlums to the ground. It made his guts flutter and his heart beat faster just to be on the trail of the most dangerous, intelligent game there was. And this one was wounded, besides being mean and angry. Jenks smiled to himself as he moved into the trees. It gave him a feeling almost like going home again.

It was, in the end, almost too easy. Jenks came upon Moreau, deep in the park, leaning against a big rock and binding up a horribly scraped leg with scraps torn from his shirt.

"Hello again," he said quietly, and Moreau jerked up, startled.

"You!" he hissed.

"Me," Jenks said agreeably, holding his shotgun out and ready, pointed unwaveringly at Moreau. "I've been after your ass from Florida to Haiti and out to the Big Apple, and now it's mine."

"You're so sure of yourself, *blanc*," Moreau sneered. "You forget my powers."

Jenks nodded, never taking his eyes off Moreau. "Uh-huh. You can be in two places at once and turn into a big black dog. How's that hokey shit gonna help you now?"

Moreau smiled evilly. "You forget my mastery over the undead."

He gestured oddly with a pass of his right hand, and two zombis appeared from nowhere out of the darkness, their expressionless eyes boring into Jenks like the unwavering barrels of their Uzis. They stood about twenty feet apart, on either side of Jenks.

"My final two servants from this group," Moreau said. "But do not worry, the others have been dispersed all over the city, only awaiting tomorrow to hear the signal to strike. Good-bye, *blanc*."

Moreau gestured again, and Jenks did the only thing

he could do. He hit the ground, throwing himself forward as he went down.

He felt bullets tear through his coat and pound like trip-hammers on his chest. One went through the biceps of his left arm, another took a chunk out of his cheek, a third drilled through his right thigh.

But the zombis were too slow to track him. They'd had him in a cross fire, but he'd dropped out of it, leaving only the zombis themselves in the way of each other's fusillade.

They shot up each other a lot worse than they shot up Jenks. One went down immediately with a line of bullets perforating its chest. The other emptied its clip, reached for another, and rammed it home as it slowly turned to track Jenks as he rolled on the ground.

Jenks came up with the Jackhammer pointed at the zombi, but the thing had also taken a handful of slugs from its fellow undead. It wavered, went to its knees, and made a valiant effort to point its Uzi one-handed at Jenks. It failed and flopped facedown in the grass.

Jenks twisted around to where Moreau had been leaning against the rock, but the colonel had already disappeared.

"Damn," Jenks swore softly, half in frustration, half in pain. His chest felt as if a gang of carpenters had been beating on him with hammers. His injured arm and leg were numb. He could feel strength leaking from them as the steady pulse of his heart pumped blood out through his wounds.

He tore tourniquets from his shirt to stop the blood flow. It wasn't necessarily the best thing to do medically, but it would have to serve for now, because he had something more important to worry about.

Stop that bastard Moreau.

He pulled himself to his feet. For a moment he was afraid that he wouldn't be able to walk, but the leg wound was clean. It had missed bone and all the major blood vessels, just tearing through muscle, and Jenks discovered that he could hobble slowly along.

He went to where Moreau had been leaning against the rock, but there was no longer any obvious trail to follow, since Moreau had bound up his wounds. There was, however, a path through the park leading away from the rock, and all Jenks could hope was that Moreau had chosen the easy way rather than blaze his own trail through the trees and shrubs.

Jenks hobbled down the path. It came out of the park on Sixth Avenue, Avenue of the Americas, where Jenks paused a moment, looking helplessly up and down the street. Moreau could have gone in damn near any direction. Mumbling a prayer under his breath, Jenks chose west and continued to head toward Times Square, where he figured Moreau might try to get lost in a crowd or to find another taxi.

The streets were crowded with pedestrians coming out of late shows from the movie houses and theaters that lined the square, unaware of the battle that was being fought just a couple blocks east of them.

Everyone who noticed Jenks gave him a wide berth, even the hookers who were anxious for customers. He was pale and lurching down the street in torn and bloody clothes. He kept the Jackhammer out of sight, but no one could miss the look of desperation in his eyes and the blood clotting in the deep furrow in his cheek.

He looked dangerous—and he felt as desperate and dangerous as hell. He wanted Moreau, wanted him so bad he could taste it, but he was afraid that the bastard had hidden himself among the seven million inhabitants of the city, like a rat lost deep in a sewer.

He gritted his teeth, praying and cursing half-aloud, adding to his look of frenzied desperation. But when he'd reached the core of Times Square, in the middle of its unceasing rush of pedestrians passing by sleazy movie houses and dirty souvenir shops, his prayers were answered.

He spotted Moreau, looking even more disheveled and wild than he, trying to flag down taxis who wanted nothing at all to do with him.

"Moreau!" he screamed at the top of his lungs.

The colonel heard and turned to stare at him, and in his eye Jenks saw recognition that this was the showdown, the final confrontation from which only one would walk away alive.

The colonel whirled, going for the gun that he carried

in a shoulder rig. It was a big, chrome-plated Dirty
Harry monstrosity, and as he yanked it from his holster,
time seemed to slow for Jenks.

He felt each beat of his heart, steady and distinct. He
felt the play of muscle and tendon glide against bone as
he pulled the Jackhammer out from beneath his coat and
brought it into line. The passersby who saw the weapons
screamed and ran in super-slow motion, their cries harsh
bird squawks in Jenks's ears.

Moreau got his weapon up first and fired. Jenks could
almost see the bullet screaming toward him. He heard it
rush past his head, whining away into the night.

As pedestrians fell to the sidewalk screaming, he trig-
gered the Jackhammer. He couldn't miss from this range.

The Jackhammer's shell exploded full into Moreau's
torso. The impact lifted him off his feet and threw him
through the plate-glass window of the adult bookstore
behind him.

Jenks hobbled through the sea of screaming, baffled
pedestrians, up to the window from which Moreau's legs
were dangling. Moreau's chest and abdomen were a
bloody mess, but he was still heaving great panting breaths
as Jenks approached. Jenks batted away the inflated plastic sex-toy that had floated down and was embracing
Moreau in her plastic arms, then righted the display of
whips and leather restraints that had also fallen over
him.

His magnum was still gripped loosely in Moreau's
right hand, but Jenks plucked it away from him like
taking candy from a baby. The colonel made a strangled
sound of hatred, and blood ran from his mouth.

"The signal," Jenks said. "Tell me about the signal to
trigger the zombis tomorrow."

"All right," Moreau said with a bloody smile. "I will."
Each word cost the colonel, but he was a man with an
iron will. Before he spoke again, however, he reached up
and pulled his eye patch off. Jenks was astonished to see
that he had a normal, healthy-looking second eye.

"There," Moreau panted. "All the better to see your
face, *blanc* . . . when I tell you . . . the signal will come
. . . from Haiti. The assassins are in place . . . you

cannot find them . . . you cannot stop them . . . their work will . . . be . . . done . . ."

He started to laugh a hideous, gargling laugh, but then began to choke. He tried to sit upright, but couldn't, and coughed up a stream of blood that soaked his already bloody shirt. He stopped coughing and stared silently at Jenks through his two good, but now sightless, eyes.

"Shit," Jenks said, slumping against the window, just as he heard a cop shout, "This is the police! Drop your weapon! Drop your weapon immediately!"

"Again?" Jenks asked, dropping the Jackhammer and sliding down the wall next to the display window. He hit the pavement, hurt, weary, and almost hopeless.

XVIII.

PORT-AU-PRINCE, HAITI
2ND OCTOBER—8:19 A.M.

Justice and Kim held a war conference at their breakfast table at the Ollofson, Justice ticking points off his fingers one by one.

"First, Sardi is still missing. We have no idea where he is.

"Second, Jenks is now missing. He's presumably in America, but we really have no idea where he is, either.

"Third, we've yet to lay eyes on the zombi hit man, and he's the one we came all this way to find." He stopped, took a deep drink of coffee, and shook his head.

"But," Kim said brightly, pointing her fork at Justice with each point she made. "First, we've made contact with a local force that opposes Colonel Moreau. For some of us the contact has been more intimate than others.

"Second, we got plenty of info from Captain Shorty,

who's now stashed on the submarine. I think we should have another talk with him this morning about Moreau's headquarters in the country.

"Third, we got Jake and the submarine, and, more important," she patted the purse on the table next to her, "the guns Jake and Joachim brought with them. Now I don't feel so naked.

"Those are the good points." With that she lowered her fork, speared a bit of pineapple, and popped it into her mouth.

Justice smiled. "You're right—" he began, only to fall silent as a man approached their table.

He was short and thin, like many Haitians, and wore the old, carefully repaired clothes of the Haitian peasantry.

"You are the man called Lambert?" he asked Justice politely.

Justice nodded.

"I have come from Mambo Jennette," he said. "She tells me to fetch you, for she knows now where your friend has been taken."

Justice and Kim smiled at each other.

"She knows where Sardi is?" Justice asked, just to make sure.

The man bobbed his head. "Yes. She says we must hurry. It will take some hours to reach him."

Justice picked up his linen napkin and dropped it on his barely touched breakfast. "Great," he said, smiling and standing. Then it hit him. "Wait a minute," he told the man. "Mambo Jennette knows me by my real name. She wouldn't send someone here for Lambert—"

The messenger had half turned away from Justice and Kim's table. When he turned back, he was holding a tube to his lips. His cheeks ballooned out as he aimed it at Justice and blew. A cloud of blue powder puffed out from the tube, striking Justice in the face. He sucked in half a breath of it, then clenched his throat shut and stepped back out of the cloud. A fine mist of blue particles already had covered his face.

The man with the tube turned toward Kim, who was still sitting at the table, but she had already grabbed her purse. She pointed it at the man and shot him with the gun still inside. The bullet caught him in the forehead, punching out a third eye that weeped blood down his face and onto his freshly laundered shirt.

Kim leapt to her feet. There was instant chaos in the dining room with most of the patrons running and screaming, some staring in horrified fascination, and half a dozen pulling out their own weapons and aiming at Kim. She took no notice, however. She stared helplessly at Justice as he staggered backward, arms out as if to ward off invisible demons.

"Don't touch me," he croaked as Kim approached. "Zombi powder. Don't get it on you."

"What can I do?" she cried out helplessly.

Justice shook his head. "Help. Find Marie. . . ." He suddenly shuddered all over. "Feels like insects crawling under my skin. . . ." He rubbed one hand with the other, but seemed rapidly to be losing control of them. "Cold," he said, "cold in here," even though sweat was running down his forehead and soaking through his shirt.

Kim watched in horror as his lips started to turn blue and his fingers began to twitch uncontrollably. He slumped against a table, and she ran to him and held him by the shoulders despite his earlier warning.

He looked up at her and said with difficulty, "Floating . . . floating away." He worked his throat, but no more words would come, as if his larynx were paralyzed.

He went totally limp. Kim couldn't hold up his dead weight, but managed to ease him to the floor where she held his head in her lap. She looked all around them and shouted, "Help! Someone please get help!"

She felt someone approach and swiveled her head to look up directly into the malevolently smiling features of Colonel Moreau. "Help is here," he told Kim, "but I'm afraid that you may not like it."

He snapped his fingers, and a squad of soldiers marched up and pulled Justice away from Kim. His eyes were open, but his head was lolling backward as if he were a corpse, and he neither offered resistance nor said a single word.

Moreau looked down at Kim and grinned his evil grin. "You will accompany us, also, mademoiselle."

"To where?" she asked suspiciously.

"Why, to where you've been wanting to go for several days now. My headquarters out in the country from which we shall launch the festivities commemorating the anniversary of the Dominican Vespers."

He held down a hand, but she refused to take it, getting to her feet on her own. A squad of soldiers was detailed to keep an eye on her, and they marched out of the restaurant with Moreau bringing up the rear.

With quiet restored, the diners settled back to their breakfasts. It was a regrettable incident, to be sure, but many of those present were Haitian or had long experience with Haiti and were used to such things. They had no sooner returned to their breakfasts when a horribly disheveled person burst into the dining room from the lobby. His clothes were in tatters and stained by mud and blood, and his face was swollen and bruised.

Sardi looked around the dining room, crying "William, I have returned! William!" but he was about fifteen minutes too late.

After being patched up in the prison infirmary, Jenks was led, protesting, to a cell where he spent the night without benefit of counsel or an opportunity to make his one allowed phone call. At least he was kept in solitary, so he didn't have to worry about the unwanted attentions of a lonely roommate. It was rather nostalgic, reminding him of his days on death row in Leavenworth before Justice busted him out.

But he had no desire to indulge in memories of the past. All he did was worry about Justice in Haiti and what was going to come down in New York the next day. Somehow he managed to fall asleep, though it was hardly as pleasant as sleeping with Kim's shoulder as a pillow.

He was woken up by feet clumping down the corridor to his cell, and he was up and at the cell door before his guests arrived.

"Well," Jenks said with no attempt to keep the disgust from his voice. "I should have known that you're the one behind this."

"This?" General Freemont inquired. He was a large man, sloppy fat, who was the head of security at the

United Nations. He hated and despised Jenks, considering him a murderer for what he'd done to the drug cartel back in Kansas, and a traitor for relinquishing his American citizenship and signing on with Justice. He'd had Jenks thrown in jail once before, where he'd been rescued by an audacious acting job on the part of Justice and Sardi.

Freemont shook his head. "I had nothing to do with this. You were the one riding down Forty-second Street like a mad cowboy shooting up everything in sight."

"What about my rights—"

"You have no rights," Freemont said with a great deal of satisfaction. "You're a foreign undesirable who's known to associate with terrorists. I may have suggested to the police to keep you incommunicado while I worked out the paperwork to fry your ass, but you're deep in it because of your own fault, boy." When Freemont spoke, he purred like a great, fat cat who'd just made a most agreeable meal out of a canary.

"Too bad, General," a voice said behind him, "that you had to come down here and gloat in person. Otherwise you might have gotten away with this illegal incarceration for a few days longer."

Everyone turned to stare at the newcomers. It was Vanderhoff and Mandrake, neither looking too much the worse for the last night's wear, though Vanderhoff did have a flesh-colored bandaid plastered over the left side of his forehead.

"You've overstepped your bounds, again, General, by ordering the secret incarceration of an alien," Mandrake said.

"Who," Vanderhoff added, handing a sheaf of papers to the policeman who accompanied them, "as a member of the Haven UN delegation just happens to have diplomatic immunity."

Freemont puffed out his cheeks in exasperation.

"Open the cell," Mandrake ordered the policeman, "and free Mr. Jenks."

"Don't do that!" Freemont said.

The cop glanced through the paperwork, then glanced at General Freemont. "Sorry, sir," he said, "but these gentlemen have some papers signed by some very important people." He turned and shouted down the corridor, "Open cell thirty-eight!"

After a moment a short reply of "Right!" came echoing eerily down the empty corridor as the guard outside the cell block electronically opened the door to Jenks's cell.

It slid back with a clanging slam, and Jenks walked as tall and straight as he could out into the corridor. He stopped before the general and stared right into his eyes. "Someday, fat man," he said, "we're going to meet where it'll be just you and me. There'll be no rule book, no one with uniforms and guns to come between us. It'll be just you and me, and I'm going to hang you with a rope made of your own guts."

Freemont glared back, but much of the steam had gone out of his look.

Vanderhoff grabbed Jenks by the arm. "No time for pleasant daydreams," he said. "We have to move."

Jenks, Vanderhoff, and Mandrake hustled up the corridor as fast as Jenks's injured leg allowed.

"I've got to get on the next jet down to Haiti," Jenks said. "We've got to discover how they intend to set off their damned assassins before they wipe out half the leaders of the free world. Not to mention a couple of hundred innocent spectators."

"Right," Vanderhoff said. "I put out some feelers about canceling the event, or at least bringing it indoors where all spectators could be searched, but the UN organizers wouldn't hear of it. As you know, we're not too popular with most of the members anyway, and my political clout is almost nil."

"And try explaining that we're afraid that things are going to be disturbed by gun-toting zombis." Mandrake rolled his eyes. "*Nobody* would buy that."

"A plausible cover story—" Jenks began, but Mandrake shook his head.

"I'm trying the one we hit upon last night. Drug smugglers out to disrupt things. It's barely plausible, but," he jerked his thumb back down the corridor where the general was leaning angrily against the cell door, looking like an enraged bull elephant frustrated to the point of tears. "You know who's in charge of security."

"They'll be careful," Vanderhoff added, "but I have the horrible feeling that careful isn't going to be enough. People will die, Bob, unless you can find a way to stop them on Haiti."

Jenks nodded. "I'll do my best." He glanced down at his wrist, realized his watch had been taken away when he'd been checked into the jail. "What time is it, anyway?"

"Almost nine," Vanderhoff said.

"Eight hours until the ceremony starts?"

"That's right," Vanderhoff said.

"Five hours to reach Haiti?"

"Three. We've got a Lear waiting at La Guardia."

"So that gives me five hours to crack this thing," Jenks said.

"That's right."

Jenks shook his head. "I guess we'd better hustle then."

Jenks got his belongings back at the desk when they checked him out, then they took a cab to the Island Heliport. They shook hands all around, and Jenks left without saying a word. There was nothing to be said. Jenks knew what had to be done and would either succeed or die trying. The others knew that. There was no sense in wishing him luck.

The Lear was gassed up and waiting on the runway at La Guardia with a Haven pilot at the controls. They took off almost immediately after Jenks strapped in. Once they were airborne, the copilot came back to see if there was anything Jenks needed.

"Some food, then rest. Then a parachute."

"Parachute?" the copilot asked.

Jenks nodded. "I've got to get through the bull and contact Lambert immediately. See if you can reach him now. But first check the refrigerator and see if you got any grub on this baby."

Jenks was still stuffing himself with deli sandwiches they'd loaded on while in New York when the copilot came back shaking his head. "No one is answering pages at the hotel. In fact—and this sounds rather fantastic—the person at the switchboard says that Mr. Lambert and Ms. Bouvier got into some kind of altercation in the hotel restaurant this morning and were carried off by the local

authorities. In fact, Mr. Lambert was literally carried
off. It seems as if he'd suffered some kind of attack or
something."

"Damn!" Jenks said, pounding his fist softly against the
padded armrest of his seat. He was feeling the seconds
slipping out of his grip like grains of sand.

"But," the copilot went on, "Mr. Ousteoputcha is lying
offshore with the submarine. We can easily drop you off
with him. Perhaps together . . ." the copilot shrugged,
but Jenks knew what he meant.

It was a chance. Not a good chance, but his only one.

Christ, he thought. First he had to find Ousteoputcha.
Then Willum. Then wherever the hell it was they were
going to send the signal from to set off the zombis. Then
stop them. All in somewhat less than, he glanced at his
watch, seven hours. He shook his head and thanked the
copilot, who went back up to the cockpit to do whatever
mysterious copilot things copilots had to do.

He finished the last sandwich and drained the last can
of beer. There was nothing to do now but wait. Wait and
sleep. He closed his eyes, thinking that it would be
impossible to sleep, but he was much more tired than he
realized, still riding the ragged edge of exhaustion.

He fell asleep almost immediately, and as he slept, he
dreamed. He dreamed of the undead armed with automatic weapons let loose in an open city square crowded
with tens of thousands of people. He dreamed of Colonel
Moreau embracing an inflated sex-doll and laughing and
lifting up his eye patch to show a perfectly good, perfectly normal eye hidden by the oval of cloth.

Even in the middle of the horror of his dreams, Jenks
stopped to wonder why in the hell a man would cover a
perfectly good eye with a patch.

He wondered, but caught deep in the coils of his
dream, he had no answer.

XIX.

CHRISTOPHE'S CITADEL
2ND OCTOBER—NOON

The unexpected grandeur of Christophe's citadel would have taken Kim's breath away if it wasn't for the seemingly desperate situation she and Justice were in.

They'd left the hotel in a four-wheel-drive Cherokee, with a driver and Colonel Moreau in the front, two armed soldiers behind them, and Kim and Justice, who was stretched out in a deathlike trance, occupying the rear.

Justice lay perfectly quiet, totally rigid, with staring, glassy eyes that looked as if they belonged to a corpse. The only thing that gave Kim any hope was the fact that very occasionally Justice's chest would slowly rise and fall in a long, shallow breath, showing that he still lived.

Kim did all she could to bring him back. She wiped the sweat that beaded his forehead and continually murmured to him in a low, gentle voice, but nothing she did seemed to help.

After several hours on the bumpy, winding, potholed Haitian roads, they finally came to a level plain. As Kim glanced out the window, she saw peasants working flourishing fields, the first real sign of prosperity she'd seen in Haiti. But mild interest in the country scenery turned to horror as she realized that the peasants working the fields weren't human. They were zombi automatons with the staring eyes and expressionless faces of all their kind. Of, she observed, Justice himself.

The Cherokee climbed the foothills of the mountain range behind the agricultural station, but stopped some distance from the top when the road dwindled to nothing more than a footpath.

Moreau turned to her and spoke for the first time in hours. "Now we walk," he said. "It is wonderful exercise."

Justice, of course, couldn't walk. Two soldiers dragged him out of the back door of the Cherokee and let him lie in the dust while they fetched a stretcher, his wide-open eyes staring up at the sky.

They rolled Justice on the stretcher and then hefted it. Justice's right arm flopped off as they started after Moreau. Kim reached over and put his arm across his lap. She looked at Justice and saw a tear run out and over his right eye and trickle down his cheek.

The sight almost made her cry herself, but she clenched her teeth and refused to let the tears come. She wouldn't let her captors have the satisfaction.

Moreau, who was leading the procession up the mountainside, called out to her, beckoning her to join him. At first she resisted the idea, not wanting to be anywhere near him, but then decided that she could possibly learn something of value from the colonel.

"See the citadel?" he asked rhetorically, pointing a meaty finger at the ruins ahead of them.

"Very impressive," Kim muttered.

"Oh, they are indeed," Moreau said. Despite his huge size, he was marching easily along as if they were on a Sunday picnic, setting a pace that had many of the soldiers following them puffing and panting. "They were built by Emperor Christophe I, way back a long time ago. Men say that Christophe was a great *bokor*, a—how you call it?—a warlock."

"Very interesting," Kim said in the same tone of voice.

If the colonel noticed her lack of enthusiasm, he didn't show it. "Did you know," he said slyly, "that I am descended from the great Christophe, and that I am a *bokor* too?"

Kim shook her head, letting him boast on, hoping that he'd say something meaningful before they reached the summit.

"Christophe was a great man," he confided to Kim.

"Once, when he was building his citadel, he had a whole company of men march over the edge of the precipice, just to show a visiting *blanc* how much his men loved him." Moreau smiled, and Kim had to look away from the evil glee his smile displayed. "Well, I have troops of such great devotion now, myself, and before this day is done we will avenge the great indignities done on Haiti in the past."

"You and your zombis," Kim prompted carefully.

"Of course," Moreau beamed. "They are beautiful troops, my children, and in"—he checked his wristwatch— "little more than five hours we shall be standing on the soil of our most hated enemy, bringing justice and retribution that has waited for more than fifty years."

"You're going to invade America?" Kim hazarded a guess.

He laughed then, so hard that they had to stop for a moment while he leaned forward with his hands on his knees and regained his breath.

"Oh, I am ambitious, mademoiselle, but not that ambitious." He paused for a moment. "Not yet, anyway. No. We strike at the Dominican to pay them back for the pain and terror of the Dominican Vespers."

A light dawned suddenly on Kim. The signs that festooned the city weren't announcing a memorial service or mass protest, but an invasion of the Dominican Republic by zombi forces led by a power-mad—or perhaps just mad—colonel.

"You'll never get away with such a crazy plan," she told Moreau. "The outcry from the United States alone—"

Moreau looked down at her and smiled smugly. "The United States will be too busy with its own problems to worry about occurrences on a small, insignificant Caribbean island. You see," he said with great glee, "we've sent representatives to the economic summit at the United Nations. Representatives who will pay back the United States for occupying us, France for making us slaves, Great Britain for turning away when Christophe called for help—"

Again a horrible light dawned on Kim, and she said, "The zombis at the airport—"

"How did you know about that?" Moreau interrupted with a frown. Kim looked at him without saying anything, and he shrugged his massive shoulders. "Well, that's just something else to talk about when we reach private quarters. But yes, you are correct. At the moment I signal the start of the invasion of our hated neighbor to the east, I will also activate the assassins at the ceremony commemorating the opening of the summit." He smiled with immense satisfaction. "The death toll will reach the thousands, I should think."

"That's monstrous," Kim said.

"Yes it is, isn't it?"

They passed the rest of the climb in silence. As they went through the portal cut through the citadel's massive walls, a man in a white linen suit was waiting for them. Kim recognized him immediately, despite his sweaty, nervous appearance, which was in direct contrast to the cool urbanity he had exhibited the last time she'd seen him.

It was Calloway from Lifeline. But even more interesting was the man standing a respectful two paces behind him, the zombified hit man they'd all come to Haiti to find. Too bad Justice couldn't see him as they carried him past on the stretcher, his eyes still focused on the blue, vacant sky.

"What are you doing here?" Moreau asked Calloway as the other stood fidgeting nervously before him.

"Bad news, Colonel. Lambert's man, the one called Sardi?"

"Yes?" Moreau said, rage already building on his face as if he suspected what Calloway was going to say next.

"He escaped."

"How?" Moreau asked, his voice soft and deadly.

"Well, I know it doesn't make much sense, but the soldiers guarding the dungeon said that when they were feeding him, he turned into a giant rat and ran out of his cell among a horde of rats he'd summoned from the bowels of the citadel."

Kim didn't even attempt to hide her elation at the

news of Sardi's escape, while Moreau managed to control himself only with a massive effort.

"Those fools are lucky that I have more important concerns," Moreau finally said. He looked at Kim. "Your friend may have escaped, but he has nowhere to run to. His escape was all a waste of effort. We shall track him down at our leisure."

This time Kim fought to keep a smile off her face. Moreau, despite his vaunted intelligence and his supposed psychic powers, obviously knew nothing of the submarine hiding off his shores with Joachim One Eagle and his company of Haven commandos. If Sardi could only connect with them, they'd quickly be able to put a stop to Moreau's mad plans.

The colonel stared at Calloway, anger still smoldering in his eye. "I see that it is useless to entrust Lambert's people to the citadel's dungeons. Do you think you and your *blanc* zombi can watch over an unarmed woman for the space of an afternoon without losing her?"

Calloway bobbed his head in the affirmative.

"Very well, then. Take her."

Calloway gestured at his undead servant, and it stepped forward and grabbed Kim by the upper arm. Its hand was stronger than any Kim had ever felt. Its grip was as unbreakable as tempered steel.

"Come along," Calloway said, and the zombi followed after him, dragging Kim behind.

As they passed by the interior courtyard of the citadel, Kim saw an area the size of five football fields, totally jammed with rank upon silent rank of unmoving, unwavering men in plain khaki uniforms. Zombis, Kim realized, and the closeness of so many of the pathetic creatures and the realization of what Moreau intended for them made her quite sick.

Kim suddenly realized that Calloway had been speaking to her, had been keeping up a running monolog since they'd left Moreau.

"—came here to get away," he was saying. "It's not much, of course, but I do have a private room where we won't be bothered by anyone."

Kim didn't like the direction his conversation was taking, but said nothing for the moment.

They went down a covered walkway open to the interior of the citadel on the west side, passing through a room block that ran north—south against the citadel's eastern wall opposite the cliff face.

"Here it is," Calloway announced, and opened a thick plank door with a flourish. The zombi dragged Kim into the room, her upper right arm bruised numb from the strength of its grip. Calloway followed them into the room and closed the door after them.

Kim looked around. The room was small but immaculate. Interesting native paintings hung on the whitewashed walls. There was a small wooden table, a comfortable-looking chair, and a bed with a flowered bedspread set into a niche in the wall.

"Why don't you make yourself comfortable?" Calloway suggested. "Would you like a glass of white wine?" he asked, pointing out the bottle that sat on the table next to a basket of fruit and a pair of wineglasses.

Kim looked at him and laughed. "You think it will be that easy?" Kim asked. "If you want me, you'll have to fight for it. Your zombi slave will have to hold me down!"

Calloway looked at her blankly for a moment, then laughed aloud. "Look, Ms. Bouvier, you are very attractive and all, but I'm afraid that you have nothing to worry about in that direction from me."

"I don't?" Kim asked, faintly surprised.

"Not at all." Calloway went up to the zombi and placed his hand on its patch of bare chest revealed by its unbuttoned silk shirt. "You see, Walter and I are very happy together, aren't we, Walter?"

The zombi never looked at him, never changed expression. "Yes," it said in its deep, toneless, hollow voice.

Sardi was all out of ideas, and nearly out of hope.

He'd managed to escape the citadel and the zombi work camp, and then he'd survived a hazardous four-hour trip over roads that were more like donkey trails. He'd made it back to the Ollofson with the location of

Moreau's secret headquarters and information about Moreau's planned invasion, only to discover that he'd missed Justice by a scant fifteen minutes. Worse, he'd discovered that Justice had been taken prisoner by Moreau himself and was probably headed right for the place that Sardi had just escaped from.

Kim had been captured with Justice. That meant, Sardi assumed, that Jenks was still on the loose, but upon questioning hotel personnel, Sardi discovered that the ex-lawman hadn't been seen for more than a day.

He thought about searching for Jenks around the town, but couldn't think of anyplace to go. The sensible thing, Sardi decided, would be to stay put at the hotel and wait for Jenks to come to him. If he was able. And then . . . and then, Sardi thought, they would *do* something. Just what they would do he wasn't sure.

It may have been the sensible thing to do, but it was also the most nerve-racking. He took a bath, cleaning himself from the filth and stench of his imprisonment, then he went down to the dining room and ate a decent meal for the first time in almost forty-eight hours. After that there was nothing to do but wait, which he did in the lobby.

It was difficult to just sit and do nothing, but in truth there was nothing Sardi could do. The tension was horrible, but so was the creeping weariness, the lassitude that threatened to overtake him despite the worry and racking nervous tension that he felt.

He was tired out from two nights without sleep compounded by the terrible physical trials he'd undergone. He felt himself nodding off once or twice and immediately straightened up and tried to combat the growing fatigue through harsh mental discipline, but failed. He realized that he had fallen asleep again when someone shook him gently awake.

It was a young Haitian woman, lithe and beautiful and familiar looking, though Sardi couldn't remember where he'd seen her before.

But she certainly seemed to know him.

"Monsieur Sardi!" she cried softly. "My mother's people have been searching for you all over the countryside."

"Your mother?"

"Mambo Jennette," she said, and suddenly it all came back. The *hounfour*. The girl who danced with fire.

"You were the dancer—" he began.

She nodded, cutting him off. "Yes, that's right. My mother's society has allied itself with Justice to battle the *bokor*, Colonel Moreau. She and I have just finished a powerful weapon to use against him, and I have come to Justice to tell him of it—"

"He's been captured," Sardi told her quietly. "Moreau and his men dragged him from the hotel dining room just this morning."

She looked stunned and dismayed.

"But I think I know where they've taken him," Sardi said.

Hope returned to her face, then died again suddenly as she stared past Sardi. He turned in his chair and saw three men standing before him in dark glasses, porkpie hats, and ill-fitting suits, the sure signs of the SD. The one in the middle had a *cocomacaques*, the ubiquitous baton that the SD favored for beating prisoners.

"What do you want?" Sardi asked wearily as he turned to face them.

"There is a warrant out for your arrest," he said, pointing the baton at Sardi.

"What have I supposedly done?" Sardi asked with resignation.

"You are a terrorist and leftist agitator."

"That's news to me," Sardi said.

"Me too," said a familiar voice.

"Jenks!" Sardi cried, leaping to his feet.

Jenks stood in the doorway to the lobby, grinning his crooked grin. He nodded at Sardi and Marie.

The three SD men half turned to the newcomer, and their spokesman nodded his head. "Yes, you are on the list too."

"And you're going to take me in, you goddamned refugee from a rummage sale?"

The SD man nodded. "Most certainly."

"Well, I hope you've brought along a couple extra

pairs of handcuffs, because I've got a few friends with
me."

Joachim One Eagle silently appeared in the doorway
behind Jenks.

"We are police—" the man began, but Jenks interrupted him with an outraged exclamation.

"Bullshit! You're not police. The police enforce the
laws impartially. They protect citizens from thieves, rap-
ists, and killers. You know, scum like you. You've never
acted like police. You don't deserve the respect and
obedience that a policeman should command. You don't
deserve anything but a short rope and a long leap."

The man raised his stick and pointed it at Jenks. "We
are a sovereign nation with our own laws—"

Jenks laughed aloud and snatched the *cocomacaques*
from his hands. He broke it over his knee with a loud
snap and threw it down at his feet.

"Your laws are the laws of the dog pack. And a new,
stronger dog has just come to town."

The SD man reached into his coat, but managed to
draw his pistol only halfway before Jenks planted a right
to his jaw, knocking him down. He screamed something
in Creole, and the other two reached for the sawed-offs
they carried under their coats.

That was a mistake. One Eagle silently lifted his right
arm, and a squad of Haven commandos swarmed into the
lobby. Their FAL assault rifles thundered an angry burst.
When Joachim put his arm down, none of the SD men
remained on their feet. There was a sudden, profound
silence in the lobby. The clerk standing behind the counter
stared at Jenks with terrified eyes.

"Sorry about the bullet holes and bloodstains," Jenks
said. "Put it on my bill."

Sardi lunged forward and grabbed Jenks's forearms in
a strong embrace. "It is good to see you, my friend. I
can't say how good."

Jenks nodded. "It's good to be back. But listen, we
ain't got much time."

"I know. We've got to rescue Justice," Sardi said, just
as Jenks blurted out, "We've got to stop them from
issuing the kill command."

Sardi looked at Jenks and said, "Kill command?" just as Jenks said, "Rescue Justice?"

"I will explain," Sardi said, and told Jenks how he'd just arrived at the hotel to learn that Justice had been drugged, and that he and Kim had been carried off by Colonel Moreau.

"Moreau?" Jenks said. "That can't be."

"Why?" Sardi asked.

"Because I killed the son of a bitch last night in New York."

Jenks told Sardi about his adventures in New York, and then he and Sardi looked at each other for a long moment.

"You don't suppose it's possible?" Jenks asked.

"His powers are great," Marie said.

Jenks nodded. "The bastard's been claiming he's a bucket, or whatever—"

"*Bokor.*"

Jenks nodded again. "—with the ability to be in two places at once."

Sardi shrugged. "This is a strange place, my friend. I have seen people eat glass and dance through fire. But to be in two places at once?"

"Yeah," Jenks said. "Sounds like bullshit to me too. We can ask him about it, if we ever find his secret headquarters."

Sardi smiled. "I was there just last night."

Jenks smiled too, a smile of eager anticipation. "Great! Let's get moving."

"The only problem," Sardi said, laying his hand on Jenks's forearm as he turned to go, "is that it's at least a four-hour trip over these terrible Haitian roads. We'll never make it before the zombis left in New York achieve their terrible goal."

Jenks's smile only widened. "Oh yes we will," he said. "The high roads may be terrible, but we'll take the low road."

Sardi frowned. "I don't understand."

"Jake Ousteoputcha is here, and he brought his submarine."

Sardi smiled. "Now I understand," he said.

"I will go with you," Marie said, "but first I must send a message to my mother. She and the Bizango Society are closer to the citadel than we are. They may be able to get there before us."

"How you gonna send a message?" Jenks asked.

"How we always have," she said, making drumming motions with her hands.

Jenks nodded. "Okay. Let's do it. Hang on, Willum, here we come."

XX.

UNITED NATIONS PLAZA, NEW YORK CITY
2ND OCTOBER—4:49 P.M.

It was a glorious autumn day. The sky was clear blue—or at least as clear as it ever gets in New York City—and the sun shone down in gentle beneficence. The crowds were already building to record numbers in the United Nations Plaza as nearly one hundred thousand people jammed the flat concrete plane in the hope of catching a glimpse of one of the political superstars who would be present.

Perfect place for a massacre, Charlie Mandrake thought sourly. From what Jenks had told him at least forty zombis armed with Uzis remained on the loose. He could imagine—just barely—what horrible damage forty conscienceless assassins could inflict on such a crowd with automatic weapons. Hundreds would die from the gunfire. Thousands more would certainly die in the ensuing panicked stampede for safety.

"See anything?" he asked Jorge Vanderhoff, dropping the binoculars and letting them dangle from their carrying strap.

"Nothing yet," Jorge replied.

"What garbage," General Freemont said. "This is just another wild story by that idiot Jenks. I can't believe I let you talk me into this."

Vanderhoff sighed and looked away from the window overlooking the square below. The three of them were in the security command post in the UN building.

"Rasta drug-dealer plots," Freemont continued to mumble. "Who'd ever believe this crap?"

Vanderhoff and Mandrake exchanged glances. They'd decided to stick to the story of drug-cartel plots and terrorism, rightfully afraid that Freemont would totally balk if he was presented with a tale of zombi assassins.

Mandrake was about to give a soothing reply to the general's grumblings for the fortieth time since they'd started their vigil, when the walkie-talkie on the table next to them suddenly crackled.

"Unit Green-Three here. Unit Green-Three."

Freemont lunged for the walkie-talkie and beat Mandrake by half a step. He glared at the State Department man for a moment, then thumbed the send button. "Freemont here. Go ahead, Green-Three."

"Sir, we've got this strange guy here. He's high on something, we figure. He's wearing a Walkman like you said to be on the lookout for, and he's carrying an Uzi in a briefcase."

The three man looked at each other, the general's mouth sagging with astonishment. Vanderhoff and Mandrake nodded with satisfaction. Mandrake plucked the walkie-talkie from Freemont's slack grip and spoke into it. "Bring him to the command post immediately. Repeat, immediately. Use clear, firm commands, and he should obey."

They waited a tense ten minutes, the general refusing to meet anyone's gaze. Finally there came a quick rap on the door, and it opened. Two security men were herding a short, thin black man into the room. He was wearing a long trench coat, and there was absolutely no sign of emotion or intelligence in his eyes.

"Here's the briefcase, sir," one of the security men said. "Gun's still in it. And here's the Walkman."

Mandrake opened the briefcase and held it out so that Freemont and Vanderhoff could see. The case had been stuffed with foam-rubber padding, and the Uzi was nestled in an Uzi-shaped hole that had been cut into the padding. Mandrake nodded at the security men. Freemont caught his gesture and said, "All right, men, good work. You can go."

The general walked up to the zombi and glared down at it. "All right, you," he barked in his most military voice, "what's your name?"

There was a long, slow silence. Freemont, getting visibly agitated, shouted, "Look at me when I speak to you!"

The zombi swiveled its head slightly and put its dead eyes upon Freemont's. Freemont glared at him for ten seconds, then shuddered and looked at Mandrake and Vanderhoff. "This guy's really on something."

Mandrake only nodded.

Freemont turned back to his examination of the zombi. "Don't you know your name?" he asked in a somewhat less harsh voice.

There was a pause, and the zombi finally moved. It shook its head slowly back and forth.

"Christ," Freemont said. "This zip's really far gone."

The general prodded it in the chest with his forefinger, but the zombi showed no reaction. The general circled it, humming and humming, and suddenly, when he stood directly behind it, clubbed it hard in the back of its neck with his forearm. The zombi still showed no reaction.

"Whatever they've given him is great stuff," Freemont commented.

Mandrake and Vanderhoff exchanged sickened glances. Mandrake looked at his wristwatch. "It's five o'clock," he said, "but they haven't started yet."

Vanderhoff nodded. "These things never start on time."

"Maybe they'll cue in the assassins before the politicos show up."

"Maybe," Vanderhoff shrugged, returning to stare out the windows with his binoculars. "In that case some politicians would live, but thousands of innocent civilians would still die."

"True," Mandrake said, crestfallen.

There was a moment of silence, then Freemont said in a strangely quiet voice, "Guys, hey guys." They turned to look at him. He was staring at the zombi, who was staring at something in its own private hell. "This man's not breathing. I've been watching him for a couple of minutes now, and he hasn't taken a single breath. He looks goddamned dead."

Vanderhoff and Mandrake shrugged and returned to their vigil. "Tell me something I don't know," Mandrake said in a low voice.

The walkie-talkie crackled again. "Blue-Four to HQ," it said. "Blue-Four to HQ. We got the damndest thing out here. Some stoned bum wearing a Walkman, like you said, carrying an Uzi in a brown paper bag."

"Bring him in," Mandrake said into the walkie-talkie.

"We got another one," Vanderhoff said, "maybe given enough time—"

"If Jenks was accurate in his count," Freemont said, shaking his head, "there's about thirty-eight more of those suckers out there."

Mandrake and Vanderhoff looked at one another. They had another believer, but it was too damn late to do any good.

Justice lay trapped in his own body. He couldn't move a muscle. He could barely drag in enough air through his laboring lungs to breathe. He couldn't talk, but he could hear, and through his dead, staring eyes he could see. Every now and then a tear would automatically well up in his eyes to flow over the eyeball to keep it moist, then roll down his cheek.

He lay on his back in a small chamber off the citadel's interior courtyard, staring at the stone ceiling. All around him he heard an incredible hustle and bustle, but he couldn't even turn his head to watch what was going on. It was like his previous paralysis, only this time the clamps drilled through his skull to keep his head immobile were invisible. Again and again he willed himself to move, but he couldn't feel his muscles, bones, or flesh. It was as if he were a disembodied intelligence captured in a jar of clay, anchored to one point, doomed to stare forever at the same section of dirty, cobwebbed ceiling.

He heard approaching footsteps, and suddenly a face thrust itself into Justice's field of view. It was Moreau, grinning like a gargoyle.

"You were foolish to become involved, Mr. *Blanc* Businessman," Moreau said. "You should have packed up and gone home when you had the chance. Now, before this afternoon is over, you shall become my undying slave."

Justice made a supreme effort to rise, to move, to even twitch his lips to form a reply to the murderous madman, but nothing would work. He lay there seething with impotent rage, and Moreau, as if sensing his outrage, chuckled softly and patted him on the cheek as if he were a little boy. Then, with a final laugh, the colonel stepped out of Justice's field of vision and strode off.

Justice lay there utterly helpless, utterly unable to visualize the invisible chains that kept him in thrall.

Kim sat on the edge of the bed, watching uncomfortably as Calloway's zombi massaged his neck and shoulders. Calloway sat in the room's only chair, eyes closed, a look of dreamy ecstasy on his face.

"They're very strong, you know," he told Kim. "It took a while to train him, but since I've made him understand my needs, Walter has been the perfect companion."

"Is that his real name?"

Calloway opened one eye and peered at her. "Zombis never remember their names," he explained. "They have no sense of ego, no concept of 'I.' That's what's been taken away from them. That's why they're so easy to dominate. But Walter here had done some, um, work for Lifeline when we were establishing our plant in Florida, so we knew all about his name and background, didn't we, Walter?" The zombi said nothing, but continued to rub Calloway's neck and shoulders. "He's very quiet too. I like that."

"Why'd he get turned into a veg?"

Calloway smiled. "Oh, he was a greedy, ambitious boy. It seems that he wanted to retire from the field and move up in the company. Well, Colonel Moreau didn't think he was executive material. He tried to blackmail us. Threatened to go to the police and tell about the drugs, so Moreau made an example of him. Killing him would have been wasteful, so he transformed him into what you see now. That quelled any hint of labor unrest. I'd always, well, admired the boy, so Moreau gave him to me to be my personal attendant."

"I see," Kim said, choking back her rising gorge. She looked around the room and tried to keep her voice very casual. "I haven't eaten anything all day," she said. "What're the chances of getting a meal?"

Calloway sighed. "I could send Walter down to the kitchen."

"I'd appreciate it."

"You should. It'll probably be your last meal."

Kim sat silently on the bed as Calloway gave detailed directions to the zombi. The zombi left on its errand, and Calloway tried to engage her in conversation about the latest Broadway shows, books, and popular movies. He truly seemed to be a man starved for cultured conversation, but somehow Kim didn't feel like talking to him. They'd lapsed into moody silence by the time Walter had returned with a covered tray.

"Very good, Walter," Calloway told him. "Put it on the table."

It did, and Kim rose eagerly to pull off the covering cloth and look at the food it'd brought. There wasn't much. Just a bowl of stew with hunks of fish and a few limp-looking vegetables floating in it, a chunk of thick dark bread, and a few squishy fruits that were well past their prime.

Calloway looked it over and sniffed. "Standard fare around here."

She spooned up a portion of stew. It smelled terrible. She tried a sip, and it tasted worse than it smelled. The fish, it seemed, hadn't exactly been fresh when added to the stew. "Mmmm," she said, trying to keep a look of distaste off her features. "Good."

Calloway nodded. *"Bon appetit,"* he said, and tried to interest himself in a well-thumbed copy of *GQ*.

There was a knock at the door before Kim could force herself to down another spoonful of the vile concoction.

"Enter!" Calloway called, and a soldier stuck his head in the door.

"The colonel desires to see you," he told Calloway, and left without waiting for a reply.

Calloway stood and sighed. "No telling what the brute wants." He turned to Walter and pointed to Kim. "She is not to leave this room until I return. Do you understand?"

The zombi grunted a reply that could have been yes.

Calloway turned to Kim. "You won't do anything foolish, will you?"

Kim shook her head.

"Good. I'll be back."

Calloway left the room and closed the door behind himself. Kim heard a key turn in the door's lock. She looked at the zombi. It was staring off into space, pondering whatever thoughts there were that entered into its zombi head.

"Walter?" she said. It turned its head, putting its dead eyes on her. "I have something for you." She pushed the bowl toward it. "Come. Sit down and eat."

The zombi, as always, did what it was bid. Kim sat at the table with it, watching it consume the bowl of fish stew.

"Now," she said when Walter was done, "let's see if that little witch was right about zombi diets."

Walter, sitting imperturbably at the table, belched.

Calloway hurried out onto the inner courtyard of the citadel where Moreau was supervising the preparations for the huge voudou ceremony that would consecrate the invasion and sanctify the assassination squad already in place in New York City.

Moreau was watching his tame *houngans* lay down the *veve* designs around the special *poteau mitan*, or wooden pillar, around which his dancers would later dance while calling on the *loa*. The *veve* were intricate symbols of special, finely ground cornmeal. Each *loa* had its own special design fashioned to invoke it and it alone. The *veve* that Moreau's *houngans* were laying out now were the symbols of Ogoun, the *loa* of fire and war.

Calloway coughed gently to get his attention. "You wanted to see me?"

Moreau looked up at him. His one visible eye was gleaming and bloodshot, alive with evil knowledge. He held a half-filled bottle of rum. As Calloway watched, Moreau put it to his lips and swallowed three huge gulps. Calloway didn't like it when Moreau drank. He was even more violent and more unpredictable.

"The actors are all present, the stage is nearly complete." Moreau reached down to a duffel bag at his feet and pulled out a red satin dress that would have looked a lot more at home at an elegant cocktail party than in its present surroundings.

"Ogoun will want a sacrifice this evening to insure his appearance. Make sure it is wearing that." Moreau tossed Calloway the dress.

"Are—are you sure?" Calloway asked.

Moreau glared at him with his one visible eye. "After all we've done, after all we've planned, you hesitate at the death of one stupid woman?"

"Well, when you put it that way . . ."

"I do." Moreau looked past Calloway to the zombis waiting patiently in the northern half of the citadel's courtyard. "After today I will put anything any way I want to. General Belloc crouches in the Presidential Palace like an old woman, afraid to take part in today's historic events. As soon as our hold on the Dominican is consolidated, as soon as the entire West is thrown into chaos and mourning, Haiti too will become ours to do as we see fit." Moreau put the rum bottle to his lips and drained it with a series of prodigious swallows. He was drinking as if he were already possessed by the *loa*.

And he's already using the royal "we," Calloway thought. That wasn't a good sign. "I'll take this to the woman," Calloway said, but he didn't think the colonel heard.

He was far away, somewhere in his own world, watching scenes in his head of past glories and future horrors.

"Big doings tonight," Calloway told Kim. "You'll get a chance to witness a zombification ceremony firsthand as my honored guest."

"What if I don't want to go?" Kim asked.

Calloway smiled. "I'm afraid that that's not an option. Look, I've even brought you something to wear." He held up the red dress. "Pretty, isn't it?"

It was, but Kim wasn't prepared to accept anything from Calloway, Moreau, or their cronies. "What's wrong with my clothes?" she asked.

"Wrong color," Calloway said flatly. He held out the dress. "Put it on."

Without a word she peeled out of her jumpsuit and slipped on the red sheath dress Calloway offered her. It was a tight but inviting fit, long enough so that its hem touched the top of her shoes, but with a slit up each side that ran nearly to the tops of her thighs. The gown had a low neck and thin shoulder straps. As she pulled the straps down and slipped off her bra, she caught Calloway eyeing her closely.

"I thought you didn't like women," she said.

Calloway shrugged. "True. But I can appreciate beauty of any kind."

"I'll bet," she muttered, slipping her breasts into the gown's built-in supports.

"Very elegant," Calloway said. "You may watch while I dress, if you like."

"No thanks," she said, pointedly turning her back.

Calloway shrugged. "As you will." He turned to Walter, who had been stolidly observing all this in typical zombi fashion. "I think the black tonight, Walter." The zombi still sat in place, ignoring Calloway. "Walter, I said the black."

It turned its head and stared at Calloway. For a moment Calloway thought he saw a flicker of something that could have been defiance in the zombi's eyes; then it was gone, and Walter stood up and shuffled over to the small dresser that stood next to the bed. It laid out fresh clothes, including black cotton trousers, shirt, and casual jacket.

"Now," Calloway said after he'd dressed. "Shall we join the festivities? I believe they've started already, and we don't want to miss anything, do we?"

"Not if we can help it," Kim said drily.

By the time they reached the inner courtyard, huge bonfires were already blazing in the pits that had been dug on the four points of the compass and oriented on axis lines using the *poteau mitan* as a center point.

At least twenty of Moreau's *houngans* and *mambos* were already dancing around the blaze. They were watched by a hundred or so human troops and the several hundred zombi soldiers huddled together in the north half of the courtyard. The dancers all wore their normal Haitian peasant garb, but they also had red bandannas tied around their heads and multiple red scarves tied on their arms that flapped and fluttered as they pirouetted around the *poteau mitan*.

"The dancing gets the blood flowing before the zombification rites," Calloway said. "By the way, there's the zombi in training right there."

Kim looked at the altar near one of the blazing bonfires that Calloway pointed at. Lying on it, still as death, was William Justice.

XXI.

CHRISTOPHE'S CITADEL, HAITI
2ND OCTOBER—5:30 P.M.

Justice could feel the warm air blowing off the nearby bonfire as it caressed his chained body. Out of the corner of one eye he could see the leaping dancers gyrate around the wooden pole. But he still could not move. He still had no control over his body.

That was intolerable for Justice, for whom absolute control over mind and body was an essential part of living. He had conquered his body before, but now he had more to fight than just his own recalcitrant flesh. Now he had to fight an insidious invader that had taken control of every nerve fiber. He had to fight a terrible poison that had clamped invisible bonds on his muscles and denied him their use.

Eventually, even if he did nothing to fight it, the poison would leave his system. Under normal conditions that would probably take days, but at best he had minutes. If, however, he could speed up the metabolism of his body, if he could convince himself that he was participating in some grueling physical event, if he could fool his own flesh into believing that he was sprinting through a marathon, then perhaps his heightened metabolism would burn through the inhibiting poison. Perhaps.

Justice knew he had to do it. In any case he had little to lose if he was wrong. Perhaps only his life.

He began to concentrate, to throw himself into his task with every fiber of his being. In a few moments he began to sweat, and it wasn't from the heat of the nearby bonfire.

"Let's get a little closer," Calloway urged, "so we can see the dancers better."

Kim looked at him. He seemed nervous. "I can see just fine."

"I *said*," Calloway repeated, "let's get a little closer to the dancers. Walter."

The zombi was staring fixedly at the dancers. Such a display of interest in anything was rare for zombis, Kim knew. Maybe the stew was starting to take effect. Kim didn't know why food would have such an effect. Perhaps feeding it protein enabled it to break past some of the inhibiting chemicals that infested its bloodstream and nervous system. In any case, Walter was starting to act strange. For a zombi.

It slowly turned and looked at Calloway, who gestured at Kim. The zombi made a slow-motion grab at Kim's arm, which she easily eluded. Now, though, was not the time to start anything. She wanted to give the stew more time to work on the zombi's system.

"All right," she said. "If you feel that strongly about it."

Calloway led the way as they pushed through the soldiers watching the ceremony, heads bobbing in time to the drum and conch music.

The dancers were really into it. They stood with their bodies leaning forward, their knees bent. Rippling undulations seemed to start at their shoulders and travel all the way down their backs as they moved on sliding feet sideways, back and forth, back and forth, as they traveled around the *poteau mitan*. Their steps were rapid, almost violent, and interrupted by numerous pirouettes and shoulder tremblings accompanied by a swinging of hips that required tremendous muscular suppleness. It was an odd, but beautifully athletic, dance. Kim would have enjoyed it tremendously, if not for her horrible surroundings.

Suddenly, as the dancers circled the *veve* that had been carefully sown around the *poteau mitan*, another dancer leapt into their midst. He was a huge, fat, but well-coordinated man wearing a long red robe that fell nearly to the ground, and a strange little cap. The cap was also red. It was flat and circular with a spade-shaped visor. It was a kepi, a French military cap like ones she had seen worn by French soldiers who had fought in her homeland in the 1950s.

The man was also carrying a machete in one hand, which he twirled in great arcs and circles as he leapt and gyrated among the dancers. It was a miracle that he didn't decapitate any of his fellow performers. In his other hand he had a bottle of rum, which he put to his lips and took great gulps from, even in the middle of his most fantastic moves.

He suddenly broke away from the circle of dancers and moved closer to the *poteau mitan*, where he danced among the *veve* that had been so painstakingly drawn on the ground. He hit the empty spaces among the designs, careful not to obliterate any of the lines.

He suddenly stopped, turned, and yelled something while looking directly at Kim. His one eye was bloodshot and blazing with crazed energy. His face was frozen in an expression of utter mania.

"Hey!" Kim exclaimed. "That's Moreau!"

"Right you are, my dear," Calloway said, and shoved her toward the gyrating dancers.

He caught Kim totally off guard. She stumbled forward a few feet, then was grabbed by a man from the circle. His eyes gleamed with religious fervor, his chest and face were smeared with chicken blood.

Kim tried to pull away from him, but without missing a beat in the dance he flung her forward in the circle, where she was grabbed by another dancer and flung forward again before she could catch her balance.

They kept this up until she was dizzy and out of breath. They threw her like a rag doll caught in a hurricane, around and around and around, and then finallly tossed her into the center of the circle, right at Moreau.

He held his machete up and over his head, ready, Kim knew, to chop down into her as a butcher would cleave a helpless pig.

Justice clenched his teeth and, in clenching them, realized he was winning his battle. But he had little time left.

Sweat soaked his body as if he were exercising in a sauna, and hope flared briefly when he saw Kim leap into the circle of dancers, disrupting them. But the hope died when he saw that Kim was nearly as helpless as he, as she was tossed back and forth by the dancers like a leaf blown in a wind.

He made a great effort, his temples throbbing with pain, his vision blacking out, and finally the muscles worked in his neck, and he turned his head a little so that he could see the entire circle of the dance.

He made a hoarse, strangled sound deep in his throat, which nobody but he himself heard. He laughed softly and heard that too. His eyes gleamed as savagely as

Moreau's, and the animal madness threatened to burst from them as he struggled like a beast with a leg stuck in a trap.

He knew, then, what he had to do to win. To defeat the poisons enslaving him, he had to let the beast loose.

Walter watched. Walter knew it was bad. They were going to do bad things and make more Walters. Walter could see vague flashes of things in Walter's head. They were memories, but Walter had no word for them. They were pictures of Walter, before. They were Walter doing things. Simple things. Things Walter liked. Eating. Swimming. Shooting people. No one told Walter to do these things. Walter did these things because Walter wanted to do them.

Walter looked at the man standing beside Walter. Calloway. Calloway told Walter to do things. Walter didn't know why, but Walter knew Walter didn't like some of the things Calloway told Walter to do.

Walter marveled for a moment at the concept of "like" and "didn't like." Walter realized, like a great sun dawning, that Walter didn't want to do the things Walter didn't like. Things Calloway made Walter do.

Walter did want to do things Walter liked. Like killing people. People who made Walter do things that Walter didn't like.

Walter reached for Calloway.

Kim stumbled toward Moreau. Suddenly she felt strange. It was more than the dizziness from the whirling dance. It was more than fear of death looming over her like a mad butcher. She felt faint but distant, and suddenly very powerful.

She reached for Moreau's massive arm as he started to swing the machete at her.

Justice let loose his humanity. He howled like a timber wolf with a paw caught in a trap and heaved and pulled and suddenly something gave. Something snapped, and he felt as if he'd left the paw behind in the trap, but he pitched himself off the altar and fell face first on the ground.

He fell hard, not breaking his fall, and the bruising pain jarred him even more. He looked up, the madness dancing in his eyes, and the few soldiers who saw him screamed. They thought it was the *loup garou,* the Haitian werewolf, come among them tear them to pieces.

But most of the soldiers and even the dancers were watching the strange scene that was being enacted in the empty space surrounding the *poteau mitan.*

Moreau held the machete triumphantly, ready to bring it down upon the woman and slice her from shoulder to belly button. Ready to bring the red juice of her life showering outward, ready to bathe himself in it and thereby call upon the *loa* of Ogoun, the war spirit, to enter him and sanctify his bloody plans of war and assassination.

He swung the machete, but the woman's slim hand was reaching up for his. She caught his wrist and stopped the blade before it could strike. He couldn't break free from her grasp. It was impossible. He looked down at her face and recoiled from what he saw there.

Her eyes were glassy and staring, her face dreamy and faraway. She twisted her wrist with fantastic strength, and Moreau had to drop the machete. She flicked her arm and threw him aside. He fell to the ground and howled in anger and fear.

He knew that he was in the presence of the spirits. The question was, Which one?

Calloway watched in astonishment as Kim bested Moreau in a trial of strength. He felt utterly bewildered, as if night had turned to day or as if he'd been presented with irrefutable proof that the earth was flat. His bewilderment was compounded as he felt a hand close on the back of his neck with the strength of a vise, and he twisted his head to see Walter holding him with its inhuman zombi strength.

"What are you doing? Let go, Walter, let me go!"

Walter just looked at him, then intoned, "Walter not like."

Calloway knew he was in trouble. He twisted, turned, and kicked. The collar tore from his jacket, and he was free. He ran blindly, which turned out to be into the circle of dancers. He burst through them and ran right into Moreau, who was still crouched on the ground.

"What's happening?" Calloway screamed.

Moreau pushed him away and stood up, his face twisted with hatred and fear.

"The woman has been mounted by a *loa*," he growled.

Everyone in the place watched her as she dreamily reached down for some of the corn powder that had been used to make Ogoun's *veve* and used it to color her own face. When she turned back to Moreau and Calloway, her face looked like a skull.

When she walked, it was with a shambling, unsteady gait, not her usual graceful stride. She went right up to Calloway and stripped the jacket from his body. He sank to his knees as she put it on, and he whispered, "It's Baron Samedi."

Kim laughed. It was deep, booming, masculine laughter. "So you recognize me?" she asked, and laughed again.

Samedi was the most terrible of the *loa*. He was the god of death, the protector of the graveyard. Bodies of dead Haitians were his to do with as he would. Dead virgins were routinely deflowered before burial so that they would escape the Baron's attentions. He was mean, cruel, powerful, and vicious. He stared at Moreau with hate in his eyes.

"I see you recognize me too," Kim said, as she approached Moreau, who was still crouched on the ground. "I am surprised. I would think you don't know me. You have never sacrificed to me. You have never called upon me. Yet day and night you have robbed from my kingdom. You have stolen things that were mine and sent them to foreign lands where they will never know my domain."

As Kim approached, Moreau scuttled backward, desperate fear on his face. He broke through the circle of dancers, and into the front ranks of watching soldiers, who also crowded back, fear in their eyes.

"You have stolen from me for so long, that you may think yourself safe. Well, Colonel One-Eye. That is not the case. I already have your twin. Now I will take you!"

Kim thrust her arm out dramatically, just as Moreau, backing away frantically, touched the first rank of soldiers. He gripped one of the soldiers by the legs and shouted, "Kill him! Kill him!"

There were frightened mutterings in the ranks. Moreau pulled himself to his feet and glared wild-eyed at his troops. "Kill him, or I shall imprison you all with the rats! I shall strip the flesh from your backs and make you eat it! Kill him!"

Stuck between the unknown retributive powers of the *loa*, and the very well-known powers of their colonel, some of the soldiers decided to throw away their guns, but some decided to make a stand. They pointed their weapons at Kim, who was staring at them with her hands on her hips and a haughty look on her face.

Justice had forced himself to one knee. His mind had cleared during the last few moments, but his body was still not totally responding. He knew that he could crawl, but that was about it. He started to drag himself toward Kim when the first shots rang out.

He swallowed a string of curses in his throat when he realized that Moreau's soldiers who had run away were now surging back toward the center of the courtyard, screaming and dying.

Justice stared at the ragged peasants chasing them back into the courtyard and suddenly recognized the bulky figure of Mambo Jennette in the lead, weaponless, but urging on her Bizango Society to the attack.

There was sudden and complete chaos. Some of the soldiers started to fire back, some just panicked and ran. Moreau stood there, eye bulging, foaming from the mouth. He seemed caught in the grip of utter insanity.

Kim stood in her haughty posture, caught in a deadly cross fire as the soldiers pulled back to the cover of the ruined chambers in the citadel's eastern wall. Bullets whizzed around her like swarms of bees, but none hit her.

Moreau suddenly ran to the northern end of the court-yard where his zombi troops were waiting impassively. Justice thought he knew what Moreau was planning.

He stood shakily and waved his arms, more feeling and control coming back with every moment. "Mambo Jennette!" he shouted, "Mambo Jennette!"

She finally heard him in the midst of the chaos and carnage. He pointed to the single figure running toward the zombi ranks and shouted, "Stop him! It's Moreau! You have to stop him!"

She nodded and shouted out orders to the squadron around her, who concentrated their fire on the retreating figure. But Moreau had the luck of the damned. He staggered once before reaching the zombi ranks, but then they closed around him, shielding him with their bodies.

And then the ranks began to move and fire.

"Christ!" Justice swore. Mambo Jennette's people were caught in the open and were taking fire from both sides. They'd killed more than half of Moreau's regular troops, but the soldiers were now firing from concealed positions among the ruined chambers of the citadel's east wall. The zombis too were in the open, but they were damned hard to bring down. They kept advancing until they were literally blown to pieces by the automatic weapons that Justice had given to the Bizango Society.

And unlike their human foes they had no fear. They simply marched stoically forward, firing at will, their own automatic weapons taking a heavy toll on the Bizango Society.

Mambo Jennette's people were falling back, withering from the heavy fire that struck from both sides. Justice, inching forward on stiff legs, made his way to Mambo Jennette.

"We have to find cover, or we'll be cut to pieces!" he yelled above the gunfire.

She shook her head hopelessly. "There is nowhere to go. We are caught in a trap, but at least we shall die fighting."

Justice shook his head. "There is always a way!" he said fiercely. He gestured toward the east wall. "We have to concentrate fire on the soldiers and storm their position."

Mambo Jennette nodded decisively. "We shall do it." She paused, then reached out and touched Justice gently on the cheek. "Thank you."

"For what?" Justice asked.

"For at least giving us a chance."

He nodded, and she turned and called out to her troops. Their numbers had been slashed to a third, but they all responded instantly to her commands. They were concentrating their fire on Moreau's human soldiers and preparing for their death charge, when they stopped, halted by a hideous sound that only Justice recognized.

It was a horrible, screeching yell, and Justice turned to see Joachim One Eagle astride a galloping horse burst through the portal in the citadel's west wall, the Haven commandos streaming behind him. Joachim had the reins in his teeth and was firing braced Uzis two-handed. His horse was foaming from weariness. He turned it smartly and swung his leg over and leapt to the ground. The other commandos were less theatrical, but just as efficient in their dismounting. They hit the ground firing. Justice saw Jenks and Marie among them.

Justice turned to Mambo Jennette. "Now!" he shouted, and the Bizango Society charged Moreau's soldiers.

It was all too much for them. To a man they'd had it. They dropped their weapons and ran into the interior of the citadel, and it became a rat hunt.

The zombis, of course, marched imperturbably on, but now they were facing even heavier firepower, and the grenades and light machine guns of the commandos blasted them down by the droves.

Jenks and Marie ran up to Justice. Jenks grabbed his arm and looked at him concernedly. "You all right, Willum?"

"I was in trouble for a while, but I'm getting back to normal," he said.

Jenks nodded. "We've got a problem," he said, then told Justice about the assassination squad ready and waiting for a signal to attack.

"We've stopped them here," Justice responded, "but Moreau is damned insane. He'll probably issue the signal anyway."

"Damn," said Jenks, "I killed the bastard once. What's his story?"

"He is two," a deep voice said.

They all turned to look at Kim, who was standing before them with a strange expression on her face and a strange light dancing in her eyes.

"Are you all right, darlin'?" Jenks asked.

She ignored him. "He is two," she repeated. "Twin brothers who have pretended to be one, and in this way fool the people into thinking they have great power."

"How do you know this?" Justice asked.

Kim ignored him and pointed. "There he is."

He had broken away from the main body of zombis, whose advance had been stopped by the well-trained, heavily armed Haven commandos. Keeping a squad of zombis around him for protection, he moved off into the warren of chambers in the east block of the citadel.

"Let's get the bastard," Jenks said. He turned to Marie. "You look after Kim."

Jenks and Justice moved off together. The chambers were littered with bodies. They searched dozens of blasted rooms. In one Calloway was sitting in a chair with his neck at an odd angle and his white zombi bodyguard standing over him, smiling. It was a chilling sight.

"Maybe we'd better separate," Justice said. "There's a lot more territory to cover, and we don't know how much time is left."

Jenks nodded. "If you're sure you're okay."

"I'm sure."

They separated. There were still dozens of rooms to check, some of which still had battling knots of soldiers and Bizango Society troopers rioting through them.

Think, Justice thought to himself. Where would Moreau go? The assassins, Jenks told him, were radio controlled. Where—and it suddenly dawned on Justice. The citadel's tower was fourteen stories high on one of the highest Haitian peaks. It would be the most logical place to set up any electronic gear.

He headed toward the tower, leaping across the bodies bunched around the first-floor landing.

Fourteen stories, Justice told himself, and no elevator.

He took the stairs at a shambling run, but as he forced himself up higher and higher into the tower, his breath came more naturally, his muscles responded more normally to his demands. He was breathing deeply when he reached the top, but it was natural breath. His muscles quivered, but from natural exhaustion. He'd burnt all of Moreau's poison from his body.

The top chamber of the tower was one big room with several open windows, and an open doorway for an entrance. He could see Moreau fumbling with a radio set inside the chamber. There were two zombi guards outside the chamber.

He had no time to batter them into submission. He ran toward the first one, who reached out with typical zombi slowness, then he changed direction and grabbed the second one. The zombi looked at him without surprise as he hooked its feet, then pushed hard. It didn't make a sound as it tumbled down the stairs.

The first one, though, had grabbed Justice from behind. It had him around the neck and was trying to squeeze the life from him. Justice tensed his neck muscles, but the zombi's fingers were like steel cables. He drove his elbow back again and again until he heard ribs break, but still the zombi squeezed. His vision started to cloud. He couldn't break free. So he went limp.

The zombi continued to squeeze for another moment, then dropped Justice disinterestedly and turned to go back to its post.

Justice leapt to his feet. He grabbed the zombi from behind and pinwheeled it down the stairs after its companion, then dashed into the room.

Moreau was standing before the radio set, looking toward Justice. His face was calm and composed. It was as if he had gone beyond madness and broken through to a new plane of terrible serenity.

"Well," he said calmly. "I see you have disposed of my guards. That means you'll have to deal with me."

Then his placidity burst, and with a horrible scream he charged at Justice with an utterly inhuman face.

They collided, and the force of Moreau's insane charge bore Justice back until he slammed up, hard, against the chamber's stone wall.

Moreau wailed like a banshee, wrapped his massive arms around Justice's body, and squeezed. Justice pulled his left arm free, but the right was pinned against his side. He chopped Moreau in the side of the neck, but the madman seemed unaffected. He continued to squeeze while uttering animalistic howls and growls. Foam flecked his lips and ran down his chin as he bit at Justice's free arm with his teeth.

Justice could feel the pressure building up on his ribs and inner organs. He didn't have any doubt that Moreau was strong enough to squeeze him to death, but he remained calm and considered his possibilities.

In the end, though, there was only one thing to do. He put his thumb against Moreau's remaining eye socket and pushed. Moreau screamed and dropped Justice. He put his hands over what had been his one good eye, now leaking scarlet and clear fluids all over his cheek.

Justice waited until he was in the right position, then came in low, caught him around the knees, and heaved. It was a tight fit, but the window was pretty big.

Moreau howled all the way down.

XXII.

CHRISTOPHE'S CITADEL, HAITI
2ND OCTOBER—6:35 P.M.

There was no need to hurry. The sounds of gunfire had stopped shortly after Justice had heaved Moreau through the window. He went down the stairs slowly, almost casually, thinking of nothing at all except the fact that he was bone tired.

Jenks met him at the foot of the stairway. "Did you get to him in time?" he asked.

"Yeah. Just barely."

"What'd you do about the zombis in New York?"

"Gave them an order. Told them to go to sleep and never wake up. Told them they'd earned their rest."

The courtyard was littered with bodies. Some zombis, shot to pieces, were still twitching. Mambo Jennette was moving about them and giving them their final rest. Moreau's wounded soldiers were being given their final rest with single shots to the head by the Bizango Society troopers. Justice couldn't find it in himself to blame them.

Joachim One Eagle was seeing to his men. There were a few dead and a few wounded, and that's the way it always went. Joachim waved at Justice, who waved back. Joachim wouldn't have time to talk things over until all his men were cared for.

They met Marie and Kim standing near the *poteau mitan* with the white zombi. The man Justice had come to Haiti to find. He was still obviously in thrall, but there was a little more alertness about him than in most zombis.

"What happened to him?" Justice asked.

"He is a *zombi savane*, now," Marie explained. "Some of his soul has been returned to him. With more treatment he may get even better, but he will always be . . . impaired."

"Someday I'll be able to question him about his past?" Justice asked.

"Perhaps, someday," Marie said.

Justice nodded. "We'll take him to Haven and see what we can do for him. There're an awful lot of questions I'd like to ask him."

They'd come all this way and had gone through so much, and they had finally achieved their objective, but somehow it all felt hollow to Justice. Perhaps he was tired, or perhaps the continual darkness and misery of Haiti had taken something out of his soul. He would, he supposed, find out which was true eventually. He looked at Kim. "That was some act you put on there, Kimmie. It even had me convinced."

Kim shook her head. Her eyes were troubled. "I don't

know what you're talking about, boss. I just blanked out when I was being tossed around by those dancers. When I came to, I was standing next to Marie."

"You mean you weren't pretending to be Baron Samedi?"

She shook her head. "I wouldn't even know how to start."

Justice looked at Marie, who threw back her head and laughed. "I told you that you must know voudou to know Haiti's heart."

She laughed again, and as she laughed, Justice saw a big black dog running frantically, dashing around the bodies piled in the courtyard. It reached the unguarded portal and ran from the keep.

Justice made a move to go after it, but Marie put her hand on his forearm.

"Haiti shall take care of its own," she said, and from somewhere on the mountain came the sound of a dog yowling in despair. Its howls sounded vaguely, frighteningly human.

ABOUT THE AUTHOR

Before turning to writing, Jack Arnett led a varied and interesting life in Southeast Asia and the Orient working for the U.S. Department of Defense. Disillusioned by the system, he left the government and became a political organizer and speechwriter before expatriating in the early eighties to pursue his own visions. The BOOK OF JUSTICE comprises the bulk of his message to the world.

Arnett is forty-two years old, single, and living somewhere in the Caribbean, where he writes sporadically and lives the life of a beachcomber.

William Justice bounced uneasily behind the wheel of the Panamanian National Guard jeep, the verdant, vibrant green of the jungle on either side of the dirt road turning darkly ominous as night crept in behind a diversionary light show of pale blue sky streaked with pastel pink. The man glanced quickly at the rearview to see if the deuce-and-a-half filled with Guardsmen was still pacing them before returning his gaze to the pitted and muddy dirt road that was the only access to this part of the Tabasara Mountains.

Frank Merriman sat beside him, all keyed up. He kept tapping his fingers like a drumbeat on his leg or on the seat between his legs as he chewed gum, head bobbing in syncopation to his imaginary beat. "We gonna make it before dark, kid?" the man asked, holding his arm up to read his watch in the dying light. "This'll be tougher in the dark."

"We're close," Justice said, once again checking the rearview, catching sight of the stoic, angry-eyed mestizo sitting beside the driver, the one referred to by most of his numerous enemies as *cara piña*—pineapple face. "How come the colonel's here? He wasn't a part of the original deal."

"He's Torrijos's boy, Will," Merriman said, turning to smile broadly at Justice. "He's head of NERI. Hell, he's entitled. What's the problem?"

Justice looked quickly at Merriman, trying to peg the feeling that rolled off the man like noxious swamp gas. "I don't like him, Frank," he said, gearing down as the road began to drop sharply off, the jungle giving way to rocky hillside. "I don't trust him. Back in '68 he was stationed out here. He ran the Chiriquí garrison."

"So?"

"So, the Guaymis hate him. He raped their women and stole their cattle. My contacts out here aren't going to be any too happy about it."

"Fuck it," Merriman said, going back to his drumming.

"Easy for you to say, fuck it," Justice replied angrily. "This Hate del Volcán warehouse is going to be a major bust, one that I engineered. I did it through establishing good relationships with the Indians out here in the mountains and by being as good as my word. I don't want *cara piña* screwing it up for me."

Merriman jerked his head to watch the truck behind them, no trace of the previous amusement in his wide eyes. "Don't you *ever* call him that," he whispered. "Jesus Christ, you'll get us both killed on the spot."

"I'm not afraid. . . ."

"Can it," Merriman spat, "and listen to me. You work for the Company, not those goddamned Indians. Since Noriega took over G-2, he's been our best source in the whole stinking country. We *need* him, Will, and if the man likes to play hide the stick with teenage Indian girls, by God, I'll help hold them down while he nails 'em."

"You're sick," Justice said.

Merriman just stared at him, Justice catching the man's looks out of the corner of his eye. Merriman held anger in check, his tight lips slowly curling into a cruel smile. "Why, I'm just a poor white boy tryin' to make a buck in the cold, cruel world," he said in a fake accent. "I never did go to college like you, so you'll have to excuse me if I'm not up on all the social graces."

The road narrowed to the width of one car, the open drop-off beside Justice a straight plunge downward over a hundred feet to a narrow valley below where a score of scrawny cattle grazed on bright green grass. Large hills and small mountains cast long, fingerlike shadows across the open, rugged landscape, the sun setting fat and blood red between two hills, glowing like a monstrous furnace, stoking Justice's unease. And always they wound, a wide spiral around the hillside, circles and circles. Justice had never thought much about gut feelings before, but he had one now, and it scared him half to death. There was something about Merriman's eyes. . . .

"What's going on that I don't know about?" he asked, watching the curving roadway through the dirt-spotted windshield, his headlights defining the potholes far too late to avoid them.

"It's just politics," Meriman answered. "Don't worry about it. It's all in the best interests of the United States. Leave it at that."

At that instant they curved into the monstrous shadow of Volcán Barú, the extinct volcano dominating the landscape. Its first sight, as always, was a shock to Justice. It was simply too big, too massive, for the country around it. Like some alien anomaly it rose arrogantly into the heavens, many thousands of feet taller than anything within a continent of it. It was the pride of the Tabasara range, a boulder in the land of pebbles and, as such, was a holy place for the Indians of the region.

"There," Justice said, pointing toward the volcano's base. "Hate del Volcán."

The village sat at the base of the volcano, tucked delicately into its folds. It was a tiny hamlet of bamboo-and-thatch huts, a self-contained tribal unit. In class-conscious Panama, the Guaymis, descendants of American Indians, were the next-to-lowest rung on the social ladder, barely a step above the descendants of blacks imported from the West Indies to build the Panama Canal. Panamanian Indians lived in primitive conditions on the frontier, eking out a living from the land, from trading and from cattle raising. The Guaymis of Hate del Volcán were no exception.

The roadway dropped sharply, descending at a sixty-degree angle to the mouth of the village. Justice could see people gathering in the dying light, pointing in their direction, several of the men mounting horses and riding toward them.

"All right," Merriman said, the excitement back in his voice. "The ball's rollin' now."

The man wet his finger, then used it to wash a small circle on the windshield before him. He took out his gum and stuck it on the spot, then reached inside his windbreaker, removing a nickel-plated .45 automatic and ejecting the clip into his hand.

"You're not going to need that, Frank," Justice said. "This'll be simple and straightforward."

"You sure the Cubans will be there?" Merriman

asked, checking the load, then shoving the clip back into the butt of the automatic with a loud click.

Justice geared down to first to slow their descent, unable to take his eyes off the now treacherous roadway. "My people tell me they're always here the first week of the month. They take in a cocaine shipment from the Medellin cartel on a nearby airstrip, then sit on it for a week until American buyers fly in and take it from them. All Communist activities west of the canal are financed from this village."

"Must be a lot of nose candy," Merriman said, snapping a round into the .45's chamber and sticking it back in his belt.

"I estimate a good five hundred pounds a month," Justice replied. "Something over half a million bucks."

Merriman clucked his tongue. "It's a start," he said.

"What do you mean by that?" Justice asked, the hairs on the back of his neck bristling.

"Not a damned thing, college boy," Merriman said. "You just worry about getting us to the bottom of this hill alive."

The road was awash with mud, a perennial condition in Panama's breadbasket with its 150 inches of rain a year. It was all Justice could do to keep from sliding over the edge and making it to the valley the quick way.

By the time they made it to road's end, the valley had been swallowed by the night, only the barest hint of pink visible between the distant peaks. Two Guaymi cowboys, wearing straw hats and T-shirts, were waiting for them fifty yards outside the village. Justice recognized Mata, his village contact, the man smiling wide and dismounting when he saw Justice.

Justice was out of the car, the truck pulling up on Merriman's side, Guardsmen jumping quickly and silently out of the back, their M16s off their shoulders and loaded with banana clips. They were Noriega's personal strike force, called Dobermans because of their viciousness.

"My friend," Mata called, meeting Justice with an extended hand. "We do good work tonight, huh?"

Justice shook the man's hand as his partner dismounted and joined them. Though Spanish and English were the official languages of Panama, the Guaymis retained their own Indian dialects. Mata was the only English speaker in the entire village, a job entrusted to one villager per generation.

"Are they there tonight?" Justice asked, Merriman coming around the rear of the jeep to join them.

"Yes . . . they are there," Mata said, pointing toward the darkened village, his own features nearly lost in the night. "They stay in a cave dug into Barú. Two nights ago they leave in their truck . . . varoom, varoom . . . go away, come back with the nose powder."

"How much . . . nose powder?" Merriman asked.

The man shook his head. "Lots. Whole truck full."

"Bingo!" Merriman said, turning to the deuce-and-a-half and jerking his thumb into the air.

It was only then that Noriega climbed out of the truck, barking orders quickly in Spanish to his men.

"*Van . . . van!* Apurate, *hombres!*"

The troops took off running, dark figures rushing past Justice, boots loudly trampling the underbrush as the colonel moved up to shove Justice out of the way and confront Mata, the Guaymi's eyes opening wide, standing out boldly in the rising moonlight.

"Cara piña," the man whispered urgently, his eyes, now accusing and filled with fear, turning to Justice.

The two men stared at one another for an instant, and in that eternal second Justice realized what a fool he'd been to trust . . . to trust . . .

Noriega grunted like an animal, a bayonet coming out of his uniform belt and whizzing past Justice's ear on its quick arc to Mata's throat. He struck home solidly, jamming the blade up to the handle in the man's neck, blood immediately gushing out of his mouth as he stumbled backward, weakly, a strange somnambulistic dance.

"No!" Justice yelled, Mata's partner turning to run as Merriman, laughing, pulled out the .45, aiming at his retreating back.

Justice tried to grab Merriman's arm, but he was clipped from behind by a rifle stock that took him to his knees. And if he'd had the forethought to pray, he'd have prayed for the peace of unconsciousness that eluded him.

He hunched over weakly, his mind bright colors and slow motion. Merriman's gun exploded loudly beside him, a scream telling him the message had found a receiver. He tried to rise, fell again, Noriega and Merriman laughing beside him.

He crawled to the jeep for support, grabbing the rearview mirror to pull himself painfully up.

Then he heard it—gunfire. Gunfire all through the village, the screams of women and children telling him the massacre wasn't limited to Cuban infiltrators. They were slaughtering the entire village.

Through waves of pain he looked at Merriman, the jeep's support the only thing keeping him on his feet. Merriman's .45 was leveled at him. "W-why?" he asked. "Why, you son of a bitch?"

"Such language," Merriman smiled. "And directed toward a senior agent. I told you it didn't concern you. It's politics, that's all. This will be good for America."

The fires began then, the village put to the torch as the screams of women being raped ripped like nails into Justice's head.

"I'll k-kill you," he growled. "So help me God."

Merriman nodded thoughtfully, fires blazing magnificent red-orange behind him. "Be a good trick, kid," he said. "You see, it was unfortunate. We came out here to bust this operation, but the Cubans had already burned out the village. We took care of them bravely, after a huge firefight; but unfortunately, you didn't survive the battle. I hope you appreciate the fact that I'm doing you a favor here. You'll be a real hero. I'll see to that. Don't worry."

Merriman smiled, then pulled the trigger. Justice saw blazing light; then it was as if someone had hit him with a baseball bat across the chest. The shot turned him around, leaving him draped over the still-hot hood, his cheek searing, the smell of his own burnt flesh filling his nostrils.

Merriman fired again, then three more times, Justice not feeling any of the bullets. In fact, he couldn't feel anything. He assumed he was dead and that his hell was having to remain conscious to see the results of his actions. His eyes were open, staring at the windshield, at the reflection of the village fires, at Merriman's gum wad still stuck to the glass. His brain spun wildly, time losing all meaning as he was sucked farther and farther into a vortex of destruction brought on by his own naive innocence. Nothing in his experience prepared him for the sounds of burning, screaming death that surrounded him, all of it final, all of it his fault.

He heard the troops as they returned, laughing, drunken with animal passion. They were carrying bags of white powder, which they began loading into the jeep, Justice's eyes bearing witness to the price of human life. Then he saw Merriman moving to the passenger side to take his gum off the windshield and put it back in his mouth. Noriega walked up and embraced the man warmly.

"We are now partners, my friend," the colonel said. "The beginning of a lasting and beneficial relationship."

"I thank you," Merriman said. "The United States government thanks you."

"And our little agreement . . . ?"

"Done and done," Merriman said. "My people will take care of Torrijos, and my government will back you as his successor."

"*Bueno*," the man laughed. "*Muy bien.*"

"We'd better get back and report the . . . battle," Merriman said, walking around to the driver's side of the jeep. "We wouldn't want to arouse any suspicions."

"This is my country," the man answered, "my world. There will be no suspicions."

Justice saw Merriman's hands on his shoulders, then felt himself jerked off the hood to crumple on the ground. Within minutes all the cocaine was efficiently loaded, the vehicles departing without fanfare, leaving him alone to face his death.

He lay on the muddy ground, bugs crawling freely over him, accepting him as a new component of their atmosphere. He could still hear the cries of the dying from the village, but after a few minutes, those stopped also, leaving only the night. His eyes stared straight up, the monolith of Barú a silent god standing watch over him. And as the vale of unconsciousness finally, mercifully, embraced him, he thanked whatever power it was that was removing him from the horror of life in the human jungle.